DESTINED
TO
KILL

JOURDYN KELLY

JADED
ANGELS

ISBN Number - 978-0-615-82348-5

This is a work of fiction. Names, characters, places, and incidents either are the product of
the author's imagination or are used fictitiously, and any resemblance to actual persons,
living or dead, businesses, companies, events, or locales is entirely coincidental.

Cover Art by Jourdyn Kelly
Interior Design by Melissa Tereze

DESTINED SERIES

EVE SUMPTOR NOVELS

THE LA LOVERS SERIES

THE SOCIETY

Hunters were born out of necessity, revered for their protection, and loyal beyond all else. They are bound by the rules of the Society. The rules are few, but they are strong. First, your fundamental duty is to protect innocents at all cost - even if it means your own death. Second, you *must* kill any Cursed Ones you come across. It does not matter if the Cursed One is your family. If someone you know is bitten, you must make sure they are dead by either beheading them or setting them on fire. Third, never, under any circumstances, kill an innocent. And, finally, never break any of the rules. What would you do if circumstances had you needing to break all of them?

CHAPTER ONE

"Anala!"

I clap my hand over my mouth and giggle quietly when I hear my father yelling for me. I know how much he hates when I take his frogs from his laboratory. But they are too cute to let him keep doing experiments on them!

"Anala! Bring me those frogs!"

I quickly let them go and shoo them away with my hand before tucking the jar I carried them in back into my pack. I am not afraid of getting in trouble. Papa would always pretend to be upset with me, but I know he loves me too much to stay mad.

"It is your own fault, you know." I hear Mum telling him as I sneak back into the house undetected. "You taught her to be headstrong."

"Ha! You dare blame that on me, woman! She is *your* daughter for sure!" He retorts playfully.

"I say it is both of you," I laugh and skip by both of them to grab a biscuit from the plate Mum holds.

"Anala, do not ruin your appetite."

"I am starving, Mum. Do not worry. I will eat more. Besides, your biscuits are the best." I smile sweetly at her, and the stern look on her face wavers into a small smile.

"Did you take my frogs, young lady?"

"No sir," I lie, knowing he knows full well I am lying.

"Anala, what have I told you about taking my frogs? I need them."

"But I did not take them," I insist. "They must have... hopped away."

This gets laughter from Mum and even a little amusement from Papa.

"Headstrong." I hear him mutter as he shakes his head and gives up. Aloud he says, "Eat your breakfast. We will train once you have finished."

I am a Hunter. I enjoy everything about being a Hunter. I never complain or argue when it comes to training. I love training with Papa. It is a time for us to connect with one another, and it's fun. Learning how to wield a sword, fight hand-to-hand combat, ride horses, and be quick on my feet is something I look forward to every day. Mum never complains about my training either. She, too, is a Hunter and knows what it takes day in and day out to stay alive. There are times when she joins us. These are my favorite times of all.

Hunters are a necessity during these times. Our village is in danger. I am only ten years old, but I can hear what the elders say, even if I do not understand everything. My parents try to explain "The Cursed Ones" to me. How they're evil and kill people because they cannot help it. That part, I do not understand. How can someone not help hurting another human? But my parents tell me that something happened to the Cursed Ones that made them that way. They are stronger and faster than regular people and have bigger teeth. I have yet to see one, but I have been training with my parents since I was five. I bet I could beat them.

Papa tells me that my arrogance will one day get me killed. I know he says it to scare me (and sometimes it does), but I wish he knew how strong I really was. I can almost beat *him* when we spar! He says he is proud of me and that I have learned more in my young years than most Hunters do their whole lives but that I have no idea what we are really up against.

Of course, I focus on the positive - Mum says that is one of my best qualities - and only hear how proud Papa is of me. It means a great deal coming from him. Henry and Eleanor Geil are the Hunter elders. Their abilities with swords and hand-to-hand are unparalleled. Considered the leaders of the Hunters, my parents are revered. Other Hunters from all over the land seek them out for the honor of being trained by them.

I think of that as my sword clangs against Father's. I know it is wrong to think of anything except what is happening at this moment, but I cannot help it. I *am* honored to be able to train with the best - even if they embarrass me sometimes.

"Anala!"

Father has my sword in his hand and his blade at my throat before I can even think to counter the move.

"What have I told you! Always be present!"

"I am sorry, Papa! I was just..."

"You were just about to get killed, is what you were!" He grumbles.

"Yes, sir. I will do better." I know better than to pout, so I hold in the tears I want to let flow for disappointing him.

"Henry, she is just a child. Perhaps you should be less harsh with her."

"No, Mum, he is right to push me. I want to be like you and you, Papa," I say, turning to him. "I promise I will do better. I will not let anything distract me again."

CHAPTER TWO
"EVERYTHING CHANGED"

"Your father is not going to like this," Thomas whispers to me. Thomas Lagan arrived in our village with his family three years ago. They were Hunters called here to help with the surge of Cursed Ones coming our way. He was cute enough with his sun-kissed hair, just a tad lighter than the wheat that grew here in our fields, and his beautiful golden eyes. He was built as a Hunter should be. Strong and tall, but also graced with such agility. We hit it off pretty quickly when he got here - despite my trouble understanding his Irish brogue. I attribute it to the fact that he was the only Hunter around my age with any measurable amount of skill. I refuse to believe it is because I think he is cute. The world could come to an end at any moment. I can not think of things like that! I promised Father no distractions, and I meant it (damn).

"Well, it is good that I am eighteen now, is it not?" I say defiantly. I tie my hair back with a leather tie and can't help but think of how opposite Thomas and I are. Where his hair is light, mine is dark, almost black. My eyes are lighter and clearer than his. And, even though I, too, have the slim, athletic build of a Hunter, my body has the soft curves a woman should have.

"Eighteen or not, your father is the leader of the Hunters. You could be kicked out for this," he reminds me.

I whirl on him. "I am better than half the men he has out there!" I whisper angrily, poking him in the chest with each word. "Hell, I am probably better than *anyone* he has out there! He should let me go hunting!"

Thomas grabs my hand and holds it.

"I agree," he says softly. "But you are his daughter. Do you not think it is difficult for him to put you on the front lines?"

For a moment, I am confused and conflicted. Confused by the way Thomas strokes my hand gently with his thumb (and how that makes me feel). Conflicted by guilt in thinking my father would worry about anything but my safety.

"Still," I say, by way of debate. I draw my hand back and turn away. I have no argument other than 'still' (as lame as that is).

"You know, one of the most important jobs for a Hunter is protection. Perhaps your father feels you can protect the village better than anyone else while they are away."

"I know exactly what the most important job for a Hunter is!" I scathe. I know he's trying to help, but it only serves to make me angrier. "My parents are the *leaders* of the Hunters! But I can do more good *out there* than standing around here *waiting*!" I turn and squint at him suspiciously. "Why aren't *you* out there?"

Thomas blushes slightly. "It is not because I did not want to be. My parents asked me to look after my sister and protect her while they were gone." He shrugs a little before continuing. "I found out you were staying here, so I told them I would."

Again, I'm speechless. That is not an easy feat, but Thomas seems to do it without much effort. All I can do is just stare at him. When he begins to lean in, I put my hand on his chest - his very muscular chest - and push him back.

"We are on patrol."

"One day, Anala, you will let me kiss you."

I possibly would have choked on those words had I not heard a sound in the bushes 100 yards ahead of us. Silently I motion for him to circle around until we can close in on whatever is out there.

I draw my sword and noiselessly start toward the rustling. Catching Thomas's eye, I count down with my fingers 3, 2, 1. We pounce simultaneously, both ready to slice into our first Cursed One when the little girl shrieks and falls to the ground covering her head.

"Bloody hell, Emma! What in God's name are you doing out here!" Thomas sheaths his sword and yanks his sister up by the arm. "You know full well you are not supposed to be running around out here by yourself!"

I replace my sword and put a hand on my heart to ensure it is still beating. Again! I could have killed this little girl all because I broke my promise to my father and was distracted.

"I apologize, Anala. You say you are sorry, too, Emma."

"Sorry," Emma cries, her accent even heavier brogue than her brother's.

"It is fine," I tell her. I wish she would not cry. I like the girl and do not want to make her sad. "Perhaps you could take her back to your home, Thomas."

"I cannot leave you alone out here, Anala," he objects. "You should come with us."

"No. I want to stay here and keep watch. I will be fine. Just go." When he hesitates, I glare at him. "I know what I am doing, Thomas! I have been training since I was five, and I am the best!"

"I do not doubt your abilities, Anala. I think we should stay in groups."

"Well, Emma should not be out here," I reply haughtily. "Take her home. I am sure I can manage without you for ten minutes."

"Fine." Thomas takes Emma's hand and pulls her along. "I will be right back," he calls as he starts running with Emma trying desperately to keep up.

"Whatever," I mutter to myself. I tire of people not taking me and my exceptional skills seriously. Yes, I am sure my parents worry about my safety, but they cannot keep me out of the way of danger forever. Eventually, I must go out there and fight with my fellow Hunters. Why can that not be now? I am old enough, skilled enough. Hell, I even want it enough. But, no, I am stuck here, 'patrolling' the outskirts of the village, looking for my own trouble. And I am not even supposed to be doing this!

Distracted again, I do not sense the Cursed One until he is right upon me. I feel his arms tighten around me, and I struggle, but he is so strong.

"A Hunter's daughter," he hisses in my ear. "You could be helpful to us."

"What are you talking about?" I struggle more, but his hold only tightens. I need to think, not just react. Papa has taught me this many times. *Think, Anala. Cursed Ones do not have our ability to rationalize the situation.*

The Cursed One only growls in response to my question. I had no idea they could even speak, and this one knows who I am. It is information the other Hunters could use. If I make it out of this alive. I feel the Cursed One release me with one arm to push my hair - which had fallen out of the tie with my struggling - back from my neck. He's going to bite me. With the Hunters training, I learned how they killed their prey—or turned them. I pray for death if I cannot find a way out of this mess I've got myself into.

My mind races with what I could do, going through hundreds of hours of training in a mere fraction of a second. Then, as I feel his teeth sink into my skin, I remember the small dagger hidden in my coat. I reach for it, surprising my attacker with the sudden movement. His teeth tear at my throat, and I can feel the warmth of my blood as it runs down my neck. I spin, ducking as he swipes his long fingernails toward my face. When I come up, I bring the dagger up and plunge it into his heart. It won't kill him, but it will incapacitate him. His eyes, an eerie white with the only color seeming to be a thin red ring around the iris, widens with shock and fury. His teeth drip with my blood as he tries lunging at me before falling to the ground.

I frantically look for my sword while trying to stop the bleeding from my neck. When I find it, I take it in my shaking hands and walk back to the Cursed One. He doesn't move, but I can still see how he looked when he faced me. I raise my sword and, refusing to close my eyes, bring it down with a powerful blow. His head rolls away from him briefly before turning to dust.

I take the belt from around my tunic and wrap it around my neck, hoping it will help. I don't know if it's doing any good because my head is pounding, and I feel faint and nauseous.

"I just need to sit for a moment," I whisper to myself. I should be dead now, right? Or, maybe changed into a Cursed One? Should I not feel different? All I feel is...sick. Tired and sick, but not evil. That has to be a good sign.

I vomit violently, but it does not make me feel any better. Walk around. That is what I need to do. It has to be anxiety from my first kill that has me feeling this way. I smell something sweet and inviting, and it makes my mouth water. I do not know what it is, but it makes every nerve in my body feel alive. *Thomas.* I *do* know that smell! Thomas is coming back. He cannot see me like this! Making sure I have my sword with me and there is no trace of the Cursed One around, I run.

"Anala! Wait!"

"I am sorry, Thomas, I have to go home!"

I do not allow him to say anything else. I just need to get away from him.

I slam the door behind me when I finally get home. For some reason, it does not make me feel safe being there. The familiarity of my home, the smell of fire in the hearth, even the smell of stew mum has cooking, is all a little too overwhelming. Everything is intensified. The sun filtering into the windows is too bright. The fire is too hot. The smell of the stew, usually my favorite, makes my stomach hurt.

Gus, our housecat, pads up to me. Instead of rubbing himself on my leg, he sits before me and stares. We look at each other as if it is the first time we have seen each other. I tilt my head, and he tilts his. Then this strange feeling washes over me. My eyes start to burn, and my teeth ache. Gus hisses lightly and ambles away. I shake my head, wishing this sick feeling would just go away.

First things first. I need to clean this wound on my neck and assess the damage before my parents get home. I promptly go to the wash-basin, untying my belt from my neck. I am almost afraid to look at my reflection in the mirror. Will there be a gaping hole, a bite taken out of my nape? I think I will wait until I wash the wound before looking. Good news, if there is a wound, papa is a Chirurgeon, mum a Midwife.

Bad news, if there is a wound and I am becoming a Cursed One, my parents are Hunters, bound by the rules of the Society. I do not usually have a problem with blood unless it is mine.

Filling my hand with chilled water from the basin, I gingerly bring it to my neck and begin cleaning. Expecting to feel holes or scraps, or something at least, I am surprised to feel only the smoothness of my skin against my fingers. I look in the mirror and use my belt to wipe away the blood staining my skin. Nothing. There is nothing there. No bite, no holes. Did I imagine being bitten? If so, where did the blood come from? That certainly was not my imagination. The water in the basin is colored from it. Could it not have been my blood? Perhaps blood from an earlier prey of the Cursed One?

It does not matter. All that matters is I am not bitten! I still feel incredibly sick, but at least I am not Cursed.

I change the soiled water from the basin and go to lay down in my bed. I try sleeping, but it eludes me. I could blame the stomach ache, but my mind is still reeling from the day's events. *Turn it off, Anala*, I think. My wandering mind is what got me in this mess to begin with. With considerable effort, I finally empty my mind and drift into sleep.

"Anala! You were to take the stew off the fire..."

I vaguely register Mum's angry voice. I try to move, to sit up, but my body is not responding. It feels as though I am in a pit of mud, and I am trapped. My throat is dry and painful, and the nausea is worse. I want to tell Mum not to yell, but all that comes out is a squeak of a sound.

"Anala?"

"Thirsty," I manage.

Within minutes Mum is back with a cup of water. My eyes burn, so I keep them closed as she helps me sit up and holds the cup to my mouth. The water does nothing to quench my thirst, but I drink every drop. Mum takes the cup from me when I finish and sets it aside.

"You are so pale, honey." She places her hand on my forehead. "You do not feel feverish. In fact, your skin is cool to the touch. Does your stomach hurt?"

I nod. "I do not feel well, Mummy."

"My poor girl. I will get your father in here to examine you. Maybe he will have something to make you feel better."

She leaves to find Papa, and I use every ounce of my strength to sit up. I hate being weak in front of Papa. A Hunter must fight whether they feel sick or not. We are strong. I must be strong, but I do not feel strong now.

"He will be here soon, honey. Perhaps you should lay back down."

"No. I want to sit up. Please?" I want to look at her and tell her I am fine, but lifting my head takes too much effort.

"What seems to be the problem?" Papa is using his 'doctor' voice. Already I feel embarrassed.

"Henry, she is pale and chilled. She says her stomach hurts," she explains. "Do you feel anything else, Anala?"

"No, ma'am." I look up at her, and that is when everything changes for me.

CHAPTER THREE
"INSATIABLE HUNGER"

Mum releases a gasp and backs away from me as though I will bite her. At the same time, Papa draws his sword, and while he does not threaten me with it, he keeps it ready.

"What!" I paw at my face, my neck. I cannot feel any wounds, so I do not understand what is happening.

"Henry!"

"I see, Eleanor. I see," Papa says quietly.

"See what?" I exclaim. "What is going on!"

"What happened today, Anala?" Papa asks. "Where did you go? What did you do?"

This is not good at all.

"Do not lie to me, Anala."

"I...I patrolled the outskirts, Papa."

"I told you to stay away from there, Anala! What have you done!"

"I am sorry, Papa! But I am a Hunter, and you *never* let me go hunting with you! I needed to do *something*!"

"Clearly, you are not ready. I have told you time and time again never to be alone!"

"I was not alone! Thomas was with me."

Mum gasps again. "Thomas? Where is he? Is he hurt?"

"Of course not," I answer. God, I am so confused. First, they are scared of me, and now they ask if Thomas is hurt. Why can they not just tell me what is happening? "He should be at home."

I turn towards Papa, but I am careful not to get up or make any sudden movements. "Please tell me why you are scared of me."

Mum begins to cry silently, making me more confused and frightened.

"Did you find a Cursed One, Anala?" Papa asks.

For one moment, I think about lying, but I see in his eyes that he would know.

"Yes," I answer, seeing Mum grip Papa's arm.

"What happened?"

I tell him exactly what happened. Well, not exactly. I leave out the part where I thought the Cursed One had bitten me. How can I tell them - two of the most skilled Hunters - that their daughter may have let herself get bitten?

"Thomas just left you there alone?"

"I told him to go, Papa. I can take care of myself."

He sheaths his sword and tentatively takes a step toward me.

"Henry..."

Papa nudges Mum back and whispers to her that it is okay. He kneels before me and lifts my chin to look at me more intensely.

"Did you tell me everything, Anala?"

I hesitate, but I need to be able to trust him. Not only is he my father, but he is also my leader. If I cannot be honest with him, I have no business being a Hunter.

"I don't know, Papa." It is the truth. I really do not know what happened. I thought I was bitten, but there is no wound. I tell him as much.

Slowly, he pushes my hair off of my neck and examines me.

"Is this where it would have bitten you?"

"Yes, sir."

"I want you to stay here, is that understood? I want to speak to your mother and gather a few things from my lab." He rises to leave, turning back when he gets to Mum's side. "Stay here, Anala. Please."

I do as he asks, afraid to even move. Not that I have much strength to move, anyway. Suddenly I feel exhausted and even weaker than before. My head is throbbing, my stomach is growling, and it aches so much. The thought of food, however, is not appetizing to me.

"Did you see her eyes, Henry? What is happening to her?" Mum's voice is soft but clear to my ears. Do they not think I can hear them right outside my door? They do not have to talk about me as if I were not there.

"I saw," Papa answers. *"I cannot explain what is happening. It is not possible. If she had been bitten, she would not be as she is now. We have seen it, Eleanor. We have seen what the bite of a Cursed One does. The bitten either die or turn. If they turn, you know they kill anyone or anything they see at once. She never once made a move to hurt us,"* he says distractedly.

"But, if she has not been bitten, why would her eyes look as they do? She is sick and pale. My God, Henry, she is our daughter. What are we to do?"

"I do not know!" Papa answers angrily. *"Nothing is making sense. We will do what we can to find out what is happening."*

"We cannot kill her if she has been bitten. I will not allow you to."

My breath catches in my throat. I cannot believe they are talking about me the way they are. Kill me? This cannot be real!

"I have no intention of killing our daughter, Eleanor. She means as much to me as she does to you! If something has happened, we will find a way to fix it."

"How do you hope to do that, Henry?"

"We are Scientists, Eleanor. More than that. We will try everything we possibly can."

"Magic?" Mum asks incredulously.

"Everything we possibly can," Papa repeats.

When they fall silent, I cannot take it anymore. I know I promised Papa I would not move, but did he really expect me to just sit there after what I heard?

"Mum? Papa?"

I will give them credit for not screaming, as uptight as they were.

"Anala, I told you..."

"Not to move, yes, I know," I finish for him. "I want answers." I see them exchange a look, and I roll my eyes. "Do not pretend that I could not hear you out here. What is wrong with my eyes?"

"How...Anala, how did you hear us?" Mum asks, her face filled with concern and even a touch of wonderment.

"Please, Mum. The walls are not made of stone. I can hear you out here through the door of my room."

"Anala, honey. We were not in here. We were outside."

"No. I heard you as clear as day. You stood here and talked about my eyes. You even discussed *killing* me! I think I deserve to know what is going on!"

Another look is exchanged, and Mum picks up the mirror next to the washbasin and comes to me.

"We would never hurt you, honey," she says and hands me the mirror.

Lifting the mirror, I try to brace myself for what I might see. I have no idea what to expect, but if it scares my parents, it will likely terrify me. Finally, I look at myself in the eyes and cannot comprehend what looks back at me. Normally a cool blue, my eyes are now so light they seem almost white or translucent. There is a faint ring around my irises, not unlike those I saw on the Cursed One. Only mine is not quite as red as his.

The mirror slips through my hands. "What is happening to me?"

Papa is quickly beside me, holding me in his arms. "We're not sure, my girl. But we will find out."

"With magic?" I ask, unable to look at either of them.

"If that is what is required, yes."

"Do you even know magic, Papa?"

He laughs a little. It is a welcome sound with everything that is going on.

"I have dabbled," he answers vaguely. "Now, you must eat and get your strength up. I need you to be with me in the lab so we can..."

"Determine what I am exactly," I say what he will not. "I am hungry but feel sick when I think of eating the stew."

Papa is quiet for a moment. Then an almost painful look crosses his face. "Your mother will help you get cleaned up. I will return with something that may... help you."

Mum washes me gently, tentatively, seemingly always poised in case I make a move. It is torturous. How can she possibly think I would hurt her? I cannot blame her, of course. I would be scared of myself, too, if I were not in my body. If only she could know how I feel inside.

The smell hits me, making me feel things I never felt before. I do not know what it is, but it is glorious - and hideous at the same time. My eyes burn again, my teeth ache, and I cut my tongue as I run it across them. I feel a ravenous hunger I have never felt before, and I will do anything, fight anyone, to satisfy it. I do not realize I have hissed until Mum quickly backs away from me and grabs her sword leaning against the wall.

"Eleanor, wait!" Papa cries and positions himself between us. "Anala, fight this! Whatever it is you are feeling, fight it!"

I can hear Papa's voice loud and clear, even through the pounding in my head. I want to do what he says, but I am so hungry. I want to rip something - or someone - apart and sink my teeth into it. The thought scares me enough to try to do what Papa tells me.

"Anala, you have to be stronger than it. You are a Hunter. Use your training to help you. Use everything your mother and I have taught you. You do not want to hurt us, do you?"

I think about how I would feel if I did something to Mum or Papa. Of course I do not want to hurt them. So, I use every ounce of training I have to stay completely still. Gripping my throbbing head, I fall to my knees and begin breathing deeply. After a few intensely challenging minutes, I feel my body relax.

"That is it, Anala." Papa kneels beside me and carefully places his hand on my shoulder. "You can do this."

"Please, Papa, get away from me. Both of you, leave me until I have all of this under control."

I know Papa wants to protest, but what can he say? He has no idea what I can or will do. I do not even know that. So, they both leave, and I sit there alone. This is impossible. How am I supposed to live like this? I do not have the strength to fight this all the time. But, if I do not, it will take me over, and I will be nothing more than an evil killer like the other Cursed Ones.

Ugh, the smell is still so intense. I see the plate and cup Papa left beside the door. If I took the time to think about what I see on the plate, I wonder if I would be disgusted instead of almost drooling with hunger. I crawl over, grab the bloody slab of meat, and sink my teeth into it. A small sound of pleasure escapes as the blood satisfies what I thought was an insatiable hunger. I do not bother looking in the cup. I can smell the sweet red liquid. I drink it as if my life depends on it. Sadly, I think it just might.

I am finally beginning to feel normal again. The hunger is gone, the throbbing stops, and I feel in control enough to join my parents in the main room. They sit, huddled together, with Mum wringing her hands together in sheer anxiety. She is always so calm and collected that this is startling to me.

"Mum?"

"Anala." Father rises quickly and grabs a nearby garment. He dips it in the washbasin and begins washing my face.

I lower my head. "I'm sorry, Papa." I am embarrassed that I did not think of the mess I must have made when eating.

"Do not be, daughter. This is new to all of us." He lifts my chin and looks me in the eye. "Do not be embarrassed. We will figure this out together."

"That is right, honey," Mum says. She wraps her arms around me and holds me tight.

CHAPTER FOUR

"IN LOVE"

"Anala," Papa looks at me over the rim of his glasses. "You know you will not be able to go outside this house as you are now."

I have been sitting in his laboratory - a bit uncomfortably - as he scrutinizes me. Old books in a language I do not recognize are strewn across his desk, and he will read a page, then look up at me, shake his head, and read again. It is actually quite annoying being looked at as a science experiment.

"Yes, Papa."

He glances up again at the sound of my voice. "I understand this will be hard for you, daughter. But I fear other Hunters will only see you as... different."

"Cursed, Papa. You can say it."

"I am not even positive of that, Anala." Distracted, he searches his desk until he finds what he is looking for. The needle is large and menacing. Again, he looks me in the eye. I have to appreciate the fact that he can look at me without grimacing. "I need some of your blood."

In the years I have seen Papa at work as a surgeon, I have never seen him unsure of his actions. The request is almost timid. I outstretch my arm before him and say nothing as he ties the tourniquet around my upper arm. What follows are a series of frustrated grunts.

"I have never had problems with this," he mumbles. "I cannot seem to pierce the skin."

"Let me try." I take the needle from him, and though it grosses me out, I try. And fail as well.

"Well, this is unfortunate." Papa rises and pilfers through his extravagance of gadgets and gizmos to find something that may work on me.

"How much do you need?" I ask.

"Enough to fill that container," he gestures to a small cup on his desk, still looking around.

Without much thought, I bite into my wrist - easily and painlessly (thank God) - and fill the cup.

"Anala!"

"It does not hurt, Papa." When the cup is full, I slide it towards him and absently bring my wrist to my mouth to lick the blood.

"Give me your arm, child. Let me bandage it."

I do as he asks. He takes gauze dipped in some concoction and begins cleaning the wound. But, it is no longer a wound. The bite - like the one on my neck - has completely disappeared.

"Impossible," Papa whispers. "Regeneration does not happen until after the initial change."

I say nothing. I do not think Papa is talking to me anyway. He just examines my arm as if he were a child with a shiny new toy.

"Papa." I take my arm back. "Thomas is here."

My statement confuses him, but he does his best to hide it. "It is late, child. No one is here."

Just then, Mum rushes into the laboratory. "Henry, Thomas is here asking to see Anala."

Papa's eyes slant toward me. He shakes his head before heading out. "Stay with her," he tells Mum as he passes by her.

"He seems a bit flustered," she says with a small, nervous chuckle.

"He did not believe me when I told him Thomas was here."

"You heard him?"

"No. I. . . smelled him."

"Oh! I, well, I do not understand."

"I am learning that people have unique smells. You and Papa have your own smells, as does Thomas." I smile a little.

"But how do you know what Thomas smells like?"

"After what happened to me this afternoon, he returned before I

20

could run away. He did not see me," I say quickly. "But I remember his smell."

"Amazing. Tell me, what else is different besides the heightened hearing and smell?" Mum sits down in front of me, close enough that our knees touch. I imagine she wants me to realize she is not scared to be near me without a weapon of some sort.

I tilt my head and study her for a moment. She is genuinely curious.

"Um. Papa says regeneration, which apparently should not be possible."

"That is right," Mum agrees in awe. "From what we have seen, Cursed Ones go through a transition period. We call them Hybrids. During that time, most of the things you are experiencing now are not as magnified as yours are. We have never been aware of a Hybrid or Cursed One that could speak or even be aware that they are - or were - human. It is why we are so perplexed by you."

Papa pokes his head through the door before I can answer.

"Eleanor?" He motions for her to join him in the other room. *"He is worried about Anala. He said she ran from him when he returned to her where they were patrolling."*

I wonder if they are mindful that I can hear them or if they think their whispering is enough to keep me in the dark.

"I explained that she is ill, possibly contagious, so she cannot receive visitors. He apologized to me for letting her patrol today."

Letting me! Thomas better be glad I cannot *receive* visitors because I would happily kick his ass for that!

"I do believe that boy is in love with our daughter."

That statement rattles me to the bone. Thomas Lagan is in love with me? In *love*? Papa surely is mistaken.

"Well, then we need to work on finding a cure," I hear Mum respond. If it is possible, I think I even sense a smile from her.

They come back into the laboratory, and I pretend I don't know what they were discussing.

"Papa, Mum said something to me earlier, making me remember something." I wait until Papa is seated behind his desk again before continuing. "The Cursed One that attacked me, he spoke."

"What?" They both speak simultaneously, then Papa, "What did it say?" He grimaced a little when he said 'it,' but I let it go.

"His voice was odd, almost like a hiss. But what he said was pretty clear. He knew who I was. Said 'A Hunter's daughter,' then something about me being useful to them."

"They're evolving," Mum declares.

"They must be," Papa mumbles. He tends to mumble when his mind is full.

"Evolving or not, he still would not have passed for human," I say. "There was nothing human about his voice."

"And, yet, you speak as clearly as you did before. . ." Papa's voice trails off. It always strikes me as odd that a Hunter as great and disciplined as my father can sometimes be so absent-minded. He picks up the container with my blood and swishes it around. "Well," he says. "Let's see if we can get to the bottom of this."

Chapter Five

"The Kiss"

I have been stuck in this house for what seems like months, and nothing has changed except my patience. Every day is the same thing. Wait for Mum and Papa to wake, drink some concoction Papa comes up with, realize it does nothing to help me, wait for Papa to bring me some animal to eat, and then wait for it all to start over again. I know Papa is trying to find a way to 'cure' me, but honestly, I think it is a waste of time—his and mine. There is no cure for this curse. That is about the only thing I am convinced of. Well, that and the fact that I will go absolutely crazy if I do not get out of here soon.

The only thing keeping me remotely sane is the time I have to myself when I can practice with my sword. I have found that I do not need as much sleep as I used to, so I use the time to train. Of course, it is not the same as training with Mum and Papa, but it will have to do. Most of the time, I am able to sneak out to the stables for more room. It is one of my new abilities. Absolute stealth. Now *that* would be an amazing trait to have as a Hunter. If only I could hunt.

Oh, how wonderful it would be to get out there and put my new skills to use. I was a great Hunter before, but I would be unstoppable now! And every time I think that way, I remind myself how the first Cursed One I ever came up against turned me into one of them. Still, I really would be unstoppable now.

The horses are getting used to my presence in the stable now. It is a good thing. The first few times I snuck in here, they almost went crazy, and I was sure the noise they made would undoubtedly get me caught.

I am practicing my jabs and thrusts when I smell him. Thomas is here, near the stable I am in! Without thinking, I glance up at the loft about fifteen feet above me and jump. It hardly takes effort to make it up there, and I probably would have been impressed with myself any other time. Instead, I hide behind one of the bales of hay that fill the area up here.

"Anala?" His whisper is loud enough to annoy the horses slightly. "I saw you come in here. Where are you?"

"You should not be here, Thomas," I murmur.

He looks up at the loft, squinting in the low light, trying to find me.

Being able to see perfectly at night is another skill I have acquired. I see his beautiful face in the moonlight as clearly as if we were in bright daylight.

"Come down. Talk to me."

"I cannot. No! Do not come up here!"

He stops climbing the ladder and sighs. "I know you come in here to train," he says. "That must mean you feel better."

"It means I need to train or go crazy," I answer. "I am still - sick, Thomas. You should not be near me."

"Tell me what is wrong with you. You sound fine." He kicks the hay in front of him. "People are saying you have the black death. Are you dying, Anala?"

Ironically, I do not know the answer to that question. Hell, I do not even know if what I am is dead.

"You cannot be here, Thomas."

"You cannot die, Anala," he responds. "I have not even kissed you yet."

My heart skips and then drops. If there really is no cure for me, I will never be able to see Thomas again.

"Thomas, do not say things like that."

"Anala, you must know how I feel about you. I have been so worried about you. It has been months since I've seen you. Months! I miss you."

"So you decide to watch me and follow me here?" I know it is not what he wants to hear, but I have no choice.

"What else am I to do? Your father will not permit me inside your house, and no one will tell me what is really wrong with you. If you are so contagious, why are your parents not sick."

"They are doctors, Thomas. They know how to protect themselves."

"Ugh! None of this makes any sense, Anala!"

"Shh! If you wake Papa up, we will both be dying!"

"I am sorry, I am just so frustrated... wait! You *are* dying?"

It is silly that I can only think about how thick his accent gets when he is frustrated.

"I did not say that, Thomas."

"Let me see you, Anala. Please?"

"I cannot, Thomas. You have to go. Now. Do not ever come back."

"That will never happen, Anala. I will keep coming back until I get that kiss."

He walks out into the complete darkness, and I follow him. I take his hand when I am convinced there is no chance he can see me. I have to cover his mouth to keep him from yelling out with surprise.

"Damn! What kind of Hunter am I if I cannot hear you coming up behind me?" he asks breathlessly.

I say nothing and keep my eyes lowered on the off chance he can see. Without a word, I lean in and kiss him softly on the lips. His grip tightens in my hand, and I linger just a little too long with the kiss, then push him away.

"There is your kiss, Thomas. Now you have to stay away."

I'm gone before he has a chance to respond. I will remember that kiss for years to come.

CHAPTER SIX
"THE CLOAK"

"Anala," Papa calls from his lab.

I - with much effort - stifle a sigh and join him. "Yes, Papa?"

"Try this one." He hands me a container with yet another elixir that I am sure tastes as awful as all the others.

"Papa. . ." I want to protest so desperately, but I remember why he is doing this. I take the vial and drink it fast. Of course, I expect nothing, so it surprises me when I feel something.

I double over in pain, feeling the now familiar ache in my teeth and burn in my eyes. Papa runs to my side, but I hold him away with my arm outstretched. The sensation inside me is so odd. All of a sudden, memories flood my mind, and my heart feels - full. There is no other way to explain it.

"Anala, are you ill? What can I do?" I hear the panic in Papa's voice and hear Mum rush in.

"What is it? What happened?"

"She turned after drinking the elixir. I am afraid I may have done the one thing we did not want to do," Papa tells her sadly.

"Oh, Henry! What will we do?"

"Stop! Both of you. I am fine." I look up at both of them, knowing full well I still have the eyes and teeth of a Cursed One. I need them to know I have not been lost despite looking like this. "I am not sure what you did, Papa, but I am still here."

Relief floods both of their faces. I think they are actually getting used to how I look when I 'change.' How strange my life has become.

"Can you explain what happened?" Papa asks.

"I - I am not sure." I can feel myself returning to 'normal' as I speak. The bizarreness of it is reflected on Mum's face. "I think the pain is what made me change."

"A defense mechanism," she says quietly.

"Hmm. After the initial shock," I continue, "the pain became tolerable. Then these memories inundated me."

"Memories?" Papa puts his glasses on and searches for his tablet to take notes. "Memories of what?"

"Me," I answer. "From when I was a baby until now. It was as if my entire life had rapidly passed through my mind. But I could vividly see each and every detail." I pause while Papa writes his notes, continuing only when he looks up at me. "Then my heart...." I place my hand over the beating in my chest. I wonder if it is odd that it still beats.

"Did it hurt?" Mum asks.

"No, Mum. It was - happy. Light and free." I look at Papa. He needs to record this part for sure. "I think. . .I think I was feeling my humanity," I say softly.

Papa's hand pauses. He looks at me, and his mouth holds the slightest of grins. "It is a start," he says, continuing his writing.

Mum kneels in front of me, her eyes shimmering with unshed tears. "I do not feel your humanity will ever leave you, honey," she says as she places her hand on my cheek. "Your heart has always been strong."

I smile. I do not know if she is correct, but I do know that as fantastic as the elixir was, it was not a cure.

"I am still Cursed, Mum." I know they disapprove of that name for me but let us be honest. It is what I am, humanity or not.

"We will keep working," Papa says as he labels the elixir and stores it securely in a lock box.

"Papa, do you actually think there is a cure? We have been doing this for months and found nothing."

"That is not true, Anala. We have discovered that your blood can cure wounds."

"I make a great ointment. Wonderful." My sarcasm is not received well by Papa, but I do not care at this point.

"Anala, we are learning much more than that. Research and experiments take time, child. It does not just happen overnight. We wait for the frogs or rats to react with your blood and keep preparing things for you to try. We do not give up. I only wish I had a Cursed One to experiment on...." Once again, his voice trails off as it does when he is distracted.

I am Cursed, but I know what he means by wanting one to test on. With that, I see my opportunity and grab it quickly.

"Let me hunt, Papa, and I can bring you one."

"Absolutely not. It is out of the question."

"But, Papa, you need a Cursed One, and only I can get you one."

"I will find another way."

"How? You are constantly here in your laboratory. Mum has not hunted since I... changed. Other Hunters will not bring you a Cursed One alive, as it is against the code. You certainly cannot tell anyone what you would need it for. I am the only choice."

"She has a point, Henry," Mum says.

"She also said why it is impossible. Hunters cannot know what has happened to you. If you go out to hunt, you will be seen. I cannot allow it."

I begin to protest, and Mum leaves the room - thank you for the support. "Papa, I can stay out of sight. No one will know I am out there or what I am."

"Anala. . ."

"Wait, please. I have skills that no other Hunter has, Papa. I could be an asset to the other Hunters without them even knowing."

Mum walks back into the room, holding a stack of what looks to be black clothing.

"She can help, Henry. Without you and me out there, the Hunters are losing hope and patience. Cursed Ones are growing in numbers. I hear what is going on out there," Mum answers Papa's unasked question. "Our Hunters think we have abandoned them, Henry. They say they understand we must look after our daughter, but these men and women leave their children daily to fight with a chance of never returning. We could send Anala out there in our place. Henry, with her skills and strength, she would be better than both of us put together."

I let the slight feeling of pride course through me as I wait for Papa to consider Mum's argument.

"There is too much risk, Eleanor. Do you know not what they will do if they find out about Anala?"

"I have thought of that, Henry, and I know the risk. I believe Anala knows the risks as well. She will be careful."

"She allowed herself to be bitten. Do you think she is ready for battle?"

Ouch. Hurtful or not, he is right, and remembering that will serve me well.

"I am ready, Papa. I made a mistake. It is something I will not allow to happen again. I have learned my lesson, I assure you."

"Henry, before you say more, I have been working on something," Mum interjects. "I knew the day would come when Anala would need to get out. You knew it as well. She is a Hunter in more ways than one now, and we must not keep her locked up. I think it would not be good for any of us." She turns to me and holds the clothing out. "If your father approves, you must always wear this when you are out hunting. There are no exceptions, Anala. You are no longer a part of their group out there. You are on your own."

I understand what Mum is telling me. It stings hearing I am no longer a member of the Hunters Society in the basic sense. I can help them, but no one will be there to help me if I am ever in danger. I will take that chance.

I unfold the clothes and find fitted trousers and a tunic. The belt that accompanies them is also black and wide, specially made to house daggers or other small weapons of my choice. Leather knife sheaths, again black, are fashioned to strap around my thighs.

"You will wear this cloak at all times, Anala." Mum hands me the garment that is surprisingly light despite its appearance. "I have ensured the hood covers most of your face, but you will still be able to fight with it on."

"You have thought this through, woman," Papa says in wonderment.

"I have."

Papa rises from his chair and steps to Mum, giving her a small kiss. Without a word, he retrieves a box from his workbench and brings it to me. "Open it," he orders.

Obeying, I open the box. Inside are what looks like two hilts from swords. Odd, there are no blades.

"I do not understand, Papa."

He takes one 'hilt' and holds it out. With a push of a button, a blade appears as if it were magic. I gasp in awe.

"How?"

"I have been working on this for a time now," he answers. "Hunters' swords have become cumbersome. I wanted to develop something that would give us more of an advantage. These would allow us to hide our weapons easily. We could perhaps catch Cursed Ones unaware." He hands me the sword. Expecting it to be as heavy as my sword, I overcompensate.

"Careful," Papa says and steadies my hand. "If this is what you want, I will agree. However," he continues before I can celebrate, "you will need to train with these new swords first. I do not anticipate you having trouble, but you will give me a week or two nonetheless."

"Yes, Papa." I am no fool! I would agree to almost anything as long as I got to hunt!

"I will also need to take you out hunting... for food. You must be able to take care of yourself out there."

Well. That is something I was not anticipating. I suppose I do need to learn to hunt for my own food. Having Papa teach me should be natural, but this is not natural. Set it aside, Anala, and do what needs to be done, I tell myself.

"Yes, sir. But, Papa, what of your experiments? If you are busy training me, how will you be able to work in your lab?"

Papa considers for a moment. "I suppose I could get word to Bernard. He could help until I can get back to it."

Bernard Luxford is Papa's former apprentice. I do not know much about him other than he and my father had a falling out years ago. I wish

I knew now what the feud was all about. Maybe then I would understand Mum's disapproval of Papa's suggestion.

"Like it or not, Eleanor, he is talented. We can keep an eye on him, but I need someone who knows my methods."

"You have me, Henry. I can help."

"You do help, my love, but this is turning out to be more than you and I can handle alone. I had this thought before agreeing to train Anala to go back out. Bernard is our only choice."

"I do not like it, Henry. But we will do what we must to help our child." Mum puts her hand on my shoulder and squeezes. "Go try on your clothes so that I may do alterations if needed. Then, you and Papa can train."

The week of training with Papa has made me feel. . .normal again. Of course, I am stronger and faster now, but Papa seems to be able to keep up with me without much struggle. That should not surprise me, being who he is. Everything feels right when I am training. I do not have to think about anything that is going on in my life. I only have to focus on what I am doing now. And, at this very moment, I am finally about to defeat Papa in our sparring contest. Unbelievable. Yes, it took me becoming Cursed to do it, but I will not think of that in the days to come. I will only think of finally besting the leader of the Hunters.

"Well done, Anala." Papa wipes sweat off his brow and smiles. "I think you have finally learned to concentrate on the fight and put everything else aside."

That is the best compliment Papa could give me. My skills were almost unparalleled, but my mind was not ready. Until now. With everything that has happened and everything I am putting my parents through, I have vowed never to make the same mistake that got me into this mess. I am focused. I am ready.

That is until I have to hunt for food with Papa. If training makes me feel normal, this makes me feel like the abnormality I am. It is an odd feeling to have your father watch as you hunt for animals with your bare hands and then let instinct take over when you catch it. I am unsure whether I should be embarrassed or if Papa is embarrassed enough for the both of us. These times together are often spent in complete silence. Neither of us knows what to say, so we say nothing. But Papa always acts as if nothing is out of the ordinary when we get home to Mum, and she asks how everything went. Eventually, even hunting for food will become somewhat routine.

"Someone is here, Papa." I stop short of our home, returning from our last training day when I smell the different scent. "I do not know their smell."

"You are sure? We are not expecting anyone."

"I am sure. I can hear Mum talking to him." I tilt my head and listen. "She does not sound as though she likes him."

"That must be Bernard," Papa says, a hint of a smile touching his words.

"Will you ever tell me what happened with him?"

"One day, child," he answers. There is something in his voice. Anger, but also - guilt? That does not make sense, but I do not question him now. "Now, we must get you inside undetected."

"That is not a problem, Papa. Go ahead. I will make it to my room unnoticed."

Papa only hesitates for a moment, then shrugs and walks away. Obviously, he trusts that I can do what I say. It is a fine day. My first spar win and the trust of my father. A fine day indeed.

When I do slip into my room - undetected, of course - I hear angry whispers coming from the other room.

"You bring me here when your daughter may have the black death?"

"She does not have the black death, Bernard," Papa retorts.

"That is not what I heard. No one has seen your child for months. How am I to know she is even still alive?"

"My daughter is none of your concern. I asked you here to help me. I am experimenting on Cursed Ones. I intend to find a cure."

"A cure! For Cursed Ones? Are you mad? There is no such thing! You should know that better than anyone."

"You do not know that! If they can be turned, they can be cured!" Mum whispers heatedly. "You know how talented Henry is. I told you this was a mistake, Henry."

"Are you dabbling in magic again, Henry?" I do not miss the fact that Bernard ignores Mum's interjection. I cannot say I like the man much.

"Magic is only a small part of it, Bernard," Papa answers. "Do not get any ideas. We do nothing but work on a cure."

"Do you realize what we could do with a cure for Cursed Ones? We would be rich!"

"This is not for the money, Bernard!" Papa snaps. "This is to save my - village. To save those poor souls who are Cursed. You would do well to remember that. If you expect something more from this, you can leave and never return."

"Fine, fine. We do it for the village. I think you are missing a tremendous opportunity here. But, I will do as you ask and help."

Perhaps it was the Hunter in me, or maybe the Cursed One in me, but something did not feel right to me where Bernard was concerned. There was something in his voice that was - off.

CHAPTER SEVEN

"FORGIVE ME"

P apa finally thinks I am ready to go hunting - real Hunters hunting - by myself. It is absurd for me to be nervous, but it is true none-theless. I dress carefully in the garments Mum made. They are indeed form-fitting but surprisingly easy to maneuver in. I tuck stakes into the belt at either side of my torso, making sure they are easily accessible. I place my dagger in my belt, as well, and use the sheaths on my thighs to hold the special sword Papa made. He trained me to use both at one time. It was difficult to get used to at first, but now, I almost feel unarmed without both.

I pick up the cloak and slip it on. Behind this cloak, I will be a Hunter, not the hunted. I feel safe and protected - even a bit powerful as long as I have this.

"Anala, oh!" Mum's hand flutters to her mouth, and her breath catches on a small cry.

"Do not cry, Mum. Everything will be fine." I smile sweetly at her, as I did when I was younger.

She comes to me and fiddles with the cloak. "I know, honey. It is just - I have never seen you look so grown up. And formidable." She touches my cheek. "You must remember to keep this on, with the hood. Do not let anyone see your face. And, please, come home to us."

"I promise. Is Papa coming to see me off?"

"He and Bernard are working in the lab. He wants to make sure Bernard stays busy while you go out."

"I see." It hurts a bit that Papa is not saying goodbye to me on my first night hunting. I promised Mum I would return, but that is not guaranteed.

"He loves you, Anala. He has taught you everything you need to know to survive. Do not devastate him by not coming home."

"Yes, ma'am." With a quick hug, I pull the hood over my head, concealing my identity, and hurry out.

Papa had secured a horse for me that was not my own. He said we could not take chances that someone would recognize my personal horse. The stallion I ride now is solid. I do not spend much time getting acquainted with him, but he does not seem to mind.

I ride up the mountain and stop at a ledge overlooking the village. It is a good vantage point for me and out of the way enough that other Hunters would be scarce here.

It is quiet. Too quiet. This stillness could put me in much danger if I allow it to. I must not let my mind linger. Stay alert, Anala. I scan the village and its surroundings. I can see Hunters patrolling, even some fighting Cursed Ones. I contemplate going down to help, but they seem to have everything in control. Using my knowledge of my abilities, especially the stealth, I concentrate harder on my surroundings. Listening so intently, I can hear my stallion's heart beating. If I am not mistaken, I can even hear the rustling of small insects roaming the ground.

Being Cursed, I hear the subtle whisper of sound, but the Hunter in me feels my visitors are Cursed Ones. That they are still a distance away and in no hurry means they have not sensed me yet. In a deft move, I bounce to my feet on my steed's back and leap to the tree branch above me. I click my tongue, and my horse trots off—no need to lose a perfectly good horse to those things. I crouch on the branch — and wait.

The wait is not long. In moments, a group of Cursed Ones - six that I can see - saunter up under my branch. There are no words between them, only occasional sniffs in the air. How they do not detect me above them is beyond me, but I use it to my advantage. Silently, I grasp both swords and, in a single movement, jump out — doing a pretty impressive flip mid-air — while my blades slide gracefully from their hilts. On the way down, I take out two of the Cursed Ones with a quick slice across their necks. Then — as they say — all hell breaks loose. The others turn on me with their agile speed. But I am faster. Cursed Ones fall at my feet in a flurry of ducks, spins, jumps, and expertly placed lunges, twists, and strokes of my blade. One grabs me from behind, and I feel it going for my neck as another runs toward us. I flick my sword toward the running one, and it finds its target, piercing through the heart. He goes down, paralyzed. I grab the one currently fighting for my neck by the head and flip her over my body. She fights like a brute warrior, hitting and snapping at me with her long teeth. I cannot get my sword around fast enough to end her, so I fight back with everything I have.

She kicks me in the stomach — lucky shot — and I soar in the air. With a swift jerk, I manage to land on my feet about one hundred feet away from her. She is on me in less than a second, and I must duck to avoid the swing of her arm aimed at my head. Kneeling, I turn my sword around and thrust it behind me into her chest. When she falls, I take a second to catch my breath.

"Bloody fierce, aren't you?" I say to her still figure. I wipe the blood from my mouth and roll my shoulders. Placing a foot on her stomach, I grab the hilt of my sword. I draw it back out of her chest and force it across her neck. Doing the same with the other, I wipe the blades, retract them and place them back beneath my cloak. A quick scan finds my horse not far below me, but as I am about to descend, I smell that familiar smell.

"That was amazing."

I freeze at the sound of his Irish brogue. Say nothing, I warn myself. Do not turn around. Do nothing that will expose you.

"Six. I counted. And you took them all out by yourself." His voice holds an awe that I should have been delighted by. Instead, I am annoyed that he just watched rather than jump in and help me. As Mum said, I am alone out here.

"I should have helped," he says, mimicking my thoughts. "But I was. . .mesmerized. That is the only word I can think of as to why I did not act." He comes closer, and I ready myself to flee if needed.

"Who are you?"

Slowly, he steps even closer. That is enough for me. I jump from my spot, landing smoothly on my stallion's back. I only hesitate for an instant before I ride off in the opposite direction of home.

Hours — and countless Cursed Ones — later, I finally arrive home, confident no one notices me. It is almost dawn, but I still have the darkness to shadow my movements. I return the steed to his pasture and amble home, lifting the staked Cursed One over my shoulder.

Papa is waiting for me. He pretends he is sleeping, but I hear his breath and heartbeat return to normal when I walk in. He was afraid for me.

"Anala!" He rises, then stops abruptly when he sees what I carry. "You were able to secure one?"

I choose not to be insulted by his amazement. "Of course. You said it would help you."

"I take it you did well on your first night?"

He sounds almost envious. I cannot blame him. He is a Hunter, and that need to be out there never disappears. It is my fault he is stuck here; I am sure I will feel guilty about that forever.

"Yes, sir." I want to tell him all about it! How incredible it felt to fight, to hunt. How strong I felt, and how the Cursed Ones did not stand a chance with me. Mum said the ones in transition were called Hybrids. But I felt like the perfect Hybrid. Part Hunter, part Cursed — all intimidating. "The swords were amazing!"

"They worked, then?" The excitement in his voice is exactly what I am looking for.

"Oh, yes! They are magnificent! You should think about making many of them for the others."

"Well, that will come in time, daughter. My schedule is a bit full." He smiles at me, then realizes I am still holding the Cursed One. "Oh! Here, let me. . ."

"No, I have it. Just tell me where you want me to put it."

It must be extraordinarily bizarre to see your eighteen-year-old, thin and not overtly muscular daughter holding a grown man twice her size as though he were a sack of flour. With a slight shake of his head, he leads me to the back of his lab and pushes the wall. It opens with the abrasive sound of stone on stone.

"I have lived in this house my entire life. How do I not know about this?" I ask.

"I am allowed to have secrets, am I not?" Papa teases. "Put it here in this chair. We will chain him to the wall."

"Papa, do you really think this will hold him?"

"Would you like to try it out? The chair and chains are made of pure silver. The chains go beyond the wall into the ground more than six feet deep and wrap around a silver pole. From what we have learned, silver weakens the strength of Cursed Ones."

"Silver?" I carefully sit the Cursed One in the chair, propping his slumped body up. Picking up the chain, I instantly feel a change in my strength. "Such a normal feeling chain for such an extraordinary feat."

I pull the chain with all the strength I can muster. The links stretch slightly but do not break. I am convinced that if I cannot break it, my prisoner cannot. I help papa chain the Cursed One to the silver chair, ensuring it is completely secure. I do not want to take chances with the lives of my parents.

"I want to be here, Papa, when you take the stake out."

"I am a Hunter, child. I am sure I can take care of myself." He sounds almost annoyed by my request.

"I do not think you are not capable, Papa. I just want to make sure the chains are strong enough."

He looks as though he will argue, but he nods instead. "Very well. Get cleaned up, and we will see what this one offers us."

Our prisoner offers us nothing for a long while. Even with Bernard's help, Papa comes up empty regarding a 'cure.' The closest he comes is formulating a potion that curbs the hunger and need for blood and one that helps mask the eerie color this curse makes the eyes. The latter is still too unpredictable for me to come out of hiding, as it can wear off without warning.

I have been in hiding for so long that word is beginning to spread that I have died. Mum and Papa can no longer dispute it because they cannot show anyone I am alive. I even have to hide myself from Bernard, which is, I admit, increasingly tricky since he is constantly in my house. I notice that his interest in the Cursed One I captured is increasing daily. I will hear him trying to engage it in conversation — to no avail. His pressing question is always, 'who captured you?'. I have yet to figure out why that would matter to him.

When Bernard finds out that my blood — though he does not know it is mine — can heal, he and Papa begin arguing frequently. Bernard wants to sell the cure to the highest bidder. Papa forbids it. He does not know what the blood will do to humans in larger doses. Would it create more of me? More monsters? It is not something Papa wishes to find out.

I hunt longer and longer, pushing the limits of sunlight as far as it will go. Being in the house while Bernard is there makes me uncomfortable, and hunting keeps me occupied with more than the thought that this is how I will be for the rest of my life — however long that will be.

I have not run into Thomas again since my first night out hunting. Secretly, I wish I would, even if just to see for myself that he is doing well. I hear Hunters telling stories during their patrol of how the Lagan boy went into a depression when he heard of my death. I prefer not to believe it. Thomas is strong in mind and body. I am sure I could not be the cause of such depression. Maybe I just do not want that responsibility hanging over me.

I think of Thomas as I ride home. Tonight has been a quiet night, hunting-wise. If I allow myself to think carefully about that, I will find it odd, but my mind is on Thomas. I wish I could kiss him again. I laugh quietly at that. My entire life has been about hunting and being the best Hunter. I never thought a boy would be as important to me as that. This is certainly not something I can talk to Papa about. Mum would understand, I am sure.

After returning my horse, I make my way home, staying in the darkest shadows I can find in the dawning day. It is about time for Mum and Papa to be up and cooking breakfast. Oh, how I missed Mum's biscuits! Perhaps I shall try to eat one this morning.

"Mum? Papa?" It is eerily quiet in the house. I do not hear or smell Bernard, so it should be safe for me. I take a step toward the lab and stop abruptly. I begin to feel the change that occurs in me now as a Cursed One. The ache, the burning. That unmistakable, enticing smell of blood fills my nostrils. So much blood, I think as I take a deep breath.

"Papa?" Is he using more blood from the Cursed One I brought him? No. That smell. It is familiar. Too familiar. But, too muddled for me to define the origin. "Mum? Are you awake?" I call out as I continue to the lab. The odor gets stronger as I get closer. Silence still fills the air, and dread fills up inside of me. Hurrying now, I push through to the lab — and see them.

"No!" I run to Mum, lying so still, surrounded by the blood that I have no desire for. "Mummy? Please wake up!" I shake her gently, but she does not respond. "You have to wake up!"

Crawling over to Papa, I check for a pulse, listen for a heartbeat — any sign that he was alive. There is none. "Papa! Mummy is hurt. You have to get up and help her!" He does not move. My mind knows I can do nothing for them now, but I do not want to believe they are gone. I sit with them, holding their hands in my bloody hands. Soaked in their blood, I let out a wail filled with agony and guilt. I want to lay down with them, join them wherever they may be now. Unfortunately for me, I cannot die now, but, oh, how I want to. How am I supposed to go on without my parents? What am I to do?

"You know what you must do, Anala," Papa's voice fills my head, and I hope against hope that it is really he who is talking. Yet, when I look at him, he still lies lifeless and pale, his cold hand in mine. I see the bites now. Bites that I missed or perhaps refused to see before. They were

attacked! They are so skilled. How could they let this happen? The irony of my question is not lost on me. I check Mum, seeing the bites on her as well. The Cursed One! I scramble to my feet and run to the back wall, pushing it open.

It is gone. The silver chair is empty, the chains limp. Is this my fault? Am I to blame for my parents' death by leaving them with this — thing?

"Focus, Anala. Think only of this moment and what you need to do." Papa's voice invades my mind again.

"Yes, papa," I whisper and study my surroundings. Things were a mess in here. There was obviously a struggle.

"Look deeper, Anala."

I shake my head. If I thought the silence was eerie, having Papa's voice in my head as he lies dead before me was scary. I take a deep breath and 'look deeper.'

"Things are missing," I say aloud. The vials of my blood, potions, notes — all missing. Why would a Cursed One steal Papa's work? Could it really have had the mental capacity to have done this? I run to Papa's secret compartment. This is where he kept most of my blood, along with elixirs and notes that recorded any changes in me. I crush the lock with my bare hand and open it.

They are still here. Obviously, the Cursed One — or someone else, as I am not convinced it was the prisoner — did not know about this. I gather everything I possibly can out of Papa's lab, my room, and around the house, packing them into a sack I can carry. After washing up, I go back to where my parents lay slain.

"Forgive me," I ask them silently. "I love you both."

With that, I say my last goodbye and set my childhood home and my parents on fire. I watch long enough to make sure no one would show up to stop the blaze, and then run towards the pasture where I steal the stallion. Of course, I feel bad about that, but it is a necessity. I do not know where I am going, but I cannot stay here and watch my life go up in flames.

I spend the next several years killing every Cursed One I came across, wondering if I had killed the ones that murdered my family. Will I ever know for sure what happened, or will I spend the rest of my immortal life questioning if I could have done anything, anything at all, to save my family's lives?

IMMORTALITY

Immortality. Humans would sell their souls for it. Immortals would steal souls to keep it. Infinite life is too seductive and powerful to resist. But immortality is more like a bad drug habit than a gift. Immortals can't give it up because, after living for so long, they don't know how to face death. You see, living forever isn't all it's cracked up to be. Sure, you have your pros, but it's the cons that can make an Immortal wish for death that will never come.

CHAPTER EIGHT
"THE WATCHFUL EYE"
CALIFORNIA - PRESENT DAY

"Ana Gale?"

Mr. Galloway's monotone voice grates on my nerves as he calls attendance.

"Here," I answer in the same manner. If he's not excited about teaching, I will not be excited to be taught by him. Besides, this is history class. It's a subject so excruciatingly easy for me that it's tedious. Luckily, it's film day, so I can spend the hour reading my entertainment magazines. Sure, it's a frivolous thing, but hey, I'm a teenager. What do you expect?

When the lights in the room are turned off, I scoot my chair closer to the window for the sunlight and begin thumbing through the latest stories of the rich and famous.

"Who's doing who these days?"

I look up at Zac Connor and smile. "Are we talking about celebrities or people in this school?" I ask slyly.

Zac is the hottie of Westchester High with his sun-bleached hair, surfer-boy good looks, and golden eyes. He has a nice smile, which always lights up around me. He isn't exactly my type, but I enjoy flirting with him.

"The only people's sex life I am interested in is yours and mine. And only if it's with each other." He chuckles, clearly appreciating his cleverness.

I roll my eyes. "Cute, Zac." Not to be conceited, but I'm used to guys showing interest in me. I'm not your typical teenager, especially here in sunny, plastic California. My English accent makes me a bit more mysterious and exotic to those here. My hair is still long and dark — an enigma itself in a school full of blondes or those who pay to be blonde — as for my eyes, well, I no longer try to hide what being Cursed does to them — though I still take Papa's elixir every once in a while to dim the red rim. Cursed Ones — or the effects of being Cursed — never existed for this generation, so I'm not worried about being 'discovered.' Besides, I like the fact that my eyes often reflect whatever color I happen to be wearing that day. Today, I have on a red tank top with faded jeans. My eyes hold a red tint to them, which always catches the attention of those around me.

My full lips are another feature the guys think is fascinating - which Zac is currently demonstrating by alternating staring at them and my boobs.

"Hey, the invitation is always open," he replies.

"So you tell me every day. And, as I keep telling you, 'not going to happen.'"

"Come on! What's holding you back? I'm hot. You're hot. It's a match made in heaven!"

"And that's exactly why it'll never happen, Zac," I shoot back. "You're too into yourself. How can any girl compete with that?"

I hear a few snickers around us, and Zac mumbles something I don't quite catch. But my attention is not on him anymore. I have that feeling of being watched, and I glance up to notice that Mr. Galloway is staring at me. The look on his face is odd, to say the least, and when I turn my full gaze on him, he doesn't even make an effort to look away. Maybe he thinks I can't see him in the dark classroom. But I can. And the way he's looking at me is making me uncomfortable.

"Could that class *be* any more boring?" The bell finally rings, and Amanda catches up as I hurry out the door. Per usual, she's complaining. Amanda has been my best friend since I moved here two years ago. I love her, but she complains about practically *everything*! Everything is too boring or too hard or too this and too that. I try to tell her just to take life in stride and not let things that don't matter get to her. But then I'm 'too uncaring' and never on her side. Sigh.

"Probably not," I reply, hoping I'm saying the right thing to appease her. When she slides me a sideways glance and grins, I grin back and take a small breath of relief. I am still feeling a bit too unnerved by Mr. Galloway to pay much attention to Amanda anyway. I am trying to take my own advice of not letting things get to me, but there was something too familiar in the look. I just don't know what it was.

"Hello? Earth to Ana." Amanda stands next to her locker — unsure how we got here — her hand on her hip and her toe-tapping. "I just told you the greatest news ever, and you're ignoring me!"

I put my weird teacher out of my mind and focus on my best friend, who is clearly annoyed with me. "I'm not ignoring you, Amanda," I say, trying to sound sincere. "I just spaced out for a minute. What was the greatest news ever?"

She just stands there for another moment and stares at me. I match her stare, smile and wait. Amanda never stays annoyed at me for long but always makes sure I know when I screw up.

"I *said* Robby asked me to the movies on Friday." She stops tapping her toe and squeals in delight. "Can you believe it! I mean, you said he would, but I didn't believe you!"

"I keep telling you I'm always right, but you never listen." I grin at her and do her little happy dance with her in the middle of the hallway. It's a little foolish, but it's worth seeing how happy she is (plus, it gives me extra points in the best friend category, and I need all of those I can get).

"Yeah, yeah, you're always right, Ana." She rolls her eyes a little but still smiles from ear to ear. "So, what should we see? I mean, I know I can't go see a 'chick-flick.' That's what I have you for." She bumps my hip with hers as we walk toward the cafeteria for lunch. "I don't like action or horror movies, but I don't care what we see 'cause I'm going to the movies with Robby!"

I listen to her babble on and on about what she will wear, how she'll wear her hair, and how she didn't know if she could eat in front of him.

Amanda has had a crush on Robby since the second grade, and now that he's finally asked her out, she is all but floating.

"Amanda." I don't want to interrupt her euphoria, but I notice Mr. Galloway is in the cafeteria. Normally it wouldn't be weird to see teachers in the cafeteria during lunch, but never Mr. Galloway. He is notorious for bringing a ham and cheese sandwich, plain potato chips, and a Diet Coke in a plain paper bag. Every day. Every day, except today. Today he is standing near the door, watching. He's watching me with that same odd look he had earlier in his class. Amanda is still talking, obviously oblivious to Mr. Galloway or my interruption. "Amanda!" I hiss sharply.

She looks at me with an odd expression, but *that* look I understand. I heard the power in my voice, too. I hadn't meant to sound so harsh, but I needed to get through her endless babble. "What? What's wrong?"

"Don't look, but Mr. Galloway is in here." We're standing in line, waiting for our turn to see today's mystery food, and I nod slightly toward the double doors of the lunchroom.

Amanda takes her time and nonchalantly glances in the direction I nodded. She looks a little surprised to see him, but I don't think it was a good enough excuse to cut into her 'Robby talk' from the displeased look on her face. "So what? Maybe he forgot his lunch."

"He has his lunch in his hand, but he's just standing there," I tell her.

"Well, maybe he just wanted to have some company today," she says, even though she doesn't believe it. Mr. Galloway never wants company.

"It's not just that he's here, really. It's the way he's looking at me," I whisper. "He started this whole staring at me thing in History class, and now he's followed me here."

"Are you sure you're not just imagining things, Ana? I mean, sure, you're hot, and, no, I'm not into you. I'm into Robby, but still. Mr. Galloway is a teacher."

We walk towards our table, and I steal another glance in his direction. Yep, he's still staring at me.

"Ha ha. Thanks for that, Amanda, but I'm not imagining it." We sit down, and I make sure Amanda is positioned to look over my shoulder and see that I'm not imagining anything. "Look at him. He's still watching me, isn't he?"

Amanda peeks over my shoulder, and I see her eyes widen. "Omigod, he totally *is*!" She peers at me suspiciously. "What did you do?"

"What did *I* do? I didn't *do* anything!" Okay, so I was reading a gossip mag in his class, sure, but what was he going to do about it? Give me detention when I could read magazines daily in his class and still have a perfect grade?

"He's just staring at you. It's kinda creepy." Amanda shivers a little.

"It's more than kinda creepy," I tell her. In fact, I'm getting irritated at being watched like a hawk. I turn, my eyes meeting his, and feel a jolt of recognition. There's something there, something I recognize from a distant past. Of course, that is entirely impossible. But it's enough to bring that distant past rushing to my present. "*Impossible.*"

"What?" I hear Amanda's question penetrate my thoughts, and I turn back to her, breaking the connection to my history.

"Nothing. Let's go. This is getting a little too freaky."

"But I didn't eat!"

"I'll buy you a burger at Jake's," I grab my tray and start to get up from my seat when I feel a sharp pain in my stomach. The pain disappears as quickly as it comes on, leaving me with such a sick feeling of dread. Worse, I can still feel his eyes on me.

"Ana, I'm hungry now. I mean, this isn't the greatest food, and I'd *kill* for a burger from Jake's, but I can't wait 'til after school!"

"I know, we're going now." It's my turn to get annoyed with Amanda and her stalling. I just want to get out of there and away from Mr. Galloway.

"We can't skip school!"

"Amanda, we're seniors. It's a rite of passage to skip school." I sigh when she just sits there. "Fine. I'm going. You can stay here and eat your mystery food if you want. I'll think about you when I'm eating a big, juicy burger..."

"Okay, fine! I'm coming. But, if I get in trouble and my parents ground me, and I miss my date with Robby, I will *never* forgive you!"

As I enter my small one-bedroom apartment, I throw my keys on the table. It's not the accommodations I am used to, but I'm going for modest and humble. I must sacrifice in a few areas, like my kitchen being too small. Hell, the whole apartment is smaller than the kitchen I am accustomed to cooking in. But I find that I enjoy the cramped, homey apartment. It suits the lifestyle I portray here in California. I decorated it in a modern contemporary style with earth tones on the walls, splashes of color in throw pillows I threw on the microfiber sofa, and curtains hanging from floor to ceiling. A Lucite table and chairs give the space an impression of openness. Built-in bookshelves carry my favorite books and house my flat-screen TV. I love it.

All of my friends think it is cool that I live alone. Not many high schoolers do. They, of course, don't know my whole story, only that I am emancipated, and that's why I can live alone and not be in a foster home. At least, that's what I told them. Getting into the real story would mean explaining much more than I could. I already have to deal with my friends feeling sorry for me, knowing my parents are no longer alive. Of course, they are all curious about how they died, but they are courteous enough not to ask me too much about it. Only Amanda has asked me about them, and I made up a story of how they were killed in a car accident. What else could I say? They were murdered, and I set them on fire?

Lunch with Amanda had been interesting. She stuffed her face with Jake's famous juicy burger and fries while she talked non-stop about Robby and their long, non-existent love affair. I tried to listen, but a dull ache had replaced the sharp pain I had felt in the school cafeteria. It was a familiar feeling, but I didn't want to think of why. We had left school to escape Mr. Galloway's watchful eye. However, I still felt like I was being watched for some reason. Of course, Amanda was annoyed with me because my attention was not wholly on her. I apologized, telling her I had cramps and needed to go home and rest. She reluctantly forgave me – I think.

The cramps excuse wasn't exactly a lie. I just don't know why I'm having them now. Today has been very odd, I decide. I haven't felt this connected to my past in a very long time, and frankly, I don't like it.

A nap should help. I will merely sleep off the cramps and the odd feelings. I'm feeling optimistic as I head toward my bedroom. Then I feel the pain again, and it brings me to my knees. This time, with the pain, comes a craving I haven't felt in so long that I almost don't recognize it.

"What in the hell is going on," I whisper in the empty bedroom. I concentrate on my surroundings, willing myself to remain in the present and not slip back into my past. Taking deep breaths, I wait for the pain to subside. I sit there, rocking on the floor, holding my stomach. The hunger makes my head pound, my eyes burn, and my teeth ache. Crap. This can't be good at all.

"Get a grip, Ana. You're just thinking about the past because of what happened in school today. Let it go." I crawl to my bed and pull myself up into it. Pulling the covers over my head, I wait — and pray — for sleep to come.

CHAPTER NINE
"I KNOW WHO YOU ARE"

The cool breeze caresses my face as I creep down the dark alley. Unfortunately, it carries the stench of the garbage that lines the way. My boots click on the street, eerily echoing as I hum a cheery tune that doesn't quite fit the scene. I sense the group of guys watching me from the dead end, and I know exactly what I am walking into. It's what I want.

There are five of them, and they look menacing enough with their tattoos and piercings. They're all big — either muscular or fat — and I would guess each had to be near the 300lb mark. Perfect. Their smiles are ominous, and I hear them making vulgar suggestions about what they want to do to me. They speak in broken English and Spanish, but I understand every word and their intentions. It's not too difficult to know what they want from the beautiful girl that's stupid enough to walk down the dead-end street alone. Obviously, I was asking for it.

"Hey there, Mami. You come here looking for some fun. You found it." This comes from what looks to be the ringleader of the pack. He's huge, muscular, and has a face I don't even know his mother could love. When he smiles, I can see he has a diamond grill. At least that's what he wants everyone to think, but I can tell — even from this distance — that the diamonds are fake. So, he's a guy who wants to seem more important than he is.

I force myself to look timid. "I'm just out for a walk. I don't want any trouble," I say quietly.

"No trouble here," he laughs. "Just a good time."

I start to back away as they come toward me. At the same time, I brace myself for what I know is coming. "I'm sorry I interrupted your... meeting. I'll just go back this way."

"But you came all this way," another one says from behind the leader. "Look, we got beer and everything." He lifts the six-pack he's carrying to show me he's telling the truth.

"I don't drink. But th-thank you," I say, making myself stammer with fear. I hear the faint click of one of the guys opening a knife. Even better. They start circling me like vultures and keep discussing their plans, though I'm not listening anymore. Instead, I focus on the best way to take out the biggest first, then work my way through the rest.

"I get her first," the ringleader says, quickly lunging at me. Anticipating his move, I — with blinding speed — jump up and over him. While in the air, I grab his head between my hands and, with a quick twist, break his neck. As his limp body falls to the ground, I come down beside him and sink my teeth into his neck. I can hear the rest of the gang either gagging or shouting for me to get off of their leader. My head snaps up, and I snarl at them, my white eyes a sharp contrast to the red blood dripping off my fangs.

"No!" I shoot up in bed, a cold sweat rolling down my back. My entire body is shaking as I struggle to gain control. I look around frantically, wiping at my mouth. When I see no dark alley or blood, I regain a bit of composure. "Just a dream," I say in the darkness, although it doesn't make me feel any better.

The relentless pounding that I think is my heart pounding in my ears is actually someone banging on my front door. I reluctantly get up when the noise finally registers in my cluttered mind. I wrap a blanket around me, still feeling chilled to the bone by my dream, and pray it's not the police coming to arrest me.

"Who is it?" My voice sounds like I've been gargling sand.

"Ana? Open up!"

Confused, I open the door. "Zac? What are you doing here?"

"Seeing if you're alive! Jeesh, maybe you could answer phone calls or something once in a while." He pushes his way into my apartment without invitation.

"What are you talking about? I'm not feeling well, so I'm napping. I guess I did not hear my phone." As a matter of fact, I'm not even sure where my phone is. "Why are you here?" I ask again as I begin searching for my missing phone.

I freeze in the middle of my search. If Zac is here and I've apparently missed many calls, that has to mean...

"Oh my God, is something wrong? Is Amanda okay?"

"Ana, everyone is fine. We're just worried about you." Zac looks at me as if I have gone completely insane.

Once I hear everyone is okay, I go back to rummaging around for my phone. I'm not quite sure what else to do. Zac being here and my dream still being on my mind has seriously made me feel that I *have* gone completely insane. "If everyone is fine, then *why* are you here, Zac?"

"Are you kidding? Ana, no one has been able to get a hold of you..."

"Wait. So you come banging on my door and waking me up from my nap just because people haven't gotten a hold of me for a couple of hours?"

"Hours? Ana, seriously, what is wrong with you?" Zac approaches me and puts his hand on my forehead as if checking for a fever. "You haven't been to school for two days!"

I swat his hand away from me. "Stop being ridiculous." Two days. My nap couldn't have been more than one or two hours, tops. "There's no need to exaggerate. What is so damned important?"

"I'm not exaggerating, Ana. It's *Friday*!"

I roll my eyes. "I *wish.* That would mean I wouldn't have to put up with your shit at school tomorrow." I know being mean is unnecessary, but I'm really not in the mood for his crap right now. The cramps are still there, my head is still pounding, and I am famished. *And* I still can't find my damn phone!

Zac sighs dramatically. "Look, I offered to come over here because

Amanda has her date with Robby tonight. She was going to cancel, but I told her I'd check up on you instead."

"Amanda's date is Friday night," I offer absently.

"*Exactly!*" Zac all but screams the word at me. I turn to look at him. His expression is...well, hard to describe. He gets even more frustrated when I say nothing and digs his phone out of his pocket. "Here! Look at the date!"

I take the phone — still wondering where mine was — and look at it. Stare at it. That can't be right. Friday. "Did you change the date on this?"

"Ana, you just saw me take it out and hand it to you. Turn on the TV. Call information. Do whatever you need to do to understand that it's been two days since anyone has heard from you."

"That's impossible. Zac, I don't remember..." I pause, trying to think about the last thing I *do* remember. Am I wearing the same clothes? If it's been two days, have I eaten? Have I been sleeping the whole time? Why was there a huge hole in my memory? "What was I wearing the last time you saw me?"

"Sorry, Ana, I'm a guy. I don't really look at what a girl is wearing. Maybe you could ask Amanda. I told her I'd have you call her as soon as I made sure you were still alive."

"I'm still alive," I say, even though, to my ears, I don't sound very convinced. "I'm sorry I worried everyone." I sit on the couch and push my hand through my hair – which I'm pretty sure resembles a bird's nest. Zac sits next to me and puts his hand on my thigh. Normally I would push his hand away, knowing how he'd like to cop a feel, but there was nothing sexual in the gesture. It was — concern.

"I'm worried about you, Ana. At first, I thought you were just playing hooky. No one to get on to you since you're emancipated, right? Amanda told me how Galloway freaked you out, so I thought maybe you just wanted to stay away for a while. But when we couldn't reach you...you should've answered your phone."

His reprimand reminds me that I still haven't found my phone. "I don't know where it is," I tell him wearily.

"I'll dial it," he says softly and takes his phone back from me. He punches a number and waits. "It's ringing."

I get up and walk around the small apartment, trying to listen for it, but I hear nothing. If it has been two days, the battery will be dead, or I could've left it on vibrate. Whatever the case, I don't hear it. "It's okay," I shrug. "I'm sure I'll find it." With days missing from my memory, not knowing where my cell phone was is the least of my problems. "Listen, Zac, don't tell Amanda about this."

He walks over to me. "If something is wrong, she'll want to help."

"I don't even know what's wrong. Let me figure it out first, then I'll tell her. Tonight is really important to her, and I don't want to mess it up."

"You sure?" Zac doesn't look convinced that he shouldn't say anything to my best friend about my lapse in memory.

"I'm sure. Just tell her I lost my phone, and I'm sorry I skipped out for a while." I think for a moment. "Tell her that what you thought was right. I just wanted to get away from Galloway."

"Fine. But I'm still worried about you, Ana. If this happens again, promise me you'll call me or go somewhere and get some help."

"I promise." Zac's a couple of inches taller than me, so I have to get on my tiptoes to give him a quick kiss on the cheek. Weakness — either from not eating or too much sleep — makes me fall into him. He catches me but doesn't immediately let me go, and I don't make a move to get away. Instead, I reach up again and kiss his mouth.

My kiss shocks him as much as it does me. But I can't seem to help myself. It's like I don't have control of my actions as I deepen the kiss, moving my body into his. Even if he wants to resist, I don't give him a chance. I tug him towards the couch and pull him down on top of me. This snaps Zac out of his shock, and he becomes more enthusiastic with the kissing and his hands. My own actions become more intense, and I dig my hands in his hair as he kisses my neck, nipping it with his teeth. The feeling of his teeth scraping against my skin is erotic to me, and it releases that hunger in me that I have tried to suppress for many years. I can feel the change coming on. Of course, deep down, I know it shouldn't be happening, but it doesn't stop me from feeling that familiar feeling. It's a feeling I hate and have been so glad — and lucky — to be rid of. At least, I thought I had been rid of it. But it takes over with Zac moving on top of me, kissing my neck. My eyes fly open, and I know, without seeing them, what they look like. I know they're white, rimmed with a blood red, with a hunger that can never be fully satisfied shining from them. I pull his hair, making him turn his neck towards my mouth. As I bare my teeth, ready to sink them into his golden skin, I hear the words in my head.

"*Fight it, Anala!*"

"Stop!" The familiar voice snaps me out of my trance, and I push Zac away from me. Unfortunately, I don't check my strength, and the push has Zac flying off the couch and into the wall. I try to calm myself, careful not to look Zac in the eyes. If how I feel is true — it couldn't be, could it — I don't want to take any chances of Zac noticing. I quickly get up and help him. "I'm sorry. You have to leave."

I practically run to the door, dragging Zac behind me, and wrench it open. I try pushing him out of my apartment, but he's resisting.

"Ana, wait! If I did something wrong, I'm sorry!"

"You didn't do anything, Zac," I tell him sincerely. But I can't look him in the eye to show him I mean it. If I have turned and he sees me, I will never be able to let him leave alive. "You have to leave. Please!"

"Ana..."

"Go! Now!" The hunger is trying to overpower me, and my voice holds the same power I had used against Amanda when she didn't listen to me today...or two days ago. I still can't believe that.

Zac backs away from me, and without another word, he turns and rushes out.

"I'm sorry!" I call out and quickly shut the door. He will probably not forgive me for this, and I don't blame him. But I couldn't risk hurting him. I walk slowly to the mirror that hangs near the door. Usually, I use it to check my appearance before going to school or hanging out with friends to make sure I look good. Now, I must use it to ensure I'm not going crazy. Or, maybe hoping I am. I lift my eyes and peer at myself. Everything seems normal except tangled hair and deep shadows under my eyes. I sigh. First with relief, then with utter confusion.

"What is happening to you?" I ask my reflection. Perhaps it is time for another dose of Papa's elixir. I haven't had to take it for years. I thought its effects had become permanent when the uncontrollable hunger and need for blood eventually subsided. Of course, I still need blood to sustain myself — I *am* Cursed — but I can also eat human food now to help the process. I keep bags of blood from the local blood bank for those urges that come during my weakest times, though it has not been this bad for decades.

I make my way to the bathroom and turn on the shower. Two days are gone with no idea what occurred. How does that happen? I glance once again at my reflection and grimace. A good-looking guy in your apartment, ready and willing to have sex with you, and you look like this? How does *that* happen?

I feel a little more human (ha) after my shower and even more so after I have something to eat. I try thinking about the last couple of days, or what I can remember of them, and all I can come up with is that the weird feeling Mr. Galloway gave me made me focus on my past. Focusing on my past has made me think about all the changes I underwent back then. That has to be why those feelings are so strong now. It's the only explanation.

I curl up on the couch and flip through channels hoping to find something that will catch my interest and keep me awake. I'm not quite ready to go back to sleep yet. Who knows when I'd wake up this time?

"Ana!" Amanda bangs on the door, yelling simultaneously. Usually, I am very tuned into my surroundings, and I should've known she was here. Then again, things haven't been usual lately.

I open the door and pull Amanda inside. "Are you crazy? It's after one in the morning! You're going to wake up everyone in the building!"

"Sorry, sorry. I just came by to see for myself that you were okay." She is slurring her words a bit, and I can smell a hint of alcohol on her breath as she hugs me.

"Are you drunk?"

"What? No, of course not! I mean, I drank a little, but I'm not drunk." She giggles and plops on the couch. "So? Are you okay?"

"Yeah, I'm fine. Did you talk to Zac?"

"A little. He wasn't too happy, though. Robby tried to get him to say what was bothering him, but he didn't. What happened? I mean, we didn't push that hard, 'cause we were, you know, at a party and all, but..."

"I got it!" I snap.

"Well, if you were this bitchy with him, then I understand what was wrong with him," Amanda frowns tipsily at me.

"I'm not trying to be bitchy. I'm sorry, I'm just not feeling very well. Nothing happened between Zac and me." I sit down next to her and bump her shoulder, trying to get her to stop frowning at me. "Tell me about this party. I thought you were going to the movies."

"If you'd been at school or at least *called* me, you would've heard about the party. Everyone missed you. Especially the guys." Amanda giggles again like she just told the funniest joke.

"How much did you have to drink, Amanda?"

"Not much. Really! But maybe a little too much to go home. I kinda told my mom I was going to stay here."

I quickly weigh the options in my head. If I have another 'episode' — that's the only thing I can think to call it — then she would be here and could tell me what happened. On the flip side, if something was wrong with me — really, really wrong with me, and I couldn't control it – then I could possibly hurt Amanda.

"It's fine if I stay here, right?"

"Yes, it's fine." What else can I say? She's my best friend, and she needs my help.

"Thank you, thank you, thank you! I take back my bitchy comment!"

I can't help but chuckle. "Are you hungry?"

"Nah, there was pizza at the party." She yawns, and I know there won't be any more conversation. There also won't be any television to keep me occupied. I bring Amanda her usual blanket and pillow she uses when she stays over and toss them to her.

"Sleep off the booze, lush," I tease and leave her to get ready for bed. I sit on my bed, still scared to lie down and sleep. "You never used to be this spineless," I chastise myself. Disgusted with myself, I turn off the light and lie down to sleep.

"How long does a damn hangover last?"

"I have no sympathy for you." I hide my grin from the whining Amanda and pour her a cup of coffee. "I hear raw eggs and Tabasco helps."

"Ugh! Shut up! You're making me sick," she moans, laying her forehead on the table.

"This will teach you not to drink. You're not old enough to be drinking anyway." I place her coffee down beside her.

"You sound like an old lady," she teases. Funny thing is, I feel like an old lady after the last few days.

"Drink some coffee. Maybe it'll help your head." I take a seat and study her. She looks pale from nausea, but I can still see a hint of a smile. "Do you want to talk about your night?"

Amanda's smile widens, and she lifts her head to take a sip from her cup, grimacing either at the heat or the taste, I'm not sure which. "It was amazing! Robby looked so cute! He told me I looked 'hot.' Can you imagine? He really likes me!"

"Of course he does. Why wouldn't he?"

"Please, Ana. Guys totally fall in love with you all the time. I mean, you're gorgeous, but me? It's not so easy for me."

I'm not sure whether to feel flattered or sorry. "Amanda, stop it. You're a beautiful girl and fun to be around. Anyone who can't see that isn't worth your time. I'm glad Robby sees that in you. You've been crushing on him forever."

"True, I have. I finally have a boyfriend! I mean, I think I do. I felt so great walking into the party with him. We haven't really talked about it yet, but we kissed!"

"Well, if you kissed, you *must* be dating." I grin at her.

She goes on and on about her night, how Robby thought she was cool for playing drinking games with him, holding hands, and dancing. At the end of the *long* and very detailed description of the night, she finally eyes me suspiciously. "Anyway, tell me where and what you've been doing. I can't believe you didn't tell me you were skipping out! You could've called me!"

Here we go—the talk I've been dreading. But, knowing Amanda, I know I can't avoid it. She had a knack for not forgetting things and being relentless when she wanted to know something.

"I know, I know. I'm sorry. I lost my cell." It's not much of an explanation, but it's all I know to be true. "I wasn't planning on skipping. I just didn't feel well. Besides, Galloway really did freak me out. I thought staying away for a few days would be best."

Amanda doesn't look completely satisfied by my answer, but her head is pounding too hard to care. It has to hurt. I can see the pulse beating in her temples and imagine the blood in her veins that ever so slightly protruded from her forehead. I feel the damn hunger rise in me again, and I get up quickly to find something strong enough to distract me. I busy myself by pouring another cup of coffee and practically sticking my nose in it, breathing in the bitter smell. It's not quite enough to mask the scent of blood, but it helps.

"What's with you, Ana? You've been acting kind of weird lately."

Leave it to Amanda to tell me exactly how she feels, I think grumpily.

"I told you I haven't been feeling well," I retort, immediately regretting my tone. "Sorry. I don't know what it is. I've been exhausted, and I've been having odd — cravings."

Amanda's head snaps up. "Are you pregnant?"

"Don't be ridiculous! Exactly how am I supposed to be pregnant? Unlike you, I don't even have a boyfriend."

"Well, I don't know what you do here by yourself all the time. You could have orgies for all I know."

"Orgies? Now would I do that and not invite you?"

"Okay, eww." Amanda tilts her head and studies me for a bit. "Maybe you should go see a doctor."

"Maybe." It's as non-committal as I can be, and still give her an answer she would accept.

"I thought your phone was missing." Amanda eyes me accusingly when we both hear a faint ringing from my living room.

"It is – was! Ask Zac! I looked for it everywhere." I follow the sound and find my damn phone right under my coffee table! I *know* I looked there. Didn't I?

"Right. Look, Ana, if you don't want to tell me something, just don't tell me. You don't have to lie to me."

"Amanda, seriously, I didn't lie..."

"I'm going to go now. You really should see a doctor, Ana. You're not acting like yourself."

With that, Amanda walks out my front door. I know better than to go after her now. I'll let her cool down and talk to Zac to ask him about the phone situation. Everything will be okay with her when she hears I didn't lie. If not, I'll have to worry about that later. Right now, I have to figure out what the hell is going on in my life!

I pick up my phone – still can't believe it's been here the whole time – and check it. There are tons of missed calls and texts from my friends. I already know what they say, so I don't bother going through them. I delete everything, set the phone down on the coffee table in plain view, and hear the signal for a new text message.

"That didn't take long," I say aloud. Amanda must've been on the phone with Zac the moment she walked out my door. But it's not Amanda.

I know who you are. . .Anala.

The phone falls from my hand. I can't move. This must be what being in shock is like, and it's not a feeling I like. I haven't felt this out of control since I lost my parents. It is starting to piss me off. I *will* figure out what's going on and find out what Mr. Galloway has to do with it.

CHAPTER TEN
"SOMETHING WEIRD"

The rest of the weekend was uneventful – thank God. There were no more lapses in memory (that I know of anyway), no more creepy texts. I'm feeling fine despite everything that's going on. A little...worn out, but okay. It is another feeling I'm not used to. That seems to be happening a lot these days, which is also pissing me off. To say I'm a control freak is an understatement, so I need to regain control of my life.

This morning is dragging. Mondays usually do, but this is ridiculous. I can't seem to concentrate on anything. At least Amanda is talking to me again after verifying my story with Zac. I should be mad that she didn't just believe me, but honestly, I have more important things to worry about. I just have to get through English class, and then I'll finally get to history class.

"You mourning?"

I glance up to see Zac standing in front of me. He is smiling, but it doesn't quite reach his eyes. I know he's thinking about the last time we were together. Looking into his eyes, I can tell it is all he has been thinking about the entire weekend.

"Excuse me?"

"All black today. You don't see that much here in Cali. Usually, people go for light colors."

My black slacks and buttoned-up black shirt were comfortable for me. More so than the bright colors Zac spoke about. "I'm not that usual."

"*Isn't that the truth.*" He says it under his breath, but it's loud and clear to me. I pretend not to hear him—there is no reason to make it worse between us. "Black looks good on you. It makes your eyes look almost silver. It's nice."

"Thanks. Look, Zac, about the other night..."

"Don't. Nothing happened. It's all good."

He smiles a little and then walks away. I always thought Zac Connor was a bit self-absorbed. I didn't realize until just then what a good guy he really was.

"You okay with going in here? I mean, you're not still creeped out by Mr. Galloway, are you?" Amanda is one of those who wears the bright colors you're supposed to wear. Her hot pink skirt with a soft pink baby tee is enough to make me sick to my stomach. Maybe it's because it reminds me of a certain antacid.

"Nah, I got this." My smile is confident and cheerful. When you spend most of your life pretending you're something you're not, a fake smile is child's play. I glance in Galloway's direction; sure enough, he is watching me. I match his gaze, turning up the heat until he looks away. It seems I've succeeded at making him a little uncomfortable today. Ironically, I'm unsure if that makes me feel better or more confused about what is happening.

"Have a seat, ladies and gentlemen."

Mr. Galloway stands and walks to the front of his desk. He looks the epitome of a teacher with his khaki pants and Argyle sweater vest over a light blue, long-sleeved shirt. He's one of the younger teachers here, and with his light brown hair and hazel eyes, I would've thought he was good-looking enough if it weren't for that bit of spit on his bottom lip that stretched each time he spoke.

"Today, we're going to do something a bit different. We're going to learn about vampires."

If it were possible, my heart would've stopped beating at that moment. The weirdness is getting absurd, and seriously, enough is enough.

I raise my hand. "Mr. Galloway, this is history class, not science fiction."

"Science fiction, Ms. Gale?"

"Vampires do not exist. History class is about what happened in the past, not about fictional monster stories."

I can hear the murmurs of those around me. They know, as well as I do, that this is the longest conversation anyone has actually had with Galloway.

"Vampires have not been discounted, Ms. Gale. Even if there's not much proof they existed, there's also no proof that they didn't. It is said that Vlad the Impaler was a vampire."

"Seriously? Vlad was a power-hungry monster who killed innocent people he thought challenged his authority. He killed children and women. He may have fed the flesh of his victims to their friends and relatives, but it was never said that he drank the blood of his victims."

"You seem to know a lot about Vlad, Ms. Gale."

"I know history, Mr. Galloway. Real history."

"Then you know Vlad inspired Bram Stoker's Dracula."

"That is also speculation. Bram didn't know much about Vlad. By your standards, you must think Bram's novel truly depicts vampires."

"I think, of course, that there are a lot of fabricated instances in the book. However, I do believe there are parts of truths."

"Then you're an idiot."

Gasps came from all around me.

"You are out of line, Ms. Gale." I notice that when Mr. Galloway is upset, the spittle on his lip sprays.

"Mr. Galloway, you are trying to teach these kids about monsters that do not exist. I can't imagine this is on your curriculum list to teach."

"Who is the teacher here? Can you say for certain that vampires, in fact, do *not* exist – Ms. Gale?" His pausing before saying my name and looking at me sends chills down my spine. It renders me speechless. There's nothing I can say about that—no way for me to answer. So I sit quietly, waiting, while he passes out literature on the 'undead.' The rest of the class seems genuinely excited to read about something other than "boring old stuff."

He stops at my desk and lays an ancient copy of Bram Stoker's *Dracula* in front of me. It's a first edition. In fact, it is one of the first copies ever published. I know this because it's mine.

"Where did you get this?"

"I know you've probably read this already, but perhaps you could reread it. Just as a refresher." It's all he says before giving me a creepy smile and returning to his desk.

I don't open it — yes, I'm stubborn. I refuse to be intimidated by this new, weird Mr. Galloway. I don't know what happened to him, but I will find out in — I check my watch — twenty more minutes. Geez, sometimes time goes by so tortuously slow.

I turn around and reach for the note that Amanda is in the midst of passing to me. I ignore the shocked look on her face. She's wondering how I knew she was about to tap me on the shoulder, but I'm too engrossed in my own thoughts to worry about it.

"Are you crazy? Why did you argue with Mr. Galloway like that? At least now we can read something interesting!" I have to read the note three times — I just can't concentrate.

"As I told him, this isn't science fiction class. I don't think it's right to make us read about history or characters that didn't exist. Interesting or not." I return the note to her, rolling my eyes at her annoyed look. When I get the piece of paper back, I know for certain Amanda is annoyed.

"There's something weird going on with you. You've changed. Let me know when you see my best friend again."

Before I can respond, the bell signaling the end of class rings. I don't move.

"You coming?" I'm surprised that Amanda is speaking to me at all.

"No. I need to speak to Galloway first."

"I kinda enjoy this new reading material. I mean, seriously, it's entertaining. Don't ruin it." With that, Amanda walks out.

I wait until Amanda closes the door, then turn my attention to Mr. Galloway. He rises from his seat and addresses me.

"Would you like to argue further about my choice in curriculum, Ms. Gale?"

"I want to know where you got my book, *Mr. Galloway*," I observe him carefully, trying to see anything that will alert me to what is happening. He turns quickly, however, so I don't see anything.

He begins erasing words on the whiteboard. To me, it seems like busy work. It's like he's trying to avoid face-to-face conversation with me. "I have no idea what you're talking about, Anala."

It takes me half a second to realize what he had called me. It takes me the other half of a second to reach him. With my hand around his neck and his feet inches off the ground, my eyes bore into his.

"Who are you?"

Though he looks scared, he seems even more interested in my strength and speed.

"Who are you!" I repeat. I grit my teeth, hoping it helps keep me in control.

"You know who I am. I'm Jared Galloway..."

"Stop lying!" I tighten my grip, knowing I could squeeze just a little harder and snap his neck. "Tell me who you are, or I swear I will break you."

"I can't breathe, Anala, please!" He grips my wrist with both hands and fights with every bit of his strength. It makes no difference, as I don't budge. I won't until I know how he knows my name.

"We've met, Anala. You were younger, then, but you know me!" His voice is strained, trying to take in even the tiniest of breath.

Younger? That's not possible. No one is alive from when I was younger. I look into his eyes, past the teacher, into his soul. I remember the week before when I had felt a familiar feeling as he looked at me. At that moment, it hit me. I *do* know him! I loosen my grip and set him down.

"*Bernard?*" Even to my own ears, my voice sounds small and almost inaudible. I take a step away from him, refusing to believe my eyes. "How? Why?" So many questions run through my head, yet I can't form more than these two words.

"I know you need answers, Anala, and so do I. I thought you had *died* centuries ago." He rubs his neck. "I must finish the day as this Galloway, and then I will be free to meet with you to discuss everything."

Galloway. If this isn't my teacher, where is he? Yeah, he is a loner and a bit of a bore, but I don't want anything to happen to him. "Where is he? What did you do to him?"

"He is well. I did not hurt him. I just needed to get into this class. There is a reason I chose this man, but I cannot explain yet."

My head is spinning. *Some* of what is happening to me begins to make sense: the intensified hunger, the odd dreams. I must have recognized Bernard from the beginning; I just couldn't let my mind accept the possibility. *Most* of what is happening makes no sense at all. Bernard shouldn't be here.

"Your explanation better come quick, Bernard. I have no patience left for everything I'm feeling."

I didn't wait for his response. Now that I know who he is, it only confuses me more. I need to get away from him before I do – or become – something I don't want.

CHAPTER ELEVEN
"BUILD YOUR ARMY"

I stand in front of the enormous house, just looking at it. It seems more like a castle – minus the moat. It almost makes me laugh at how stereotypical it is. The thirty thousand square foot home stands sprawled on hundreds of acres of plush green land. At least it isn't sitting atop a dark mountain with black clouds, rain, and lightning flashing every few seconds to show a sinister, dilapidated, haunted mansion.

This house could be a home. It is open, airy, and inviting despite its enormity. Yes, the gray stone it is built with lends it a cold exterior, but the inside is full of warmth. I made sure of that when I designed the place. I walk through the gates that keep curious out and up the long, well-manicured walkway. I'm smart enough to keep landscapers and maintainers of the house on the regular payroll—no need to let something so grand fall apart. Obviously, since I'm here now, it was great foresight on my part.

I see him standing at the front door. I suppose I should question how he got in the gates, but I have too many other things to worry about. Clearly, he has his ways, especially since he is still alive today. He looks like himself now, which I must admit I'm not sure if I'm grateful for. But seeing Bernard as my high school history teacher was beyond weird.

"Bernard." I walk by him and use my keys to open the door to my home.

"Thank you for meeting with me."

"Like I have a choice." I motion him inside and close the door. We stand in the regal foyer decorated in imported Italian marble and rich cherry wood. The grand staircase seems as though it could reach up to the heavens. That description is even more fitting when you look to the top of the stairs and see floor-to-ceiling windows with a panoramic view of blue skies and white clouds.

"I would offer you a drink or a seat, but I don't want to. All I want is for you to tell me what's happening."

"Maybe you should offer me a seat for this, Anala." To his credit, Bernard doesn't make a move. He just stands there, waiting for my answer.

"Ana."

"Excuse me?"

"My name is Ana. If you want me to keep talking to you, you'll call me by my name."

"Your name is Anala. You are the daughter of the leaders...."

"Stop! I don't know why you're here or what you want from me, but what I want is for you to call me Ana. No one knows me as Anala here, and that's how I'd like to keep it."

"Very well, Ana." Calling me what he isn't used to takes effort, but he does it. He follows me into the parlor, another open space with light flowing in from the vast windows. The vaulted ceilings make the furniture appear almost minimal, though there's enough seating for a group of twenty or more. More of the imported Italian marble flows in from the foyer, surrounding the fireplace that is the focal point of this room. The mantle is made of more of the rich, handcrafted cherry wood. I love how it gives the room such an artistic feel.

"Why are you here, Bernard? More importantly, *how* are you here?"

"I am guessing the same way you are, Anala – Ana." He looks uncomfortable, fidgeting in his chair. When I don't respond, he continues. "Your father's mixture of Cursed blood and...whatever else he used. Would you know what that is? Never mind, we will get to that later." He pauses.

"There have been sightings – killings, rather. I believe Cursed Ones have returned. I came here in search of Hunters. Imagine my surprise when I found you. What an added bonus to having a real Hunter helping us deal with this as quickly as possible. We cannot let it become an epidemic."

"I don't understand. It can't be possible that there are more. I took care of them myself a long time ago. I hunted down all of them, Bernard."

"It is possible that you missed one, Ana. You are only human."

"No! Bernard, no. I made sure I eradicated all of them. If your statement is true, it's not because I failed. This isn't my problem anymore. I want to live my life as normally as I can. Hunters no longer exist in this world."

"I'm sorry, Anala, it is true. Hunters do exist. You are here! Others may not have the training you have, but they are here, somewhere, born of their ancestors. I believe they go to school with you. Please, there's no other way."

"I won't do it. I will not endanger anyone else and will not return to that life."

"I'm afraid you have no choice."

I stand up abruptly, unable to sit still anymore, furious beyond belief. "I *do* have a choice, Bernard. How dare you come here and put this on me."

"*I* have no choice. I know, just as you do, what these things can do. You were born a Hunter. You are bound by the rules of the Society. You must find the rest and teach them the way of the Hunter."

"No. Hunters ceased to exist. The Society ceased to exist centuries ago when I — Hunters — eliminated the threat." I try to think back to those days. Is it possible that I missed one? Two? "How in the hell is it possible that they are back?"

"Anala, Hunters do not just go away. Being who you are, I am fortunate to have found you. You know what's happening, and you know how to stop it. Again."

"I *don't* know what's happening, Bernard!" I pace the room, fury and confusion battling for the top spot in my head. I really could rip someone's head off right now.

"I'm still trying to figure out what is happening myself. The only explanation I have is you must have missed..."

"This isn't my mistake, Bernard. I got rid of every last one of them."

"Can you be sure? Do you still have the brew your father made? You must if you are still alive. Could someone have gotten to it? A friend you have invited into your home? You seem to be very trusting of those around you these days. Maybe sold it to the highest bidder for luxury like this?" Bernard says, spreading his arms in the grand room.

"Do you think I did this? That I could do that to my father?" It's insulting that he would even entertain the idea.

"I have no other explanation if what you say is true and you killed them all." He runs his hands over his face, and I take a moment to study him. He's older than me — my actual age — but he still looks like he could be in his early forties. My keen sight notices that stress makes his features look more weathered than usual.

"You stole from him." It isn't a question. It is an accusation. Ages ago, I remember Papa telling me how he did not trust Bernard.

"I am sorry, Anala. He gave me no other option. Before you were thought to be dead, I knew your father was working on a cure for whatever ailed you. What he came up with granted whoever took it a long-lasting life. It was far too enticing for me not to want that for myself. Of course, you know that already. He must have given it to you. I do not understand why they did not stop the rumors of your death, though."

"Not aging can be difficult to explain," I say, offering him nothing more.

"That is true." He shrugs, deciding that my explanation is good enough for him.

I see him wringing his hands in obvious discomfort. "What are you not telling me?"

"My supply is running out."

My thoughts return to Papa's lab and how many vials of my blood he took. He told me once that one drop could cure a disease or stop the aging process for years. If Bernard had been the one who had my parents murdered — with as many vials that were stolen — Bernard should be well-stocked for centuries to come.

"We all run out of time, eventually, Bernard." I need a drink. All this information, thinking about the past and my parents, and having Bernard here gives me a splitting headache. Walking to the wet bar, I know that what I want and need are two different things. I choose tequila, though I know it will not quench my thirst. Only one thing can do that now, and that aggravates the hell out of me.

"Ana, I — I thought I had enough to last many more years," he stammers. "However, I barely have any left, and I already feel the effects."

He's lying. I don't know exactly what he's lying about, but I know he's lying.

"Do you have extra you can give me? I've been trying to duplicate your father's formula — with synthetic blood, of course," he says quickly. "I have not been able to. Perhaps pure Cursed blood is the only thing that works."

"I would not ask for any favors if I were you, Bernard. I am not in a giving mood." I down the first shot of tequila, relishing the burn as it slides down my throat. "What now," I ask.

He's disappointed by my rejection but says nothing more on the subject. "Now we must find the others. I suppose you would know better than I who they are since you hunted with their ancestors."

"These 'Hunters' do not know who they are or what they're up against. Cursed Ones, or vampires as they're known now, are fiction to people these days, Bernard. Made-up villains in horror movies. Or romantic figures for young, impressionable girls."

"It is your challenge to make them believe and get them ready. You are their leader now. The head of the Society."

"Awesome," I say sarcastically and take another shot.

"You seem to be popular, looked up to. It shouldn't be hard for you to get their attention."

"It depends on who *they* are," I mutter.

"Anala, you must keep an open mind. In order for them to follow you, you must be a true leader."

"This is insane, Bernard. If that's why you took over Galloway's body to look for Hunters at the school, they are just children! You cannot expect them to put their lives on the line."

"No younger than you or your fellow Hunters were before, Anala."

"The difference is, Bernard, centuries ago, Hunters knew who they were, what they were up against, and were prepared since birth for their destiny. If killings have already begun, you know we don't have the time to train mere children."

"From what I've determined, there are full Cursed Ones and Hybrids. Too many for just you, Anala. We have a little time before the Hybrids become full and are able to turn others. You can use that time to build your army, but it needs to be done quickly."

"You are asking me to lead children to their deaths, Bernard. These are friends of mine. If they are descendants, that means their parents are as well. Why can't they do this?"

"Do you think adults will take orders from you, whom they see as a child?"

"Do you think they will feel it's better to risk their children? They will never go for that either."

"The children are our best shot, Anala. I can take care of the parents. Get them out of town and occupy them so they will not interfere. All you must do is convince the Hunters to work with you. Do you know where to start?"

"Yes. Unfortunately, I do."

CHAPTER TWELVE
"SAM"

Reluctantly, I knock on Amanda's front door and wait. I have no clue how I will convince this seventeen-year-old girl – still beaming from having a boyfriend – to learn to fight 'fictional demons.' She already thinks I'm crazy. This might make her want to send me to the loony bin.

Lost in my thoughts, trying to find the right words to say, I don't notice when the door opens. But the scent I'm hit with takes me back to a boy I once knew a long time ago.

"Yes?"

He looks angry. I would think he was angry with me if I hadn't just gotten there. Irritated or not, he's pretty hot. He's tall and built quite nicely. His hair is a silky wheat color. I almost want to run my fingers through it just to see if it's as soft as it looks. But it's his eyes that intrigue me the most. It's not so much the golden color of them; it's how clear they are. They make me feel as though if he looked at me close enough, he would see exactly what I am. They also look like Thomas's did so many years ago.

I must have taken too long to answer him because he clears his throat. "Look, this isn't a good time..."

"Sorry. I'm looking for Amanda."

"As I said, it's not a good time."

I see Amanda round the corner then and roll her eyes. "Sam, stop being an ass and let Ana in."

Sam. I quickly search my memories and remember Amanda often talked about her brother. I had never met him. He had moved out by the time I entered Amanda's life. From what I recall, Amanda told me he was a cop. Isn't that just perfect.

"So... you're the infamous Ana."

"Excuse me?"

"Don't mind him," Amanda says, pushing past him and taking my arm. "He's just grumpy."

"Oh. Okay." I let her guide me to the kitchen, where her parents are bustling around like they are in a hurry. A part of me is surprised to see them there. After all, Bernard had told me they wouldn't be in my way. I don't know what I thought they would be doing, but I didn't expect them to be here.

"Good evening, Mr. and Mrs. Logan."

"Ana! It's been so long since we've seen you." Amanda's mother hugs me, then returns to writing things down on one of the many pieces of paper in front of her.

"Ma, we should talk about this, and it's a *family* discussion." This comes from the broody Sam. He looks at me when he says 'family.' Apparently, I'm not welcome by Amanda's big brother.

"Sam, you're being rude. Besides, there's nothing to talk about."

"Your mother's right, Sam," Mr. Logan says as he stuffs papers in his briefcase. "We have not been on vacation for ages, and it won't hurt you to stay with your sister until we get back."

They're leaving. I guess Bernard did find a way to distract the parents.

"I don't need a babysitter," Amanda pouts.

"We know, honey, but we'd feel better if you weren't alone while we're away." Mrs. Logan pats Amanda on the shoulder. I'm always a little envious of those who had a loving mother. It makes me miss my mother, even after all these years. Mrs. Logan glances at me and smiles. "Maybe you should stay here as well, Ana."

"Thank you, Mrs. Logan, but I'm used to being alone."

Her smile turns almost sad. She feels sorry for me. I'm unsure what

Amanda told her parents about my situation, but they are always concerned about me. If they only knew the truth.

"Well, I wish you would change your mind. It's dangerous out there. Why just a few nights ago, there was a multiple homicide!"

"Mom, they were gang members. I mean, I'm sure that happens all the time." Amanda looks at me and, again, rolls her eyes. "Sam is a homicide cop, so Mom gets a little too into all this stuff."

I try paying attention, but my mind is reeling. Gang members, homicide. It has to be a coincidence. Right?

"It wasn't gang-related, Mandy." I hear Sam say. "Unless gangs are putting down the guns and breaking necks instead."

Oh, God. Could it be that my horrible dream wasn't a dream at all?

"Whatever. I don't know anything about gangs, and I'm smart enough not to go walking around in alleys after dark." She chooses a grape from the bowl on the counter and pops it in her mouth.

"Ana, dear, are you alright? You look pale."

Hearing my name brings me back to the Logan's kitchen and out of the alley from my nightmare. "Hmm? Yes, I'm fine." Desperate to change the subject, I ask Amanda's parents where they are off to.

"It's actually a work thing in England, but we're stretching it out to make it a vacation and invited a few friends. Andrew's company is picking up the check on accommodations, so why not? Oh! You're from there, right? It just seems so delightful," she continues without even giving me a chance to answer. "Speaking of, Andrew, did you remember the passports?" With that, my conversation with them is over as the doorbell rings again, and the chaos continues.

"Hey! You should come stay with me! It'll be fun!" Amanda is starting to get excited about the possibility of a long slumber party when Sam chimes in with his cheerful self.

"Look, I don't need to look after another kid. It's bad enough I have to stay here with you. I have a life, you know." He raises his voice enough on the last part so that his parents can hear.

"Neither of us are kids, jerk." Amanda throws a grape at him. It doesn't really demonstrate her not being a kid, but it is quite funny when it hits him the squarely in the forehead. Good aim.

Just then, Amanda's parents come back in, flocked by other adults.

They all seem to be talking at once with excitement, discussing what attractions they want to visit and occasionally asking for my opinion. I answer politely and study them carefully.

"I can't believe you invited us on this trip! Oh, it's been so long since we've been away from the children." I hear one whisper. She's a slight, blonde woman I recognize from different events as Mrs. Connor —Zac's mom.

"I know. I love my children, but I am so ready to get away." I hear another say. I don't recognize everyone, but I assume these are the parents of some of the kids on the list I gave Bernard, whom I thought the Hunters were. Sadly, I doubt some of them will even notice their kids are not around when they return from vacation.

I sit on Amanda's bed and pretend to read a glamour magazine she has lying around. Her parents have already left, and I can hear her brother mumbling grumpily to himself downstairs.

"Is your brother always this charming?"

"Actually, he usually is nice. I don't know what his problem is. I mean, I know he doesn't want to stay here, but he was fine before."

Before I came over, I assume. Sam is a Hunter, and I'm - well, more - but no Hunter has ever been able to 'sense' me.

"So? Are you going to stay over?" Amanda plops down beside me. "I think it would be nice. You've been distant lately, and I think there's more to it than Mr. Galloway."

Amanda is another that I've always seen as sort of self-absorbed. She never really cares about others unless it directly affects her. Now, I see she's more observant than she appears.

"I've been going through some things," I admit. I will have to tell her as much as I can if this is going to work at all.

She looks concerned. "Do you want to talk about it?"

"I have to because I'm going to need your help."

"You sound so serious." Amanda gets up from the bed to pace. She seems more nervous than I am. I wonder why.

"It is serious. I'm just not sure how you're going to react." I see her step falter.

"You *are* pregnant, aren't you?"

"What? Amanda, no, I'm not pregnant." I stand with her and block her pacing path. "I don't even know how to begin."

"I've always heard it's easier just to blurt it out. I mean, it's like a Band-Aid, right? The faster, the better." She starts fidgeting.

"This isn't the sort of thing you just blurt out," I tell her. Yes, I'm stalling, but I honestly don't know what to say. "Okay, um, you know the books that Ber- Mr. Galloway gave us to read? All of that stuff he was trying to teach?"

"Yeah."

"What did you think of it?"

"Seriously? Ana, what does school have to do with any of this?" She grabs my arms and squeezes. "Please tell me you are not having an affair with Mr. Galloway!"

"Gross! Of course not!"

"Did he come on to you? Do something to you?"

"No. No, no, no. Amanda, please focus."

"I'm trying! It'd be much better if you just told me what's happening!"

Sigh. "Amanda, the killings in the alley that you were talking about earlier, I believe they were done by...a vampire."

Silence.

Her burst of laughter takes me by surprise. "Come on. What's really going on?"

"I'm serious, Amanda," I begin to explain to her - as best I can - how the plague of vampires roamed the country centuries ago.

I tell Amanda the revised version of the past, of course. I explain to her that Anala is my ancestor, the daughter of the leaders of the Society of Hunters, leaving out the part that I/she was also a Cursed One. I tell her about her ancestors and how they were Hunters, which also makes her a

Hunter. Seriously, explaining how Cursed Ones - or vampires as we're known today - exist and it's up to us to stop them is beyond difficult.

Amanda just stares at me for a moment, then snorts. "I knew something was wrong with you! I mean, you've been weird the past few days, but this is too much!"

I desperately need to find some way to prove this to her. At this point, I wish I could show her what I am and be done with it. "I know it sounds a bit far-fetched..."

"Far-fetched!? Come on, Ana, this is just ridiculous!"

Okay, think Anala. I scan Amanda's room for anything that can help me.

"Do you have a letter opener?" Of course, my question only garners more odd looks from Amanda.

"A letter opener? Seriously?"

Ah, yes, this was the age of texting, Facebook, and Twitter. What does this generation need with an ancient letter opener?

"Fine. Do you have anything sharp? Scissors?"

"I have a pocketknife. Will that do?" I can tell she's confused by my request, but at least she's obliging me.

It's my turn to give her an odd look. Amanda Logan is so 'girly' that knowing she has a pocketknife just doesn't fit.

"Um, yeah, that will do fine." She starts to hand it to me, but I push it back to her. "Open it," I tell her. I walk over to the opposite wall as she does what I ask. Grabbing a pen from her desk, I draw a circle smaller than a dime on the wall.

"Hey! Why are you writing on my wall?"

"Relax, it's a tiny circle." I walk back to her. It's not as far as I want it to be, but it will do. "Can you see it?"

She squints toward the wall. "Barely."

"Throw the knife at it."

"What? Seriously, Ana, this is getting really..."

"Amanda, please. Do me a favor, don't argue with me, stop thinking I'm weird, and do what I ask." I'm putting a bit of persuasion into the request, but I don't overdo it. I need Amanda to decide to believe me on her own.

"Okay," Amanda agrees with a huff. She squints again, trying to focus on the small circle.

"No. Don't think about it. Don't try. Just do."

"But..."

"Amanda, just throw it!"

I think I scare her enough that she doesn't think of anything else except getting rid of the pocketknife in her hand. To her utter amazement, the knife sticks into the wall. She runs up to the wall to see if she even came close to the circle I drew.

"Shut up! I hit it! I mean, I really hit it! Dead center!" She does a little dance while singing, 'I hit it, I hit it.'

"Do it again."

"Huh?"

"Take the knife and do it again. Hit the same spot."

"Come on! That was just luck!"

"Amanda."

"Dang! You are being mean!" But she grabs the knife and walks back towards me.

"Remember, don't think..."

"Just do," she finishes and once again throws the knife. Once again, it sticks in the wall in the same place as before.

"Holy...how did I do that?" Amanda looks at me like I'm an Encyclopedia full of information.

"I told you. You are a Hunter."

"This is real? I mean, really real?"

"Yes."

"I can't believe this. Vampires? Hunters? This is all so... Twilight."

"Well, not exactly. Vampires aren't as nice as that." Except for myself, I think.

"How are we supposed to fight them? I mean, we're only two people. Two *girls*! Throwing a pocketknife at a wall is one thing, but fighting a real vampire?" She whispers the word as if they can hear her.

"It's not just us," I tell her. "We must recruit the others, and it will not be easy. Then, we'll have to train. You and the other Hunters will have to know how to kill the vamps." I see Amanda shudder when I mention 'kill.' Not sure what she thought we were going to do. Tame them?

"Who is going to train us? I mean, you said that Hunters were no longer needed, so who would know how to train us?"

"Let's get the others on board first. Then we'll discuss that." Because *that* is a whole other can to open up when they find out I will be training them.

I end up staying the night, talking about Cursed Ones and Hunters. Luckily for me, she really is into this stuff. I can only pray that the others will be this easy to convince.

As it turned out, it *wasn't* as easy convincing the others that I wasn't crazy. If I could've just *made* them believe me, that would've been less time-consuming and fantastic. But, as with Amanda, I needed them to agree to this on their own. I thought perhaps having Amanda with me when I talked to the others would help. At times it did - she seemed to rather enjoy doing the 'throw-the-knife-to-the-tiny-circle-on-the-wall' experiment - other times, not so much. Going down the list was weird, to say the least. Most of the names I came up with from memory of Hunters I worked with in the past didn't come as a shock. They all excelled at their talents. Whether it be the fastest swimmer, the great quarterback, or – a bonus for me – the best fencers. At least *they* would come in very handy when it came time to teach the new Hunters how to wield a sword.

Some surprised the hell out of me. The cheerleader captain? Really? Sure, she was a fine cheerleader, but unless she was faking it, she was as dumb as a whip! She was conceited beyond belief and extremely difficult to talk to, especially about something as important as this. I don't know why she decided to accept what I was saying, but my biggest concern was how I would train her. Hell, I had no idea how I was going to train any of these kids! All in all, I had an extremely eclectic group of extremely different personalities. I don't even know why they trust in me and blindly follow me to what could essentially be their death.

During school, we all pretty much remain in our separate groups. Why would we want to hang out together just because we're part of some elite group?

After school, Amanda needs to stop by her house, and then we'll all meet to talk about training. I'm glad that Sam's working today. He unnerves me in ways I can't explain. I thought it was because he reminded me of Thomas, but just the way he looks at me makes me feel like I'm either being interrogated or ravished by him. Only one sounds intriguing to me, though I would never tell Amanda that.

"I just need to get a couple of things, and then I'll be ready." We stop in our tracks when we see Sam standing there, beer in hand. Damn it! He's not supposed to be home yet. "Oh! Hey, Sam, you're home early!"

She looks at me, and I read the fear and guilt in her eyes. We both know Sam would never willingly let her fight against vampires. If he finds out what she's up to, I have no doubt he'd try to handcuff her to her bed, all in the name of safety. Sam's a cop. It's in his nature to try and fight the bad guys. Unfortunately, being a cop doesn't qualify him for this fight. There's also that little detail of how he would never believe me about the vampires. If, by some chance, he did, he would never take orders from me.

"I'm home on time, Mandy. Where have you been?"

"Over at Ana's. I'm going to stay over there tonight."

"I don't think so."

"Um, Mom and Dad let me stay over there all the time."

"Well, Mom and Dad aren't here, and they left me in charge, so you're not going. If you want to spend time together, she can stay here."

Times like these make me both glad to be an only child and a little sad. Honestly, though, Sam is really annoying me with the whole 'she' thing. The name's Ana, buddy.

"*She* is standing right here," I say testily. It's petty, I know, but whatever. Sam's attitude towards me is getting old. "And *she* would like to spend some time at her own home tonight."

"Sorry, but Amanda's staying home tonight."

I really don't have time for this. I'm running out of the time I need to get these Hunters – and I use that term loosely – trained. I don't know why Sam has to be such a hard ass.

"Ugh, you are such an ass, Sam! I mean, me going over to Ana's is so not a big deal!"

"Then it won't be a big deal for you to stay here, either." He says it with such finality. Apparently, he thinks the discussion is over. He obviously doesn't know me very well.

"Sam," I walk closer to him, keeping my eyes on his. I hear his heart beat faster and louder. He finds me attractive. I'm used to that from other men, but I never expected Sam to feel that way. "You've clearly had a couple of sleepless nights." I lower my voice, putting just a touch of power and persuasion behind it. "Wouldn't you like just to have a night where you didn't have to worry about two teen girls all night? We'll be perfectly safe at my place."

I see Sam's eyes glaze over just a bit. He's stronger than I give him credit for, but those sleepless nights I know he's having are working in my favor.

"Fine. Just be careful." And, with that, he leaves us alone.

"How in the hell did you do that? I mean, he *never* backs down!"

"I guess he's just overly tired and agreed with me," I shrug. "Go get your stuff, and let's get out of here before he changes his mind." I glance in the direction Sam went. I'm not sure how long my persuasion is going to last.

CHAPTER THIRTEEN
"IT'S YOU"

Amanda and I meet up with the others at Jake's. Everyone wants to eat, and though I really wish just to get started, I agree. No one speaks of what we're all together for. I imagine they were all still having a hard time believing it, even Amanda. So, I let them eat in peace. Reality is going to be a bitch for them when they realize this is actually happening. So, after an hour of awkward conversation and stuffing our faces with food, I tell everyone to follow me. It's time to get busy.

I pull up to the gate, punch in my code, and wait for the others to enter the gate before continuing up the long driveway.

"Holy crap! What is this place?" Amanda exclaims. She, as well as all the others, look around in complete awe at the estate. I had to bring them here. There's no way I'll be able to train them all in my tiny apartment.

"This is where we're going to train. It would be helpful if everyone could come here after school every day. Maybe you guys can even stay here while we train. There's plenty of room."

"You mean to spend the night?" Zac asks.

"Yes." I raise my hand, cutting off the next question. "Let's go in, and we can discuss everything." I unlock the door and push it open, ushering everyone in. Their awe continues as they walk in. These kids had money – well, their parents do at least – still, I can't imagine they've seen the likes of this place. I let them gawk.

"Ms. Gale, welcome home."

Bernard startles me. I wasn't expecting him to be here, and I especially wasn't expecting the 'Ms. Gale'. To my utter shock, he is dressed as a butler. Having him on my property was one thing. Having him in my house was something else altogether. This time, I intend to find out how he got in.

"I imagine it will be easier to explain me as your servant than what I truly am," he whispers as the others wander around.

"How did you get in?"

"I've been around awhile, Anala. You learn a thing or two."

"I don't appreciate you using those skills on my home." One of my first projects, change the locks and amp the security. "You're not my servant, Bernard, and I don't think you should be here."

"I do not mind acting as such to aid you. I want to help."

"Bernard, training is not a spectator sport. It is customary that only other Hunters be present when training is in session." I cut him off before he can argue. "You are the one who brought the rules of the Society up when you made me do this. Deal with it."

"Right. Well, I have set up the dining room to serve as a conference room. I thought it would be a good place to teach the young Hunters or discuss plans. I also have refreshments."

I sigh. He thought of everything. Yet, I still don't feel comfortable having him here. "We've already eaten."

"Well, perhaps just drinks."

I almost groan. I really need a drink. I'm starving, and it's a hunger no burger could satisfy.

"Thank you for setting everything up, but you still have to go," I tell him. "I'm sorry. Rules are rules."

Whatever else he was going to say was cut off when Amanda came running in.

"Ana! This place is uh-mazing! I mean, totally... just amazing! Seriously, whose place is it?" Everyone else follows her back into the foyer, where Bernard and I converse. They're all murmuring about the place.

"It's mine."

Amanda's jaw drops. I'm not sure if it was shock or anger, though. Knowing her, I imagine she would be pissed at me for keeping something like this from her.

"It's been in my family for years," I say by way of explanation.

"I can't believe you didn't tell me this!"

"I'm sorry, Amanda. I've just never had a use for it until now. It's only me; it would've been silly to live here by myself."

"Could you imagine the parties we could have in this place?" This nugget of brilliance is from Jeremy, the 'genius' quarterback. Thank God he was good at football because academics are not his strong suit. His brawn and athleticism will be his most significant assets as a Hunter.

"We're not here to party," I snap irritably and sigh again. "Look, I know everyone has a lot of questions. And I want to be able to answer them for you. But for now, I think it's best to show you where you'll spend most of your time." I push Bernard towards the door. "Goodbye. I'll be in touch."

After the grand tour, I take time as the others roam around to fix a 'drink' for myself. I hate that it tastes so good and satisfies me like nothing else. It doesn't energize me like I know taking blood from a live human would, but it's good enough.

I check the clock above the mantle. It's a school night, so it's too late to start training tonight after all the 'oohing' and 'ahhing' going on. Truth be told, I don't feel motivated to start training. This group isn't anything like the Hunters from years ago. They're undisciplined and unruly. It's like taking infants and teaching them to walk and talk. Of course, there's also the fact that they have had absolutely no hunting training whatsoever in their lives, no sword training – except for the kids that fenced – no real knowledge of Cursed Ones at all. I don't know if I have the patience for this. Even after all of the years I've lived, the one thing I never learned was patience.

I take my drink outside onto the terrace and look out over the expansive yard. The yellow, full moon slowly rises in the sky and looks enormous. I wish I could lose myself in the vastness surrounding me and not have to deal with the death and sadness that would come.

"How am I supposed to do this again?" I ask the emptiness around me.

"Ana?" Amanda strolls out onto the terrace. I should've known she was there, but I didn't. Damn it! My keen sense of awareness eludes me sometimes when I'm stressed. That worries me. I'm going to need time to myself at some point to practice everything my parents taught me. My body is strong, that I don't doubt. What I doubt is my ability to be strong in my mind and soul. Quickly I drop my glass into the bushes below and smile.

"Hey. Did everyone get settled in?"

"Yeah, but, I mean, are you sure it's a good idea for them to stay here? I can see the fights now. Well, after the orgies, that is."

I can't help but chuckle at the prudish 'eww' she let out.

"Once we start training, no one will have the energy to do much of anything but sleep. Don't worry so much, Amanda."

"Don't worry? Ana, you come to me and tell me that vampires are real and that I'm one of the 'chosen' ones to fight them. I mean, how am I not supposed to worry? What if I can't do it?"

"Amanda, I know this is hard for you to understand or even believe. I get that." I look her straight in the eyes, needing her to know I believe in her. "But you're a Hunter. The ability is in you. All you need is confidence."

"Hmm," is all I get from her in return. She leans up against the balcony railing and looks everywhere but at me. "So, who's going to be training us? That old guy?"

"Old guy?"

"Yeah, your butler or whatever he is."

"Bernard?" I laugh a little at the old guy comment. Imagine if she knew how old I really am. "First, he's not my butler. He was an associate of my father's. But, no, he's not going to be here. I'll be training you guys."

Now she looks at me. "You? Sorry, Ana, I mean, do you even know what you're doing?"

I grab at my heart, pretending to pull out a knife. "Ouch! Of course I know what I'm doing!"

"How about you tell me what you're doing."

"Sam!" I hear a bit of panic in Amanda's voice when she sees her brother. Hell, I feel a little panicked myself. "How did you...why are you here?"

If Sam found out about this place, he must have been checking up on me. That's all I need. And, apparently, he likes to invite himself in. Instead of confronting him, I keep silent. For now.

"You should be at home, Amanda. It's a school night."

Well, now I know compulsion doesn't completely work on him. I will have to keep that in mind.

"You said I could stay with Ana tonight. Don't you remember?"

"Yeah, well, I changed my mind."

He looks as confused as Amanda does about him changing his mind.

"That's too bad," Amanda says boldly. "I'm staying. In fact, I'm going to have to stay here for a while."

Sam laughs. "Are you crazy? There's no way."

Amanda looks at me with an apology in her eyes. "I have to tell him, Ana."

"Amanda, that's not a good idea." Now I'm panicking.

"Tell me what?" Sam is suddenly suspicious.

"Maybe he can help. I'm sorry, Ana, but he'll never let me stay if I'm not honest with him. Besides, if I'm...what you say, doesn't that make him one, too?"

Of course it does, but...well, shit, isn't this just great.

"Somebody better tell me what the hell is going on, and soon." Sam does not look amused at all. This is going to be fun.

"Ana?" Amanda waits for me to answer.

Damn it, I don't need this! My life was so simple just weeks before. Now I have to deal with Cursed Ones, untrained Hunters, and Sam.

"Do what you must," I tell Amanda and go inside.

I can't imagine him wanting to let us, especially his young sister, put ourselves in danger. Being a cop, he will think this fight is the job of the police force. Boy, is he in for a surprise. I can't persuade him to fight with me. I can't use compulsion on him. I can't make someone risk their life. I hope he doesn't make this too difficult for me.

I look out to the terrace. I can hear Amanda telling Sam what I told her about Cursed Ones. "He's never going to believe her," I say aloud.

There is only one way he, and possibly everyone in this house, will believe me. I'm going to have to go hunting.

For now, I keep an ear on the conversation between Sam and Amanda. I have to admit, I'm a little surprised that Amanda recalled the story I told her very well. At least I know she was listening. When I hear Sam snort out laughter, I know exactly why I left him off the list. This is definitely going to be a hard sell.

"Here we go," I say as Sam comes storming inside.

"Vampires? Really? This is the shit you're feeding my sister?" He's angry – what else is new when it comes to me?

"I'm not 'feeding' Amanda anything, Sam. Just because you can't believe it doesn't make it untrue."

"And just because you say it's so doesn't make it true," he counters. He throws his hands up in frustration. "Okay, let's say it is true. You're telling Amanda that she has to fight them? If I were to believe this crap, I certainly wouldn't let that happen."

"Sam, I didn't tell Amanda she *had* to fight. I simply gave her the information, and she made the decision herself. I didn't force her or anyone else to come here and train with me."

"Anyone else? You've told others about this?" He puts up his hands to stop me from answering. "Never mind. The only thing I want to know right now is if you have proof."

I can't help but sigh. The burden is beginning to overwhelm me. "I can get it," I tell Sam. "Give me an hour, and you'll have your proof." I start to walk away, but Sam grabs my arm. I probably would've broken his hand or thrown him across the room if I hadn't been so confused by how I felt when he touched me. Okay, maybe not, but I didn't particularly appreciate being manhandled that way.

"No," he says. "If you're going somewhere, I'm going with you."

Damn, he really does think he's in charge, doesn't he? "I don't think so." Yes, I'm bitchy, and yes, I snatch my arm away. So what? He doesn't deserve any better with the way he's treating me. "If you want proof, you'll stay here with Amanda and let me do what I need to do."

I don't wait for a response; I just leave him with his sister and walk out.

I'm going to need to stop by my apartment. If I have to bring them proof, I'm going to need my equipment.

I slowly open the locked chest at the foot of my bed. I never thought I would have to wear these clothes or wield these weapons again. I dress the part, making sure all of my weapons are secure in their place. I'm nervous. Will I still be the Hunter I was almost 600 years ago? "We're about to find out," I say aloud and pull the hood of the cloak over my head.

Hunting certainly is not the same as it was so many years ago. I knew where the Cursed Ones would be then. Small villages were full of food for them. It wasn't hard to determine where they would be heading. But now, with millions of options for them, I have to think more carefully about where they may be. Where would I go if I were hunting humans for food? I take into consideration that vampires must have evolved more since I last encountered one. I expect they would use surprise, stealth, and maybe even some help from humans being silly enough to walk alone in an area with few witnesses. That's what I would do. So, I end up standing on the roof of a small bar overlooking an empty lot. The streetlamps are either not working or have been busted out. I, and those like me, will be able to see their prey, but humans will not know what is lurking in the shadows until it's too late.

Unsuspecting fools stumble out of the bar, laughing and cursing about being unable to find their car. Remarkably, it doesn't take long for me to find a Hybrid. They always were less patient than their makers. Left to fend for themselves after being turned, they usually ended up dead by a Hunter's blow before their 'life' could even begin. They were drawn to the first smell of blood and were far too eager. By the looks of it, this Hybrid has just recently been turned.

He is far enough away from the stumbling couple that I could most likely get to him before he got to them. With any luck, they won't realize anything is happening around them. I start running from my perch on the roof and jump when I get to the edge. I time my leap perfectly as I hit the Hybrid before he emerges from the shadows. With an "oomph," he falls back, and I tuck my head under, somersaulting off of him as he skids across the asphalt from the force of the impact. He recovers quickly, but I'm already on my feet and ready. I would love to take my time and see how much of being a Hunter I remember, but I told Sam to give me an hour. Being on a deadline is definitely a bummer.

I dodge his first attempt to grab me - okay, so I can't resist just a little dance with the Hybrid. He lunges again, and I grab his arm, twisting it behind him. He's strong. I'm stronger. Holding him captive from behind with one hand, I use the other to grab a stake from my belt. With a swift jab, I stake him in the heart.

At first, I think the stake has somehow gone all the way through him and into me. But I am still standing while the Hybrid slumps to my feet. I tenderly touch my chest, over my heart, hoping there is no blood. There's not. Why the pain? I shake my head. I will have to worry about that some other time. I can't just stand here taking my sweet time with this thing paralyzed at my feet. I drag him to an even darker corner of the building, leaving him until I can get my car.

My hour was up fifteen minutes ago, but I still take my time. The hell if I'm going to let Sam dictate how I do things. He will have to see that situations involving *my* Hunters will have to be done *my* way if he plans on becoming a part of this Society. I change my clothes, carefully hiding my cloak under my car seat. Now, how to get the Hybrid inside. He's not that big, but I think I'd have a hard time explaining it if I just threw him over my shoulder and carried him in. What would Papa do? He seemed to always be able to figure out how to make things easier. A wheelchair or gurney would be great right about now. Too bad you're not at a hospital, Anala.

I blow the hair out of my face with an exasperated sigh. Screw it. I hoist the Hybrid over my shoulder and run to the small building behind the house. The room I want to put him in is in the training area - thank God - and I'm pretty sure no one will be out there. I push my way through the door and unlock the room. Despite the fact that I thought all Cursed Ones were gone forever, I still had this training area built along with this room. I don't know why I did it, but I'm grateful for it now.

Glass covered by thick curtains surrounds the room. The glass is thick and impenetrable, even for me. Inside stands only a silver chair with silver chains that are encased in the wall. I know the chains are not only built into the walls but also buried six feet into the ground in cement. When I built this place, did I really think I would need this again? *Hunters are always prepared.* Mum's voice echoes in my head. They taught me well, I think, as I look around the room that reminds me of the crude room Papa had built in my childhood home.

I secure the Hybrid and take a minute to study him. Young, I think. Mid-twenties maybe. Tattoos cover most of his skin, that I can see. I wonder what he was like before this happened to him. I shrug it off. Nothing I can do for him now. He's my proof and perhaps my ticket to getting these untrained kids to take me seriously.

"It's been an hour and a half. She said an hour." Sam paces the room.

He's not worried, just pissed. I appreciate the concern, I think sarcastically.

"Do you think she's okay?" Amanda asks nervously.

Thank you! At least *someone* cares!

"I'm fine. Sorry I'm a little late, but I had to stop for supplies." I see Amanda visibly relax when I walk in.

"Supplies as in fake vampire teeth?" Sam seethes.

"Yes, Sam. Don't forget the fake blood and contacts," I retort. Wow, he is annoying. "Gather the others," I tell Amanda, "And meet me in the training area." I don't wait for a response from either of them. Frankly, I don't care what Sam has to say.

I'm standing in front of the small room when the others arrive five minutes later. The curtains are drawn, so they can't yet see the Hybrid.

"I know that most of you... and, if we're being honest, *all* of you," I glance at Amanda, "are having a hard time believing everything I have told you. Sam, our friendly neighborhood detective, challenged me to find proof." I saunter up to Sam and smile. "I'm going to borrow this," I say, grabbing his gun from his holster. I hightail it into the room and lock it before he even figures out what I did. Ignoring the banging on the door, I pull the curtains open.

Gasps came from everyone - even the huge football player. I know that what they see is different from what truly is. They see a young man slumped in a chair with a stake in his heart.

"What have you done?" Sam asks incredulously. "You *killed* someone?"

"Of course not. It is against the code of the Hunters to kill innocents. You will have to get acquainted with those rules soon." I know I'm pissing him off even more with my flippant attitude. I'm a spiteful, spiteful girl.

I walk behind the Hybrid and take hold of the stake. I fix my eyes on theirs - concentrating mainly on Sam's - and pull the stake out. Instantly the Hybrid is awake, his eyes white and menacing with a blood-red ring around them. His teeth, long and sharp, are clearly noticeable to everyone on the other side of the glass wall. He's snapping at them, at me, and struggling to get free. I see the others take a step back.

"Don't worry. He can't get free. Even if he did, he can't get out of this room."

"Ana, you're in there with him! If he gets free, he could kill you!"

"Amanda, I'm the one that brought him here." So annoying to have people *still* questioning my abilities. But I have to remember that all of this is so new to them. "He won't get free," I repeat, deliberately softening my tone. I look at Sam, who is standing so close to the glass and examining the Hybrid the best he can from the other side.

"Do you believe me now?"

"All of this can be faked," he says without looking at me. "And, if it is real, the police are the ones to handle this. Not you or the rest of these kids."

"Police? What exactly do you think cops can do against these things?"

"We take care of bad guys all the time, Ana. What makes *them* any different?"

I take a millisecond to take in the sensation of hearing him say my name gave me. Then, keeping my gaze fixed on Sam, I lift the gun, point it at the Hybrid, and shoot him directly between the eyes. With considerable effort, I ignore the instant throbbing in my own head and attribute it to the blast of the gun.

"Jesus! Are you insane? You just shot...."

Whatever else Sam is going to say is drowned out by the hisses and snarls coming from the Hybrid. Talk about being pissed off. I suppose I would be pissed, too, if someone shot me in the head.

"Cops and their guns are useless, Sam. The only ones that can fight these things are Hunters." I gesture to those around him. "These Hunters."

"You can't expect me to just sit back and let you put these kids' lives in danger!"

"You're right. I don't expect you to 'just sit back.' You are also a Hunter," I pause and let that sink into his thick head. "Cursed Ones know what Hunters are, Sam. If you don't let these guys train and learn how to protect themselves, it's not me who will be putting them in danger. It's you."

CHAPTER FOURTEEN
"IT'S ALL ON ME"

We all sit around the table in the dining room. Everyone is chattering all at once, talking about the Hybrid and how cool it is to be a Hunter. I wonder if they will still feel that way when they find out what they will have to do to get prepared. Obviously, I won't be able to put this off until tomorrow as I had hoped.

"Let's get started," I call over the chitchat, and everyone quiets. "We have a lot to cover and not a lot of time. We will spend an hour or so tonight going over some basics, then go to bed. Tomorrow, we will begin training."

"I think perhaps we should all just get some rest tonight," Sam starts. He was - shock - pacing. I can tell his mind is reeling from what he just saw.

"That isn't up to you, Sam," I say. I keep my voice level but not timid. There is power behind it. He will not try to take over. "I'm in charge here."

"You? You're just a. . .kid."

I'm unsure if it is just me or if he really stumbles a bit on the word 'kid.' Either way, I didn't like it.

"Fine. Tell me what you know about Cursed Ones." I cross my arms, sit back in my chair and wait.

"They're vampires, right? So, sunlight can kill them, and we stock up on Holy Water, crucifixes, stakes, and...."

"That's enough," I cut him off, irritated. If I weren't so tired, I'd probably laugh at him. "First, if you weren't paying attention in the training room, let me refresh your memory. Stakes do not kill Cursed Ones. They incapacitate them, which is very helpful, but not kill." I pause as I watch his brows knit. It seems like, for the first time, Detective Sam Logan doesn't have all the answers. I decide not to make this even worse for him and address the room.

"All of you will have to forget what you've learned about vampires from books and movies. Sunlight does not make them sparkle or burn. At best, the sun will diminish their abilities, but not much. Definitely not enough to let your guard down. Holy water and crucifixes will do nothing, so forget that. Garlic is silly unless you want to give them bad breath for when they bite you. Am I missing any clichés?"

"Do they really bite your neck and drain your blood?" Amanda asks quietly.

"Yes. That is true. Though it doesn't necessarily have to be the neck."

"If stakes don't work, what does?" Zac asks.

"You must either behead it or set it on fire. But unless you plan to carry a flame thrower with you, we'll stick with beheading using swords."

Amanda and the other girls shiver. The boys appear to be thinking about this like a video game.

"Um, I don't know how to use a sword. And, other than Frick and Frack over there, I'm sure none of us do." Jenna, the cheerleader, smacks her gum and looks incredibly bored on the outside. Inside, I can hear her heart pounding, and I see a faint film of sweat on her brow under her impossibly blonde bangs. Her ice-blue eyes also give away just how scared she is. She's taking this more seriously than she's letting on. Good.

"You will. All of you will." I turn to 'Frick and Frack" - the fencing twins, better known as Eric and Emily. "I hope that I can count on you two to help me teach the others when it comes to learning how to fight with a sword. However, you must remember that what we'll be using is nothing like your epée."

"We'll do what we can," Eric says quietly. He and his sister are both quiet and speak mainly to each other. I often wonder if it's because they were Asian and their English is a bit unconfident. But, after Jenna's comment, I don't blame them for keeping to themselves. Be that as it may, I've seen them compete in fencing. They're very good and intensely passionate when challenged.

"Thank you." I turn back to the group. They're so unsure of themselves. Growing up as a Hunter, we were told daily how needed we were. And, if you happened to possess skills like my parents, or even I did, you were praised above all others. I don't think any of these kids grew up thinking they were needed at all. "Each of you possesses a quality within you that makes you excel at what you do," I start and turn my attention to Jenna. "Jenna, you are an exceptional tumbler. It's what makes you a great cheerleader."

"Uh, the best," she corrects - still smacking her gum.

"It's also what will help you become a great Hunter," I continue, ignoring her interruption. "Hand-to-hand combat is inevitable. Your gymnastics ability will prove to be instrumental in your ability to evade death."

Jenna stops smacking her gum.

"Jeremy," I say, addressing the six-foot-two, 200-pound quarterback. "Your brute strength and ability to think in stressful situations are your qualities. It's what makes you a great leader on the football field. If you find yourself under attack, your Hunter instinct to think quickly will keep you alive."

Jeremy puffs his enormous chest out, and I believe he's twitching his pecks beneath his shirt.

"Eric and Emily," I grin. "I think you two know what your greatest asset is. You two are amazing fencers. I see no reason for that not to carry over into the new swords you will be training with." My smile warms as I turn to Zac. "Zac."

"Let me guess, my ability is charm," he smirks.

"Kind of," I chuckle. "Your true abilities are that you are cunning and tenacious, and you have a ferocity in you that makes you who you are. It is your love and loyalty for your friends and family that, I think, would have you doing anything to protect them."

"I like that," he says softly and blushes slightly.

"I don't have any skills, Ana," Amanda says nervously. "I mean, I'm not a cheerleader or fencer. I don't really do anything."

I beam at her. "That is where you're wrong, Amanda. You possess the most powerful ability of all. The ability to retain all of these abilities."

"Shut up! I do not!"

"You do. You've already demonstrated your skills in accuracy with the knife. I do not doubt that you will excel in weapons training. I've been shopping with you, so I've seen your finesse in acrobatics and thinking under pressure, not to mention your strength." I'm teasing her about the shopping, but it is true. When she wants something, no one better stand in her way. "And, the most important capability that both you and Sam hold is discerning between good and evil."

"What do you mean?" It's the first time Sam has spoken since I squashed his theory on vampires.

"You're young, Sam. One of the youngest to make detective. Correct?"

"Yeah, I guess."

I think my acknowledging his accolades makes him uncomfortable. Cute.

"Have you ever wondered how you did that?"

"I'm good at what I do."

"Yes, you are. But, have you ever just stopped and thought about why you're good at what you do?"

He opens his mouth, then closes it again.

"Most people don't question their success," I say, hoping not to make him feel even more awkward. "When you're out there patrolling the streets, do you ever feel drawn somewhere or to someone?"

Sam's brows furrow. "Sometimes," he says slowly.

"That's the Hunter in you," I explain. "If by chance you come across someone who means no harm, but is maybe hungry, so he steals a candy bar or something, you let him go. Right?"

"It's not right to steal," he responds in his cop voice, glancing at the others. "But, yes, I've done that before."

"And, when it's someone who does mean harm, you feel that in the pit of your stomach?"

"It's called a gut reaction."

"It's called being a Hunter," I counter. "Gut reactions can go either way, but yours are always correct. Each of you felt that reaction when you walked into the training area, didn't you?" I pause while each of them thinks about it. Yeses were mumbled by each, with a 'man, I thought that was just cramps or gas' from Jenna. "But you, Sam, you felt it in your core. Deeper than the rest. So did Amanda."

Sam looks briefly at Amanda, and she nods.

"You can sense them," I say. And, as I do, I realize how scared I am that they, at some point, will begin to sense me. "You have no idea how instrumental that will be out there."

"And, how about you? What are your abilities, Ana?"

Again, a strange sensation washes over me when he says my name. I shrug it off, refusing to be distracted by anything.

I smile at him. "You'll just have to wait and see."

There is no sign of Bernard today at school. To my utter relief - and maybe just a small bit of annoyance - Mr. Galloway is back to himself. The curriculum is also back to the 'boring' stuff, much to the other's chagrin. I'm just glad no one questioned him about the change.

Amanda had been extra quiet the entire seven hours we were there. I had given her a journal last night to read, and she was engrossed in it every free minute she had. It was a journal that I had written, chronicling my experiences. I was smart enough to generalize some of the circumstances, of course, but other than that, I made sure it was precise, clear, and informative. I told the story of my parents and me - Anala Geil - and how I/she had died (though, in this instance, I stuck with the Black Death theory, as so many in my time had thought). I also wrote about the other Hunters and what it was like to be a Hunter then. I even mentioned the 'Cloaked One' that hunted in the shadows.

I suppose - in hindsight - my writing the journal was another instance of being safe rather than sorry, as with the training room, the holding room, and the weapons I had made. All the steps I took to prepare for the 'what if' made me question if somehow I knew this would happen. My blood was out there. Enough of it to create Cursed Ones. Hell, I'm still here. I'm a liability in and of myself. The only surprise should be that it took so long to happen. One thing I'm sure of; this is my fault. Hunter or not, it's my responsibility to clean my mess up.

"This is fascinating!" Amanda is riding with me to the house to meet with the others to start training. She had been reading the whole time. I appreciated the quiet since I didn't think I'd get much in the coming days and weeks.

"What?"

"This journal! I mean, first of all, it's, like, 600 years old!"

"598," I mumble. Ugh, I don't think I've ever in my life, as long as it has been, felt so old.

"Whatever, same difference. Have you read this? I mean, of course you've probably read it, but have you *really* read it? The life these Hunters must have lived." Her voice is filled with wonderment. Have I *really* read it? Pssh! I *wrote* it!

"Do you think you're ready for that life?" I ask her, and she frowns.

"I don't know. I mean, if what you said about me last night is true, I might have the ability. I just don't know if I have the stomach."

"You just have to have the heart."

"The heart to kill someone? Isn't that contradictory?"

"You're going to have a philosophical conversation with me now?" I smile at her annoyed face. "I'm kidding. Lighten up. Look, what you're hunting, they're not human. They're not even animals. They're..." What? What am I?

"Monsters?" Amanda offers.

Well, I can't say that didn't hurt. But I also can't say it's not the truth, at least when talking about the others.

"I suppose," I answer quietly.

"I think that's how I'm going to have to look at them in order to kill them."

"You read the journal, Amanda. You know the code. The rules of the Society. What will you do if one of the group is turned?"

"Don't even say that!"

"It's a possibility. What if it were Sam?"

"Ana!"

"I'm sorry, Amanda, but you have to keep these things in the back of your mind as a Hunter."

"Well, then, for right now, I'd like it to stay in the back of my mind," she mutters.

I don't push her further. Poor girl has enough to deal with.

"What you did last night, telling everyone their abilities, is that your ability?" she asks, breaking the awkward silence.

"No. More just observations. I know who and what Hunters are, what makes them who they are."

"How?"

"What do you mean?"

"I mean, how do you know about all of this stuff? It says in the journal that Cursed Ones were eliminated centuries ago. Is it because you come from the lineage of the Leaders of the Society?"

Sure. Let's go with that. "Probably," I say aloud. "Most families stopped telling the stories. They wanted to forget what happened all those years ago. Hunters became obsolete because there was nothing for them to hunt. Eventually, we became forgotten."

"Your family didn't forget. They passed this book on to you."

I glance at her as we pull into the driveway of my home. "My parents always wanted me to remember who I was. Regardless of how far removed I am from that life and that time, I still know who I am."

Everyone awaits us in the training room. All decked out in exercise gear as I asked. Of course, I could have done without the boob-popping sports bra Jenna was sporting, but what can you do? I just hope it doesn't distract the guys too much.

I, too, am dressed and ready to train, and though I'm not showing quite as much as Jenna, I still receive appreciative looks. Even from Eric, which I find funny for some reason.

"So, where's our trainer?" Jenna asks - and, yes, she's popping gum.

I glance at Amanda. Apparently, she hasn't told anyone about me. Let the fun begin.

"Right here," I say with a smile. "I'm training you."

"You're kidding, right? We're doomed. Why can't *he* train us?" Jenna gestures to Sam, who is looking at me with a weird expression. He obviously doesn't think I'm qualified, either.

"Okay," I begin. "Sam? Come spar with me?"

"What?"

"Jenna doesn't think I can train her. I'm sure the others feel the same way. They're just too polite to say anything. So, spar with me. Whoever wins gets to train everyone else." I pause. "Though I have to say, I'm not sure how you're going to do with the swords."

Sam slowly walks towards me, unsure really of what to do.

"Lunge at me," I tell him. "Don't hold back. Use all of your strength and speed."

"I'm not going to hurt you."

I smile. "I know. I'll try not to hurt you."

He half-heartedly charges me, and I sidestep his outreached hand easily.

"No, Sam. Come at me for real."

"I can't. I'm going to hurt you if I do."

I shake my head and face the others. "I can't show you my skills if Sam is too scared to spar with me. Any other takers? Maybe you, Jeremy?"

I barely get Jeremy's name out when I see Sam coming at me, full-force, in my peripheral vision. I bend back at the same time Sam's fist comes towards my face. I push his outstretched arm forward with speed and strength (which, even when I hold back, has him whirling around). As I did with the Hybrid, I pin his arm behind him with one hand. With the other, I grab his hair and tug his head to one side, exposing his neck.

"You've just been bitten," I whisper, my breath caressing his bare neck. I briefly see goosebumps form and feel him shiver before I let him go.

Sam rubs his neck where my lips were so close. Close enough that I heard the blood pumping through his veins. I wonder, had I not had so much training, if I would have bitten him just then. Lord knows I wanted to.

I turn to Eric and Emily. "Your turn," I say. I need to get my mind off Sam's neck and back where it belongs. I go over to the weapons locker and open it. The cabinet is full of stakes, swords, and daggers. The others, who were stunned into silence before, gasped.

I take two retractable swords, fashioned after the ones Papa had developed, and hand them to the twins. They just stand there, looking at the hilts, then at me with confusion.

I take my own blades, the originals, and hold them at my sides, waiting for them to do the same. I press the button, and my blades slide out.

"Go ahead," I say and nod to the swords. They press the buttons and smile broadly when the blades glide out. "They're a bit different than what you're used to. Do you think you can handle them?"

"Yes," they say in unison.

"Good. Then come after me."

"Ana, those are real swords!"

"It's okay, Amanda. I know what I'm doing." I nod to the twins. "Don't hold back."

The look they give each other then fascinates me. I have a split second to take it in before they encroach me, approaching me from either side. With both of my swords, I'm able to deflect the blows coming from each of them. They are good. Very good. I see that look between them again before they attack once more.

I duck Emily's sword coming at my head, but they plan to come at me from the bottom, too. They hope to catch me off guard and sweep me off my feet. Good plan, but I am ready. As I duck Emily's swing, I do a front-hand spring, leaving my feet just as Eric's sword fills their space. When I land, I spin around quickly, slicing my blades toward them. I stop just inches away from their necks.

"Amazing," I say.

"Yes, you are," Eric responds, a little dejected. He's not used to losing.

"No. I mean you two. You told each other what to do."

"We...we just know each other well enough...." Emily stammers.

"You spoke to each other without saying anything," I interrupt. "It's okay," I say, answering their shocked glance at one another.

"Actually, it's fantastic! I've heard about people like you but never seen it."

"You don't think we're weird?"

I laugh. "We're training to fight vampires. What could be weirder than that?"

They visibly relax, and I turn my attention back to the rest in the room. The looks of complete and utter confusion and awe are hysterical. Oh, to have a camera at that moment.

"Are you kidding me?" Amanda is the first to break the silence. "I mean, really? With the acrobats and swords and stuff? How in the hell do you know how to do that?"

"I've trained most of my life," I answer honestly. "Did I pass the test?" I ask, directing my question mostly to Jenna, but I'm also interested in Sam's response.

Jenna just gives an unenthusiastic shrug and a 'whatever.' Sam says nothing but watches me closely, as always.

"Fine," I say. "Let's pair up. . ."

"I pick you!" Jeremy blurts out immediately.

"I thought you and Jenna would work well together," I smile.

"Are you on drugs? He's, like, twice my size!"

"Size won't matter out there, Jenna. These things, no matter how big or small, will have strength and speed that will supersede yours even as a Hunter. You will have to use your head." I turn away from her and move on. "Eric and Emily, I think you should stick together. With what you two can do, it's a great advantage for you and anyone you're hunting with. Besides, I am willing to bet you train together already in fencing."

I pause to consider my options. Training with Sam would not be exactly fun for me. Then again, kicking his ass could be quite exhilarating.

"Amanda, you and Zac pair up."

"Wait, why can't I work with my sister?"

"Yeah, Ana, no offense to Amanda, but I'd rather work with you," Zac announces.

"And that's why we should switch it up," I counter. "Sam, you will be too afraid of hurting Amanda if you spar with her. You'll never go full out. Zac, you'll be the same way with me."

Sam and Zac eye each other curiously. What I wouldn't give to be able to read minds at that moment.

"Fine," Sam says finally and walks away.

With everyone paired, it is time to start training. I almost don't even know where to begin. I was five when Papa started training me with simple kicks and punches. We don't have time for simple now. We have to go full force from the beginning. This is not going to be easy.

"Has anyone here had any kind of training? Martial arts, kickboxing. . .anything?"

"I've done kickboxing a couple of times," Amanda says quietly. "And Sam used to try to teach me self-defense."

"Good. That's good. Anyone else?" When no one speaks up, I keep my groan to myself to not discourage them. "That's fine. What we're going to have to do is just rely on what we were born with. Clear your mind of everything except what is happening right now, and do what comes naturally."

I walk up to the brooding Sam and throw a punch at him. Even though he had no clue it was coming, he managed to duck out of the way just in time.

"What the hell!"

"Good job," I say simply. "Now, the rest of you. One of you portray the attacker, the other the Hunter. Do that for a while, then switch. Don't hold back. If you get hit, keep going. You won't always come back from hunting unscathed. Learn to take it. Go."

I watch for a bit as they choose who would be who and then start training. To my complete surprise, they were quite good. None of them were particularly awful, even Jenna. Of course, that's not to say we don't have a hell of a long way to go, but it gives me hope, at least until we start working with the swords.

"Do you really believe they can do this?" Sam - with excellent Hunter stealth - asks quietly.

I'm able to control myself enough not to jump at the sound of his voice, but just barely. Honestly, if I don't get in tune with my senses, I'm not sure how good I'm going to be at teaching these kids.

"I have no other choice *but* to believe," I answer.

"There are always choices, Ana."

I turn to face him then, looking him in the eye. "What are they, Sam? Please, tell me. If there is a way to do this without them," I gesture to the group, currently yelling at each other more than sparring, "then I'm willing to do it. I think I've proven to you that the police will not be effective. No offense."

"Our parents must be Hunters if we are. That's not ideal, either. But Amanda is too young to worry about killing or being killed."

"*You* don't want to take orders from me, Sam. Do you think your parents will listen to me?"

His brows knitted together. "That trip that they're on now. Did you have anything to do with that?"

"No," I answer honestly.

"But it wasn't a coincidence."

It wasn't a question, so I didn't bother answering.

"Does Amanda have to be involved?"

"I wish she didn't, Sam. I sincerely do. But she is an asset to me and this...problem, as are you. I was telling the truth when I said you two had the greatest abilities out of the rest. Having you two here could be the difference between life and death for the others."

"No pressure," Sam mumbles.

Something inside me snaps at that moment, and I push my hands against Sam's chest more forcefully than I intend. He stumbles back and hits a boxing dummy with a thud. The commotion drew the attention of those around us.

"Pressure!" I yell. "You think *you* are the one with pressure?" I push him again. "You have been on my ass the entire time you've *known* me. Questioning my abilities, hell, let's be honest, you've questioned everything I've done!"

"Ana..."

I push him again. "No, you don't get to talk now. I do. Do you want to know what pressure feels like, Sam? Try having to tell these kids that they have to put their lives on the line in order to save humanity. Better yet, try being in *my* shoes and have to train these kids, who have *no* Hunter training whatsoever, and train them well enough to keep them alive! If they fail, who do you think that's on, Sam? You? No. It's all on *me*! All of their lives are on me!"

My breathing is heavy, and I'm shaking with rage - or fear, I'm not sure which. When I turn and see everyone just staring at me, I throw my hands up in the air.

"What! Get back to training!" I shout and stomp out of the room. I slam the door behind me and lean on it. "Stupid," I mutter, taking deep breaths to try and calm myself.

I know I shouldn't have lost my temper. Papa never would've done that. He would have just taken whatever anyone said to him and let it go. Maybe he would push them harder in training, but he never lost his composure as I did.

I'm excellent at training myself but as a trainer...I don't know if I'm cut out for that. I'm eighteen, for crying out loud. It doesn't matter how long I've been eighteen. What matters is I never got to grow up, not in the truest sense. Two more years, with my parents at my side helping me, and I would have become a trainer. I never made it that far. Neither did my parents.

"Ana?"

"You should be training, Amanda." At least my voice was calmer now.

"You're crying."

I touch my face and feel the wetness. I didn't even realize the tears had come, and I feel foolish for them.

"I'm fine."

"Look, I know Sam can be an ass. . ."

"It's not his fault," I interrupt. Of course, it was a little bit his fault, but the outburst was my inability to keep my composure.

"I can't imagine what this is like for you, Ana." Amanda lays her hand on my shoulder and gives me a little squeeze. "I mean, I heard everything you said in there, and to tell you the truth, I didn't think about all of that before. I should have."

I give her a small smile. "It's your job to train and learn how to stay alive. Not to babysit me and my feelings." I sigh. "I wish I hadn't blown up like that. Sam already thinks I'm some irresponsible kid. Now he's going to add in 'emotionally fragile.'"

"If he does, I'll kick his ass myself." She waits for a beat to see if that will make me smile even more. It does. "I think you wouldn't be human if you didn't feel pressure or even fear. Sam will understand that if he has a brain."

Human. If only it were as simple as just having emotions.

"Sam has a hard time giving up control," Amanda continues. "He's always been that way. And, seriously, I think you confuse him."

"Me? Why would I confuse him?"

"Really, Ana? I mean, I think you confuse everyone a little. You're not normal."

"Um, thanks," I grumble.

"I don't mean that in a bad way. Your looks, your abilities, the way you speak? No one around here is used to that. Maybe it's an English thing?"

"Hmm." What in the hell do I say to something like that?

"It was a compliment, I promise. Now, I'm going to go back in and kick Zac's ass. That was actually pretty fun."

"Amanda. . ."

"I know, I know, this isn't supposed to be about fun. But, I mean, come on, Ana. Let me have just a *little* fun while I can! Besides, you'll see how fun it is when you get to beat up on Sam."

She does a little dance that makes me chuckle and goes back inside to leave me alone again. Beating Sam up really did sound like a lot of fun at the moment.

"Ana?"

Damn it! There's no reason I should keep getting surprised by these people! I have got to meditate and start focusing!

"What do you want, Sam?" My inability to sense him makes me cranky again.

"To apologize."

Well, now *that* certainly takes me by surprise.

"You? Apologize to me?"

"I can admit when I'm wrong," he says dryly.

"I had yet to see it. Until now." Such pettiness. If I'm going to be half the trainer my papa was, I'm going to have to learn to keep my feelings in check. "I'm sorry, that was unnecessary."

"Now we're even," Sam says. "I never thought you'd be one to apologize either. By the way," Sam touches his chest gingerly, "you may want to go a little easier on me when we're sparring. I've trained a bit in hand-to-hand in the academy, but you're stronger than I thought."

With that, he goes back into the room but leaves the door open for me to follow. I heard the double meaning in his statement. He believes I can do this. I hope he's right. I smile a little and join him.

CHAPTER FIFTEEN

"BECOME THE HUNTER"

W e train for three hours - or what Jenna calls "forever." After letting them rest for a bit and getting a bite to eat, I summon them into the meditation room. I can already tell this is going to be a hard sell.

"Have a seat, please."

"Could you not afford chairs for this room?" Jenna whines.

Ignore her. If I want to keep my sanity, I'm going to have to look past Jenna's attitude. Once everyone is seated, I begin.

"This may seem odd to you all, but meditating is one of the most important parts of being a Hunter."

"Seriously? You really believe in this crap?"

"Jenna! Shut. Up. Ana is trying to help us, and your pithy little comments are doing nothing but feeding your own bitchy amusement."

Jenna, as well as the rest of us, stare at Emily - jaws dropped in astonishment. Honestly, I think it's the most I've heard her say. Ever. And, to have it directed at Jenna and in defense of me? Pure gold.

I clear my throat (after closing my gaping mouth, of course). "Um, thank you, Emily. And, yes, Jenna, I seriously believe in this." I sit in front of them, legs crossed, and speak calmly. "I'm not asking you to do anything except get in tune with yourself. None of you knew a week ago that you were Hunters. But that part is in you. I need you to find it now."

I take a deep breath and notice that most of them follow along. I could have bet big money that Sam and Jenna would be the only ones not following and won.

"If you don't have confidence in your abilities, no amount of training will help you. Jeremy, come sit in front of me, please."

"Pleasure." He grins and scoots up to sit knee-to-knee with me. He doesn't have to be that close, but I let it go.

"I want you to sit here and concentrate with me. Clear your mind of everything except what's happening in front of you."

"Easy to do," he says with an appreciative look. Keeping these kids alive really is going to be the most difficult thing I've ever done. There's not an ounce of discipline in these 'Hunters.'

"I'm going to put this blindfold on. When you're ready, and you think I'm not expecting it, I want you to strike out at me."

"Whoa, what?"

"Don't question it." I place the blindfold over my eyes and concentrate on nothing but the sounds around me. I will my senses to become heightened. I can hear the rustling of Jeremy's clothes in front of me.

"Don't look to them for approval or answers," I tell him, knowing full well he turned to the others, wondering what to do. "Just do as I ask."

"Ana. . ."

I sigh and take off the blindfold.

"Listen. All of you. If this has any chance of working, you will have to listen to me. Most of all, you'll have to trust me and trust that I know what I'm doing." I glance at Sam and the others. "Stop seeing me as your peer or a kid. I am your trainer. I am the Leader of the Society of Hunters, such as it is now. I don't say that to be arrogant. It's just how it is. If you trust me, I can help you stay alive."

Jeremy nods, and I look at the others. After receiving nods from the rest (a half-nod from Jenna), I replace the blindfold.

"Now, when you're ready."

My ears perk up at every sound. Jeremy's heartbeat, the sound his clothes make when he moves, even the faint sound his fingers make when he slowly curls them into a fist. His heart beats slightly faster, and

I hear him lift his right hand. As he strikes out at me, I tilt my head out of his reach and catch his fist in my hand.

When I take the blindfold off, he has a silly grin plastered on his face. "That. Was. Awesome!"

I smile in return and hand him the blindfold. "Your turn."

He reluctantly takes the mask from me.

"Jeremy, remember. Confidence."

He nods and puts the mask over his eyes.

"Now concentrate. Breathe deeply and focus your senses on your surroundings. Once you master this, you'll notice that smells and sounds will become much more amplified. You have to center yourself. Become the Hunter."

I quiet down and watch Jeremy closely. Moving my right hand ever so slightly, I see his head slant toward the sound, and I smile with satisfaction. I strike out with my left hand. He leans out of the way and catches my hand in his.

"I did it!" He rips the blindfold off and tosses it in the air. "Hot damn!"

"Very good," I smile. "You can let go of my hand now."

"Oh. Sorry."

"This is what I want all of you to work on tonight, just for a little while before bed. Meditate. Find the Hunter within you, and at the risk of sounding ridiculous, become one. This is as necessary as training."

I stay in the meditation room after everyone leaves. Still seated on the floor, I close my eyes and concentrate. I let every sense fill with such intensity it's almost overwhelming. The Cursed One in me takes these abilities to a whole new level. One I'm going to need. I can hear crickets chirping outside—the rustle of the wind in the trees. I can smell the spring dew on the grass outside and the aroma of flowers that are closing up for the night. And more.

"You should be in your room meditating, Sam." I slowly open my eyes and see him standing at the door. He tries to hide his surprise, but he is not good enough.

"I've never been good at stuff like this."

I gesture for him to sit in front of me.

"It's something you're going to have to become good at," I tell him. "Teach me."

We sit in silence for a moment, just studying each other.

"Close your eyes," I say, finally. When he obliges, I continue. "Clear your mind of everything except what we're doing."

"Clearing my mind has never been my strong point," he counters.

"Shh. Try." I give him a minute to breathe in the silence. When I see his shoulders relax slightly, I take it as a small victory. "I'll be right back. Just keep breathing and keep your eyes closed."

When I return, I carry with me vials of oils. I open one but hold it as far away from Sam as possible.

"What do you smell?"

Sam's brows knit together. "Citrus?"

"Don't ask me. Tell me."

"Grapefruit."

I close the vial and open another.

"And, now?"

"Um, mint? No. Eucalyptus."

"Good." I open another.

"Sandalwood."

My eyebrow raises at that one. I don't think I even know what sandalwood is. "Good. Now, what do you hear?"

"Beating. Like a drum, but softer. A heartbeat."

"Anything else?" I move the oils out of the way and accidentally brush his hand with mine. His eyes open, and even in the low candlelight, I can see the confusion in them.

"No." He gets up quickly. "Thanks. I'll try this out on my own now."

With that, he leaves, and I'm alone again. That was odd, I think, with a shrug. A quick, deep listen, I hear no one, smell no one. I glance upwards.

"Mum? Papa? How am I supposed to do this? I need you. Oh, how I wish you were here with me. These kids would be much better off if I weren't the one teaching them. I don't even know if I'm doing everything right." I close my eyes, hoping for an answer, a sign, anything. When nothing comes, I sigh heavily and go off to bed.

I run around with my wooden sword, swatting and swinging at everything around me. In the distance, I could see Mum waving at me and smiling. I wave back and give her a big, toothy grin.

Papa is training a Hunter close to me, and I mimic their movements. The Hunter is not very good, but Papa continues to teach him patiently. The boy misses his mark again and apologizes profusely. Papa just pats him on the shoulder and smiles. He tells the boy to go home for now, and they will start again in the morn.

"Papa," I run up to him and take a stance with my sword. "I wish I could be more like you."

Amused, he imitates my stance and lets me swat at his sword with my wooden one. "Why do you say that, Anala?"

"Everyone looks up to you, Papa. You are so good with them. That Hunter was terrible! I would have thrown him out." I kick a stone with my little, unclad foot and wince at the pain.

Papa chuckles and picks me up, twirling me around. "I am their leader, little one. They trust me to teach them and keep them safe. I have to believe that everyone I train will gain the confidence and ability I try to instill in them. That is what being a leader is all about."

"Do you think I will be like you one day?"

Papa sits me down and kneels beside me. "Anala, my daughter, you are a born leader. When the day comes, you will be better than I am. Believe in yourself. I do."

I sit up in bed and wipe the tears from my eyes. "Thank you, Papa," I whisper in my empty bedroom.

Standing under the steaming hot shower, I think of my eclectic group of Hunters. After my dream, I became more confident in myself and my training. It seems the change in me resonated with the others because they also changed. They were tired but stronger, faster, and more in tune with themselves and each other. The rest of the week, into the weekend, consisted of nothing but going to school and then hard-core training. We graduated to dull swords by mid-week and sharp, cut-your-head-off swords by the end. I admit I am rushing them a bit, pushing them, but I honestly don't think I have any other choice. The number of Cursed Ones grows by the day.

Their absence from home when their parents returned was explained by extracurricular school projects or hanging with friends. It seemed easy enough without much questioning. Such different times we're living in now. So, we spent more and more time with each other, getting to know each other (for the sake of hunting together). I actually enjoyed getting to know the others. It started feeling more like the Society of Old when we sat around the dinner table and talked. Even Jenna was becoming more tolerable (shocking as that is).

Sam's attitude towards me was still strained, but I decided to cut him some slack. I can't imagine how he's dealing with his job as a detective and training so hard to be a Hunter. Of course, there's also the fear that we are close to actually having to go out and hunt, which puts his sister in imminent danger. I know everything inside him wants to do nothing more than protect her and the others. Knowing that being a cop does nothing to help our situation must be difficult for him.

I'm scared, myself, about their first time out. I can only hope that Papa was right, and I was born to do this. I've given them all the tools they need to stay alive, but they've had so little time to come to terms with all this. If I've failed...I don't even want to think of the consequences.

I step out of the shower and tug on my robe. I can sense the others near. They all wanted to stay since it was the weekend, and I'm glad they did. They filled the colossal house somehow and make it more bearable for me to be here.

I walk into my bedroom and dry my hair with my towel when I smell the familiar scent. It's so close I frown in confusion. I walk to the door and open it.

"Sam!" He's in mid-unsure-knock, and there's no holding back the surprise from either of us. I thought everyone had gone to bed already. He looks like he's been caught doing something he shouldn't be doing.

"I'm sorry, I shouldn't be here."

I catch his arm when he starts walking away.

"Why are you here?"

"I. . ." His gaze slides down to my robe, and I almost swear he blushes. "I don't know," he finishes.

He does know. And, after the look he gave me, so do I. I step back and hold the door open. "Come in."

He wants to decline, but he bows his head and comes in.

"Sit down, Sam."

He's fidgeting so much that it's making *me* nervous. He sits uncomfortably on the bed, notices the chair next to the wall, and quickly gets up. He sits again and rubs his hands on his jeans as if they're sweating.

"I really shouldn't be here."

"You already said that. Why don't you tell me why you *are* here."

"Because I can't sleep."

"Are you worried about something?"

"No. Yes. I don't know." He pushes a hand through his hair and blows out an exasperated sigh. "Of course I'm worried. But that's not why...I can't stop thinking about you," he confesses.

Hearing him say it still astounds me, even with the inkling of why he was here.

"I know, I'm a sick man," he says, taking my surprise in a way I don't intend.

"Why does that make you sick?"

"Because you - you're so much younger than me. I shouldn't have these feelings for you."

I can't help but smile at that. If only he knew just how old I was. Perhaps he would think that was even worse.

"I'm... of age," I tell him. "Besides, you're not *that* old." I grin when he glances up at me. "Would it help you to know that I think of you, too?"

"Of what an ass I am?"

"Mostly," I smirk. "But there's more, too."

"I think it would've helped more if you yelled at me and told me to get the hell out." He sighs. "There are so many reasons why this shouldn't happen."

More than you know, I think silently. "Amanda?" I ask aloud.

"That's probably the biggest one. And, with her newfound abilities, I'm not sure I want to test her."

"Then perhaps we shouldn't tell her. Or the others. We don't need any more complications."

"Don't do that. Don't talk like this is going to happen. I can't believe you'd want to be with me after how I've treated you." Sam rises. "Damn it. This was a mistake. I'm sorry."

Once again, I catch his arm as he tries to walk past me. Saying nothing, I reach up and kiss him.

The instant our lips touched, I'm taken back to a night many centuries ago when I kissed Thomas. The taste of Sam and the way his lips felt against mine is so familiar.

When Sam breaks the kiss, he gently touches his forehead to mine. "I feel like I'm stealing your innocence," he whispers.

I can't think of one thing to say that would put him at ease, so I say the first thing that comes to my mind.

"I'm not a virgin, Sam."

Seriously? *That's* what I come up with?

"Oh. I don't think I like that, either."

Jealousy. Interesting.

"How about this," I say, pushing him towards the bed. "Just for tonight, we don't think about anyone else or anything else except each other." I nudge him onto the bed and straddle him. "Can you do that?"

"Yes."

I listen to Sam sleep quietly beside me. I don't think anything in all my years could have prepared me for this turn of events. I glance at Sam. For someone so high-strung and grumpy, he was incredibly gentle with me. Sighing, I toss my legs over the side of the bed and bury my head in my hands.

"God, what did you do, Anala?" I whisper. Papa would certainly not approve of this. Sleeping with a Hunter that I am training? That all but spelled disaster.

"Ana?"

I jump a little, even though his voice is barely a whisper. I'm also suddenly aware that I have nothing on. I slip back under the covers and face him.

"Sorry, did I wake you?"

"No. Everything okay?"

He looks at me so intently. I suppose I should be used to it by now, but it still unnerves me.

"Yes," I smile.

"Having regrets?"

"Of course not." I can't hold his gaze.

"That didn't look very convincing, Ana." He tries smiling, but I can see the uneasiness.

"Sam, I don't regret what we did," I pause, searching for the right words. "Please don't make me regret it. We are so close to having to go out hunting. The last thing you need is a distraction. Don't let me be a distraction to you."

He traces his finger down my cheek and over my lips. "Too late."

"I'm serious. Just because we're sleeping together doesn't mean I need you to be my hero. You need to stay focused and do what you are trained to do. And you need to remember that I can take care of myself."

"I understand. I do!" he reiterates when I don't look convinced this time. "Distractions are dangerous. Ana, I'm a cop, so I get it, okay? No heroics," he grins.

I can't help but smile back. "Good. Now get some sleep. We have a full day tomorrow."

"In a little bit," he says and then kisses me.

I wake up early, leaving Sam to sleep a little longer, and head to the training room. I purposefully come early, knowing I will have the room to myself for a while. I walk into the holding room, and the Hybrid is instantly alert. He gives a half-hearted hiss, then slumps back in the chair. He hasn't eaten since I brought him here. I can sympathize with how he feels and how weak he must be, but I also remember he's the enemy.

"Can you speak?" I ask, unsure if I'll get any response with how weak he is. "I know you're hungry. Talk to me, and I will get you food."

He just grunts softly.

"Who is your Maker?" Nothing. "What are you doing here? What do you want?"

"Cloak," he whispers.

The hairs on my neck stand up. Did he say cloak?

"What?"

"Need Cloaked One," he growls.

"What do you mean?" He saw me in my outfit. Does he want me - or the Cloaked One - dead because I caught him?

"Food."

I hear the others enter the training room and see his gaze shift behind me.

I block his view. "Who is your Maker?" I ask again. "Tell me, and perhaps I will spare your life."

He hisses at me again, as much as he can in his anemic state. "Cloak."

Well, this is no help at all. If they hear him, the others will only wonder what 'cloak' means. Fearing that and knowing I won't get the answers I need from him, I make the decision. The others need to know what it will be like when they kill Cursed Ones. I will use this one to demonstrate.

I feel their presence get closer. They're curious as to how our 'prisoner' is doing. Keeping my back to them, I take my fingernail and slice it against the palm of my hand, drawing blood. The smell hits the Hybrid hard, and he goes wild with need. He strains against the chains, his eyes turning white, with a thin, faded red rim. His teeth grow, and saliva drips from his mouth like a dog with rabies. I'm torturing him, but it's necessary. Hunters need reminding of what they are up against.

I lick the blood from my hand where the wound has already healed. "That will do," I tell him quietly and leave him.

"Are you sure he can't get out?" Amanda asks, looking wearily at the holding room door as if it will burst open at any moment.

I reassure her, moving past her and the others. In the middle of the room, I gather their attention.

"Today, you'll see what happens when you defeat your enemy." My words do not even come close to describing the unadulterated violence they are about to witness. "You're late," I announce when Sam walks in, purposefully voiding my voice of any emotion.

"I know. I'm sorry. Overslept."

"Whoa. Did Sam just apologize to Ana? Hell must've frozen over," Jenna quips, and the others snicker.

"Enough," I snap. "We are on the verge of going out in the real world and hunting these...monsters." I glance at Amanda when I use her word. "We don't have time to be late or to make jokes." I turn my back to them, take a deep breath and compose myself. Turning back, I say, "None of you know what you're really in for. So, I'm going to show you."

I order them to stay put as I return to the holding room. They aren't going to like what I'm about to do - hell, I'm not sure *I* like what I'm about to do. It's necessary.

"I would get ready if I were you," I announce moments before I unchain the Hybrid. I'm confident that he is weak enough that he won't be able to do much damage. But he will undoubtedly cause a bit of panic.

I heard many expletives, gasps, and even a few 'finallys' from the group. I watch for a bit, analyzing their tactics and evaluating their composure. All in all, they do pretty well keeping the Hybrid at bay. I do, however, notice that none of them go for the kill. Not even Detective Sam.

The Hybrid goes after each Hunter, only to get more frustrated at the failed attempts. Interestingly enough, I can almost see *him* analyzing the situation. Choosing the smallest, seemingly weakest, in the bunch didn't work. When none of them turn out to be easy prey, I see him considering how to escape. Cursed Ones are certainly evolving, I think fleetingly as he runs towards me.

With my swords at my sides, I press the buttons to release the blades. The Hybrid hisses, using what was left of his strength to charge me. I side-step him, spinning, I hit him, making him stumble back. He snarls with hunger and anger but doesn't charge again. Instead, he holds his ground, poised as we each weigh our options. I see him glance at the bars above me. They were used in training as obstacles the Hunters needed to determine how to use to their advantage. I see now that the Hybrid was trying to do the same thing. It's fascinating. I'm almost sorry that I'm going to have to kill him. Almost.

I drop my swords and jump to the bars at the same time he does, preventing him from fleeing. Wrapping my legs around him, I tug. We both come tumbling down, and he holds on to me, hoping this is his chance to get food. Unfortunately for him, I am ready for impact. Falling backward, I bring him up and over me, launching him into the glass of the holding room. The blow has him struggling to gain his footing. Grabbing my swords, I perform a kip-up and am on my feet, in front of him, in seconds. He's defeated, and he knows it. This isn't how it is in the field. He's just too hungry and weak to fight anymore. Once again, I have to help him - and my cause - by nicking my palm and drawing blood. Ravenous, he bounds towards me. No tricks, no fancy moves. I cross my swords like a huge pair of scissors and close them across his neck.

His head rolls once, away from his slumped body, before they turn to dust.

The others run over to me - and to their credit, none of them are too grossed out by what they see. In awe, perhaps a bit of shock, but mostly they are just trying to comprehend everything that happened.

I am disappointed in them for their lack of 'killing instinct,' but they're alive and unscathed. That's a plus. They held their own and used their skills. Still, not delivering the killing blow will not work out there.

"Why didn't you kill him?" I'm not asking anyone in particular, and they look at each other for the answer. "*Someone* answer me. I don't care who."

"He was weak?" Amanda's answer comes in the form of a question, annoying me.

"Do you think he would have given you the same consideration if he had gotten past your defenses? He would've killed you without a second thought."

"We're human, Ana. He may kill us without hesitation, but you can't expect us to be the same way." It's Amanda's turn to be annoyed with me.

"You're not just human," I counter. "You're Hunters. It is your destiny to kill these...things. It is the code."

"Ana, this is our first time experiencing all of this," Sam interjects quietly. "We haven't been prepared for this as you have. These kids, me, we're doing our best."

He's right, of course, but we simply do not have the time for 'humanity' when it comes to Cursed Ones. And, yes, I realize the irony of someone like me feeling that way.

"Train for a couple of hours. We'll meet in the dining room to eat and discuss our next move around noon."

I leave them to it, retreating to my room for time alone. I immediately remove my shirt and examine my shoulder when I get there. As expected, there's no wound, just a trace of blood where the Hybrid got a bite in. I have no idea how this bite will affect me, but I'm thankful he was just a Hybrid. They are not potent enough at this stage to turn someone, only kill them. I feel okay though, even if a bit cranky. The aftermath of letting a Hybrid get one in, I suppose. I'm better than that. Sure, they're evolving, but that is no excuse. If he can get to me, what are the chances of survival for the others?

CHAPTER SIXTEEN

"HE MADE ME FEEL"

I meet the gang in the dining room at precisely noon. Apparently, they're all cranky as well. I don't blame them. I am their trainer, the one they look to for advice and guidance. What do I do? I run off and hide. I should have been there training with them. Just one more thing Papa would be disappointed in.

"First, I want to apologize," I begin as I sit at the head of the table. "I should've handled this morning differently. Beginning with telling you how sufficient you all were against the Hybrid. I am impressed with how well you are all doing in such a short amount of time." I pause, thinking about how Papa would handle this—searching for the right words. "I know this is very new for all of you. Being a trainer and responsible for a society - as few as we are - is new to me. I don't expect you to lose your humanity," I say, holding Amanda's eye. "However, you also can't let it get in your way out there. It's your life or theirs. And I can tell you that they will not hesitate to kill you. They do not possess the humanity you do."

"None of them?" Amanda asks, her gaze never faltering.

I, of course, cannot answer that question honestly. "They are evolving," I say by way of answering. "You've read the journal. You know that a Hybrid would not quit trying for food back in the day. This one gave up and began looking for an escape. I can honestly tell you that I do not know what we're up against out there."

"So, how do we find out?" Sam asks.

"We go out and hunt. Tonight."

"Tonight!" Sam's fork clatters against his plate. "Don't you think that's a bit hasty?"

"Damn it!" Jeremy swears and drops his knife. "You scared the hell out of me, Sam!" He quickly grabs his napkin and covers the bleeding cut on his hand.

The smell hits me as hard as the first day I was turned. I feel that all too familiar sting in my eyes, the aching of my teeth, and that unimaginable hunger. I haven't felt this way in so long. Impossible! I immediately drop my gaze, grateful everyone's attention is focused on Jeremy.

"Excuse me."

I try not to run out of the room, but I can't trust myself around the others with how I feel. When I finally reach my room, I run to my bathroom, slamming the door behind me. I can't seem to be able to catch my breath or get the damn smell of blood out of my head. I open the small concealed fridge, and with shaking hands, I take out a blood-filled bottle. I drink it down eagerly, savoring the almost instant satisfaction. Something human food has never been able to do for me since turning. I chug more until the bottle is empty. The need for blood shames me. I know, deep inside, that it isn't my fault. That doesn't do anything to help my guilt.

Turning on the faucet, I rinse my mouth out, hoping to get all of the red washed away. Glancing in the mirror, I see my eyes, white with a red ring. I see my teeth, sharp and threatening. I've seen it before, of course, but it has been so long that the image shocks me. My hands shake, and my head begins to pound. Why is this happening?

I dig a locked box out of the cabinet and fumble with the key I had hidden. The pounding in my head makes it hard to do much of anything. I finally open the box and frantically look for Papa's mixture that helps me with the hunger. I down the elixir almost as quickly as I did the blood. It stings going down. Hurts actually. It feels like I am burning from the inside out.

"Deal with it, Anala," I scold myself. I endure the pain and almost appreciate it because I know what it will do for me.

"Ana?"

Amanda's voice pierces my throbbing head.

"Yes?" I pray my voice is calm and she won't hear anything wrong.

"Are you okay? You left pretty fast."

I glance in the mirror again, my still white and red eyes staring back at me.

"I'm fine," I answer. "I just wasn't feeling very well." I replace the vial I have with another. This one is filled with the liquid that would clear my eyes. It was one of the best elixirs Papa could have ever created. If he couldn't cure me, at least he could help me fit in.

"I didn't think you would have a problem with blood being who you are."

My hands freeze. Did she know? Could she sense me? "What?"

"We're Hunters, Ana. We can't be squeamish," she says through the closed door.

I relax a bit and laugh. "I'm not squeamish, Amanda. Just felt a little," I don't bother looking in the mirror again. I know what I look like. "Off," I finish. I drink the elixir and wait for its burn. It takes a lot of strength to keep in the groan as my insides, once again, feel on fire.

"Are you sure you're okay?"

Apparently, I'm not entirely successful at holding in my pain. When it begins to subside, I risk a peek into the mirror. My eyes were normal again - well, normal for me - and I'm starting to feel better.

"Yes. I'm good," I tell Amanda, locking the box back up and hiding it again. "Feeling much better," I say as I open the door and face Amanda.

"Good. I mean, you're going to have to be at your best to deal with Sam. He's not exactly happy about your announcement."

"What else is new?" I say, rolling my eyes.

"Ana, have you thought this through?" Sam - pacing, of course – drinks his drink, runs his hand through his hair, sits, and gets back up. It's all extraordinarily frustrating and stressful as hell.

"Of course I've thought this through, Sam. I'm not going to just send you guys out there on a whim." I'm insulted, especially after what happened between us. "We simply do not have the time to keep waiting. Every minute we sit in here, train here, more Hybrids are being made."

"How do you know that?"

"Because that's what they do."

"But, how did you learn that they were back?" Sam asks curiously.

"I've wondered that, too," Jeremy chimes in, and the others follow suit.

"Bernard told me," I answer. I have to keep so many things from them that being able to tell the truth occasionally feels good.

"And who is this Bernard guy? How do you know him? Can he be trusted? Does he know where they came from? Why they're suddenly back after centuries of being...well, dead?"

So many questions, I feel like I'm in an interrogation room with Sam, and he's trying to get me to confess to every bad thing happening in the world. I wonder, fleetingly, if my head would explode if I didn't have inhuman abilities. "Bernard used to work with my father. I've known him for years." I hesitate, wondering how to answer the other questions. Do I trust Bernard? No. But should I tell them that? "Trust doesn't matter," I say. "I know that what he says is true. We've seen it. I don't know how much he knows of their return. Honestly, I haven't had time to sit down and have a long chat with him. The important thing is Cursed Ones are back, and it's up to us to stop them."

"Fine," Sam says, obviously not satisfied with my answers - or lack of them, but moving on. "So, how do you propose we go about hunting? You said this isn't a whim. What's your plan?"

"I will take half of you out. . ."

"Wait, you're separating us?"

"She has to," Emily answers softly. She blushes slightly when everyone - including me - looks at her questioningly. "She can't risk losing us all at once," she explains.

"Right," this comes from Jenna - I know, I'm shocked, too. "If something happens, like, we're ambushed or something, she can't jeopardize us all."

"I get it," Jeremy chimes in. "Separate groups are like. . .back up," he says, looking at Sam, expecting him to understand his analogy.

"Whoever is left has to clean up," Zac declares. "We would have to take care of any Hunter that's been... compromised."

Amazing. My faith in them is renewed by their ability to understand what must be done.

"Exactly," I say aloud. "You are all correct." I turn to Sam. "I would feel better if our group was bigger, but we must work with what we have."

I address the whole group again. "As I was saying, I will take half of you out the first time. After that, you will choose groups with one person rotating in the fourth spot. I don't care how you choose, but I will suggest keeping Eric and Emily together. Their ability is a great advantage when they're together."

"Rotate? Does that mean you're not going to be with us?" Amanda asks.

"You can't just throw them out there to fend for themselves, Ana."

Unbelievable. Just when I think Sam is maybe beginning to understand me, he completely proves me wrong.

"I'm not just 'throwing them out there,' Sam! I will be there to make sure they can handle themselves."

"And, then what? Why wouldn't you be in rotation with us?"

"I will! As much as I possibly can, I will. However, this will never end for any of us unless I find who is *making* these Hybrids! I will be out hunting for their Maker!"

"She can't hold our hands every second, Sam," Eric interjects. "She's given us the knowledge we need. It's up to us to utilize it."

Well, holy hell. These kids are going to make me cry. I probably would cry with pride if I didn't think it would make them feel I had no faith in them before.

"Choose your first team," I tell them. "Whoever is going out tonight, get some rest. The others train. We will go out at midnight."

I do drills by myself in the training room, anxiously awaiting for midnight to come. The others had finished training and were doing their best to get sleep. I'm restless, scared, and nervous. If earlier were any indication, these Hunters finally get who they are and what they are destined to do. That doesn't mean it doesn't scare the hell out of me taking them out for the first time. Only now, it's not them I'm not confident in. It's me. My ability as a leader and trainer is about to be put to the test. God, I hope I pass.

"You should be resting up for tonight, Sam." I could smell him the moment he entered the training area. There were arguments earlier when teams were being chosen. It came down to putting names in a hat and choosing that way. I wasn't happy when Amanda and Sam's names were consequently picked, but I said nothing.

"I can't sleep. Shouldn't you be resting, too?"

"Can't sleep." I focus on the wooden dummy, practicing counterattacks and quick reactions.

"Want to spar with me?"

I stop hitting the dummy and face Sam. "You shouldn't be going out with Amanda. You know that, right?"

"I didn't choose it," he answers innocently.

"But you're glad it happened," I accuse.

He got into a fighting stance and affixed a smirk on his face. "Can't say that I'm not. You going to spar or what?"

He strikes out at me, hoping to catch me off guard. No such luck as I duck his punch, crouching and sweeping my leg at his feet. He is obviously ready for that as he jumps quickly, avoiding my leg.

"Not bad," I tell him.

Sam doesn't respond. He moves around me, waiting for me to show a weak point.

"I want to make love to you again," he says quietly, and I falter ever so slightly. He uses it against me, grabbing and spinning me around until my back is pressed against his chest. His arms are wrapped tightly around me, and he mimics having a stake. But before he can bring the 'stake' down into my heart, I break free, capturing his hand and twisting it behind him as I rotate to face him.

"Dirty move," I say, my lips close to his.

"Doesn't make it untrue," he replies before crushing his mouth to mine.

"What in the hell?"

Sam and I tear apart as though a fire has started on our lips.

"Amanda!" Damn it! I do *not* need this now. Not tonight.

Amanda abruptly turns and leaves the room - very angrily. When Sam makes a move to go after her, I stop him.

"Let me go."

"But she's my sister."

"Exactly. I don't think she will want to talk to her brother after seeing him kissing her best friend." I don't mention that I don't think she will want to talk to me, either.

"Maybe," he answers, unconvinced. He places a hand on my arm as I walk by him. "I'm not sorry. Whether she likes it or not, I'm not sorry."

I smile at him before leaving him. We'll see how long he feels that way. I step out into the hall and stop. Closing my eyes, I heighten my senses, focusing solely on Amanda's scent. She went towards the balcony. Hearing her grumbling and kicking the chairs out there only solidifies my assessment.

I step cautiously out onto the balcony.

"Amanda?"

"I don't think I want to talk to you, Ana."

"I know you're. . ."

"No! You don't know how I feel at all! Do you want to know? I don't feel like I know you at all, Ana. You have been my best friend for two years, and I don't know who you really are!"

"That's not true."

"It's not? Okay, first there's this whole Hunter thing," she starts, ticking each thing off on a finger. "Then, there's this place. Not to mention whatever the hell happened between you and Zac!"

"Wait. Zac?"

"Don't even try to say nothing happened. I mean, I've seen the change between you two. He won't tell me anything; you certainly haven't told me anything. And now, my brother? Sam, Ana? Really? You could have anyone you wanted. Why did you pick Sam?"

I sigh and pick up two of the chairs she kicked over. I gesture for her to sit with me, but she refuses.

"Amanda, if I had told you I was a Hunter, a *vampire* Hunter, you would have thought I was mad. Let's face it until you actually saw the

Hybrid, you *did* think I was mad. This place," I spread my arms, enveloping the enormity of where we were. "I never thought I would ever have to be here again. It was built merely as a precaution. I had hoped never to have to use it."

I pause. I know Sam is there. I smelled him the moment he decided to listen in on our conversation. But I don't have time to think about his feelings right now. Amanda wants honesty. I'll give her as much as I can.

"I kissed Zac."

"What!"

"That night he came to check up on me. Your first date with Robby? I wasn't feeling. . .myself. He was sweet and concerned, and I kissed him before I knew what was happening."

"Ana! How could you not tell me?"

"Because I knew it was a mistake as soon as I did it. I stopped and practically threw him out of my apartment. No explanation. I tried apologizing the next time I saw him, but he didn't want to hear it. I just wanted to forget it happened and hoped he would, too."

"He has had a crush on you since you first came here. I doubt he's going to forget kissing you."

Well, that makes me feel much better. I can't dwell on it. I can't help what Zac does. I just hope it doesn't get in the way when we're hunting.

"As for Sam," I continue, avoiding any more conversation about Zac. "We didn't tell you because, well, frankly, we thought you wouldn't like it."

"You thought right. You lied to me. How do I forgive that, Ana?"

"What do you want me to say, Amanda?"

"You could tell me why him."

Ugh. I would much prefer not to have the subject of the conversation listening.

"When my parents died, I closed myself off, Amanda. It hurt too much to care about people only to lose them." It is one of the curses of being immortal. Friendships, love, it is easier not to have them. "When I moved here and met you, I felt this - kinship. So, I let you in. Then I met Sam, and there was something there, instantly. He made me. . .feel."

"But, I thought what you were feeling was hate. Or at least dislike. I

138

didn't think you two liked each other, and now I see you kissing." She stumbles on the word 'kissing.'

"I never hated Sam. Yes, he's a frustrating, hard-headed control freak. . ."

"Ha. Sounds *vaguely* familiar," Amanda quips under her breath.

"But he still made me feel something inside that I haven't felt in a long time," I continue, ignoring her shot at me.

"Great. Now if I tell you I want you to stop seeing him, I look like a major bitch."

"Is that what you want?"

"Would you stop?"

"I don't want to."

Neither of us answered the real question.

"You know you're putting him in more danger, right?"

I know. And I know, despite my conversation with Sam, he would try to protect me, leaving himself vulnerable. "Yes."

"And, you're okay with that?"

"Of course not."

She doesn't question me anymore. Amanda knows her brother. No matter what she or I say, he will do what he wants. At the moment, what he wants is me.

"Whatever. I can't tell you not to see him. But, as your best friend, I can ask you not to let it go any further. At least until this is over."

"Further?" I frown.

"Don't sleep with him!" She answers, exasperated.

"Oh." I lower my eyes. I couldn't have predicted that she wouldn't have assumed we were already - doing that.

"You're *sleeping* with him? Geez, Ana!" She paces in a tiny area on the balcony. I wonder if pacing is a family trait.

"It just happened, Amanda," I say softly. "It wasn't something I expected. . ."

"Don't hurt him," she interrupts. Her voice is quiet but serious.

Confusion settles across my face. "I don't want to."

"Make sure you don't. I love you, Ana, but if you hurt him, I will take you down."

When she walks away, I sit there pondering her words. There seemed to be more to her threat, but I can't imagine why.

"Do you always eavesdrop, Detective?" Sam hasn't joined me since Amanda left but still watches me.

"I wasn't eavesdropping," he says, sitting beside me. "I just wanted to make sure everything was okay."

"Well, you heard. Apparently, I'm dead meat if I hurt you."

"Then I suppose we should try to make this work," he grins.

I smile back, but Amanda's words still haunt me. What does she know? Of course, I could just be overly sensitive and paranoid. There's too much on the line tonight. I must focus on that and not all of this high school drama.

"Are you ready for tonight?" I ask him.

"Yes, I think so."

"You can't have doubts. Confidence is. . ."

"Everything," he finishes. "I know. Look, Ana, I'm as ready as I can be. Unless you grew up knowing about all of this, as you did, this is daunting and unpredictable."

I stand up and start pacing. I hate feeling this way. So out of control. It's frustrating that these Hunters have no fundamental knowledge of what they're up against. They were born Hunters but grew up not knowing their true destiny. How could I possibly expect them to be ready for what they're about to do?

"I'm sorry about all of this, Sam."

He catches my hand as I pace by him. "This isn't your fault, Ana."

If only I could be sure that was true.

Amanda, Sam, and Zac - such is my luck - are the first group I will take hunting. I tell them to dress in dark clothing and choose weapons from the cabinet while I get ready. This is going to be extremely interesting, I think, as I get dressed. Amanda and Zac are upset with me, and Sam wants to sleep with me. Things couldn't get any worse, could they?

"Famous last words," I mutter to myself. I dress in my usual hunting gear - minus the cloak, of course - and head out to join the others.

"Damn. Why don't I have an outfit like that?" Amanda comments.

Obviously, my attire is somewhat of an attention-getter, even without the cloak. I admit it has undergone a few changes throughout the years. The fitted trousers and tunic have become a form-fitting body suit. A zipper, currently unzipped enough to show a bit of cleavage, adorns the front of the black suit. The black boots come up to my thighs - a decision made purely out of necessity as they can hold more weapons. I still have the original leather belt and straps that surround my thighs. Honestly, I feel much more comfortable when I have the cloak on, but I can't do that now.

"Wow," Zac whispers, then abruptly turns back to the cabinet.

Sam watches and says nothing. But I see the look in his eye and know what he's thinking.

"It's not a big deal," I move past them, hoping I'm not blushing. "My mum made it for me." Kind of. Okay, so the belt and sheaths were the only original things. Whatever.

"My mom wouldn't even let me *buy* something like that!"

"Can we get over it? Please. Let's focus. Do you have everything you need?"

"We're ready. Swords, daggers, stakes - wooden, silver, and splintering."

Sam rattles off weapons like he's reading a grocery list. He sounds confident, and Amanda and Zac seem to be exceptionally calm. I don't know if it's all an act, but if it is, it's pretty good.

"Let's get going then."

CHAPTER SEVENTEEN
"NEVER FELT SO HUMAN"

Amanda and I walk together down the dark alleyway as the guys flank us. Honestly, I think Amanda wants to keep me away from Sam. I don't mind. There shouldn't be any distractions. So, I keep the conversation to a minimum, speaking only to give them direction.

When I sense a Cursed One, I notice Amanda's reaction simultaneously. Her hand grasps her sword, and I see it tremble almost imperceptibly.

"Are you ready for this?" I whisper.

"Yes," she answers, but she's not as convincing as before we arrived.

I motion for the guys to fan out and wait for my signal. I go ahead to check out the situation. Hybrids are feeding off some poor soul that had the misfortune to cross their path. The Hybrids, I understand. The poor soul, I understand. The two humans in the mix? That I don't understand at all. Since when do Hybrids not kill any and all prey in their immediate vicinity?

I, apparently, study the scene too long as Zac runs past me toward the Hybrids.

"Zac! Damn it!" Zac's warrior cry as he runs toward the Hybrids does not help his plan to ambush, and the others - the ones not eating - are ready for him. My swords already in my hands, I release the blades, dragging one across the neck of a surprised Hybrid as he lifts his head from his meal. Zac fights a quite large Hybrid, again with tattoos - I wonder if there's a theme.

A quick check shows me that Sam and Amanda are fighting two more Hybrids and doing an excellent job. I have to believe they can take care of themselves. On the other hand, Zac just proved to me that he needs more work. As that thought enters my mind, he brings his sword up into the Hybrid's stomach. In order to incapacitate the Hybrid, he would've needed to hit him in the heart. But the blow stuns the Hybrid enough to make him hesitate in his next attack, and Zac plunges a stake into his heart.

One more Hybrid - there were five in all - tries a sneak attack on me while I watch Zac. Lucky for me, I have been honing my awareness skills, and I jump up doing a back flip, pushing myself off her shoulders. With a quick flick of my wrist, I end her just in time to see Zac slash his blade across his Hybrid's neck. I ensure Sam and Amanda are okay and see them both make the killing blow. So, this is what a trainer is supposed to feel? Pride, coupled with a feeling of accomplishment? Not too shabby.

The grunt of one of the humans brings my attention back to Zac. He pushes the other human away from him and is seconds away from killing him—an innocent. I run towards him, catching his hand and sword in time.

"Zac, no! He's an innocent!"

"They're with those. . .*things*! They're not innocent!" He's panting, high off of the adrenaline from his first kill.

"They are *human*, Zac. It is against the code," I remind him.

"But, if they're working with the enemy, that makes them the enemy."

"Their fate is not up to you. You can only slay Cursed Ones."

"Then, what? We just let them go? Let them help more of these monsters?"

"Zac, calm down," Amanda lays a hand on his arm, which is still shaking.

"Killing humans is something I can't allow, Zac," Sam mentions, then turns to me. "So, what *do* we do with them?"

"This is not common," I say, mostly to myself. "I do not understand why or how the Hybrids let these innocents live."

"They're not innocent, Ana. Stop calling them that," Zac all but growls.

I whirl on him as Sam slaps cuffs on the humans. "Enough!" I grab his lapels and push him back. "You need to get in control of yourself. No matter what you think of these guys, they are *human*. *Innocents*! You are bound by the code of Hunters not to harm humans.

"We can't leave them here, Sam. We'll take them back to the estate, and you can question them."

"Protocol says I should take them into the station, Ana."

"Does any of this look like protocol to you?" I ask him, gesturing to the bloody body at our feet. "If you take them in, what will you tell the rest of your colleagues? You caught them while out hunting vampires?"

"I can blame them for this. They're high on something. I don't think anyone will question me about that."

"Fine. See what you can get out of them here before you take them in. You," I point at Zac. "You could've gotten yourself killed running in here like you did. You could've gotten all of us killed! What in the hell were you thinking?"

"You were taking too long," he mumbles.

"What?"

"I thought you didn't trust us. We didn't make the 'kill shot' before when you tested us. I just wanted you to know we were ready."

"Zac, I wouldn't have brought you out here if I didn't trust you. I was analyzing the situation that the humans greatly complicated. If you wanted me to know you were really ready, you would've kept your cool and waited for my signal. You cannot be a rogue hunter out here. Your fellow hunters rely on everyone to have their back and work together. If you can't do that. . ."

"I can," he interrupts. "I promise. I screwed up. I'm sorry."

"Sorry won't work if you get yourself killed or, worse, turned. Get yourself together. We'll continue hunting after Sam finishes."

Sam doesn't get much from the humans. He's right. They were drugged, but with what? He calls the scene in and turns over the 'suspects' when the uniforms arrive.

The rest of the night goes on without a hitch. We found a few more Hybrids - minus the humans and prey, thank goodness - and Zac was much more restrained and focused. All in all, my group of Hunters do exceptionally well despite the little time they had to prepare.

"So? How'd we do?" Amanda asks when we get back to the estate.

I start removing all of my weapons, replacing them in the cabinet. "I'm here to train you, Amanda, not grade you." I sigh a little when she looks dejected. "I'm proud of you. You all did an amazing job, minus the little hiccup in the beginning," I say, glancing at Zac. "I am confident in your abilities, and, actually, I enjoyed hunting with you."

They smile at me, pride showing on their faces.

"Now, you should all get some rest."

"Could I speak with you for a minute," Sam asks me quietly.

"Sure."

Zac and Amanda leave, but I notice the look I get from Amanda. She certainly isn't smiling now. She really hates whatever it is I have with Sam.

"Maybe we could go somewhere a little more private?"

"You really need to rest, Sam."

Now it's Sam's turn to look dejected or rejected. "Right. Goodnight, then."

"Sam, wait. Come sit with me." When he comes back, I take his hand. "What you did out there, using the humans as suspects, was great thinking."

"Thanks. They'll do a drug test on them. Maybe I'll be able to find out what they were on. It had to be strong for them to stand there and watch what they watched."

"This is all so strange. Things have changed so much. It looks like I will have to talk to Bernard and see what he knows."

"Want me to go with you?"

I chuckle. All night, I feel he made it a point not to 'baby' me or Amanda. Now, when I need to do something as simple as speak to someone about what's going on, he wants to be there with me.

146

"This is something I have to do myself. But, thank you for the offer."

"You'll tell me. . .us, what you learn?"

It depends on what it is I learn. I can't divulge that information if it has anything to do with me or what I am.

"Mmhmm."

"Okay. Well. . .I guess I'll try to get some rest now."

He looks unsure, boyish, and impossibly cute right then. He's halfway across the room when I stop him.

"Sam. I'll be ready in about ten minutes."

He smiles broadly and picks up his pace.

I sit there for a moment after Sam leaves. I send Bernard a quick text, arranging to meet with him and giving him an abridged version of the night's events.

Oh, how I wish Papa were here. He and Mum would know how to determine what is happening now with humans and the Cursed Ones being so evolved. Papa could assess whether cursed blood is what the humans were 'high' on. I wonder what the crime lab will find.

I took the second group out the next night. I'm happy to say it was uneventful compared to the first group. We had our fair share of Hybrids, but the humans were missing from the equation this night. I don't know whether to be thankful or curious about why there were none.

This group was a bit more timid but highly efficient. Eric and Emily were marvelous in the way they used their ability. Whoever went out hunting with the two of them certainly had an advantage.

Even Jenna was strong and confident. I gave myself a moment to feel the pride in my small society and even a bit of pride in myself. I've managed to take this eclectic group and turn them into bona fide Hunters.

"I want to tell you all how very proud I am of all of you." I stand at the head of the table with my glass - of tea, since Sam thinks we're all too young to drink - lifted. "You have impressed me. Hunters would train since birth, knowing from an early age what they are up against. You were thrown into this life believing vampires were nothing but fictional stories. And yet, you have made the transition into this world seamlessly. I congratulate you and humbly thank you for what you have done." I lift my glass a bit higher, salute them all, and then drink. They all look completely satisfied with themselves, as they should. To be able to do what they've done takes immense talent and concentration. I couldn't have asked for a better group of people - much to my surprise.

"We owe it all to you, Ana," Emily stands and raises her glass to me. "Without your training and believing in us, we couldn't do this."

The others chime in their agreement, and I think if I could have blushed, I would have.

"You owe it to yourselves," I tell them. "Don't underestimate your abilities." I pause, unsure of the reaction I will receive with what I have to say next. "You're ready to go out on your own."

Silence.

"Will you at least be watching from a distance?" Amanda asks timidly.

I wish I could tell them I would be, but I can't. They need me to trust them as much as they need to trust themselves. The "Cloaked One" will never be too far away, but they don't have to know that.

"No."

Amanda nods as though she understands why, but I catch Sam's eye, and he doesn't look like he understands at all.

"Confidence," I say quietly. "Patience. A fierce need to stay alive. That's all you need. Well, that and your abilities. I have faith in you." I hold Sam's eye for a brief moment and then make eye contact with the others. "You can do this."

"And you're sure this is the only way?" Sam asks. It isn't meant to be mean or undermining. I'll give him that.

"Yes. If I don't find the Maker, Sam, no matter what we do out there, how many Hybrids we kill, it'll be a never-ending circle. We'll get nowhere."

"Are there more of us?" Jenna ponders. "Couldn't we train more of us?"

"Not here. It would take me more time than I have to find others. Not to mention the time it would take for me to train them. That's assuming they don't laugh in my face."

"Do we know if they are contained here?"

I bring my attention back to Sam. "I don't know yet. I will talk to Bernard and find out what he knows. They tend to start in one place, build their army and then move on. But, as we've seen, nothing has been typical lately."

When it seems no one else has questions, I relax a bit. How daunting it is to be the leader of an albeit small society. They look to me for so much. Information is something I am going to need to get from Bernard, and I'm pissed that I haven't heard from him. I'll try one more text, and then I will hunt him down if I must.

"Get some rest. Meditate. And I mean that, Jenna."

Jenna rolls her eyes at me, but I see the seriousness deep in her blue eyes. She now understands this isn't a game. Finally.

"Can I talk to you, Ana?"

Once again, Sam asks for alone time in front of Amanda. He really is not helping my situation with her.

"Of course."

I catch Zac's eye before he leaves, and he looks disappointed. With a shrug, he walks out with the others.

"You're not giving Amanda a chance to stop being mad at me, Sam."

He frowns as though he doesn't understand.

"She's still mad?"

"We're still sleeping together," I answer matter-of-factly.

"I'm sorry." Sam is distracted and starts his patented pacing.

"What can I do for you, Sam?"

"Let me go with you."

Now it's my turn to frown with misunderstanding.

"Go where?"

"Hunting for the Maker."

"No."

"Ana."

"No, Sam. The Maker is the strongest Cursed One." Other than me, I think silently. "You are not ready for that."

"If it is so strong, you'll need backup."

"This is not up for discussion, Sam. I need you here with the others. They see you as a leader, as well. I need you to lead them."

"Ana, they can handle themselves. You've said that yourself."

"Sam," I hesitate, hoping I'm saying the right thing. "I told you not to make me regret it when we got together. Please. Don't make me."

He blanches as though I punched him in the gut. "I'm not trying to make you regret being with me, Ana." He sits heavily in the chair in front of me. "I'll stay with the others. But, if you need me, I'm here."

"I know that," I say, softening my voice. I walk behind him and lay my hands on his shoulders. Leaning down, I whisper in his ear. "Thank you for that, but I have to do this myself."

He nods. I know he still doesn't agree, but he will concede.

"Should I go to my room?" He asks, sounding almost shy.

Once again, I lean down, kissing him softly on the cheek.

"Go to my room," I murmur. I smell Zac then, and he's close. Backing away from Sam, I smile. "I'll be going to bed soon."

Sam's confused by the abrupt change until he hears Zac himself.

"Right. Goodnight, then." Sam turns on his heel and brushes by Zac. "Zac."

Hmm. Judging by his tone, Sam is unhappy that he's leaving Zac and me alone. I'll have to remind him that there's nothing between us. I think I know just the way.

"Ana?"

Zac interrupts my little fantasy, and I have to force myself not to sigh.

"Why aren't you meditating?"

"Is Sam the only one who can talk to you alone?"

"No! Of course not! I'm sorry, Zac. What do you need?"

He wavers, uncertainty shining in his eyes for a brief moment.

"Let me go with you."

What? You have got to be kidding me with this. Is he really here asking me for the exact same thing Sam asked for? There's no reason to prolong this by asking him questions I already know the answers to.

"No, Zac. I need you here."

"Is Sam going with you?" He asks, not able to mask the bite in his voice.

"No." I, in return, can't help the terse response that escapes.

"Shouldn't someone. . ."

"Enough, Zac. You're not ready to hunt for something like a Maker. You will stay with your team. They need you. I need you here."

"I'm just worried about you."

My annoyance alleviates a bit. I know he means well. "I know. But you don't have to worry about me."

Zac steps closer and, to my utter shock, raises his hand to touch my cheek.

"I don't think I could stop if I wanted to," he says softly.

Oh, Zac. I pull his hand away from my face, squeezing it briefly before letting it go.

"This can't happen, Zac."

"Because you're my leader?"

Because I'm with Sam. "Not just that." Oh, I have to tread so lightly here. If I upset him, it may affect him while hunting. "These are very tense times, Zac. I need you to focus on hunting, nothing else. Do you understand?"

"I think so. But I still think I should go with you."

"Zac, I'm not used to being a leader, so I don't know, really, how to handle this stuff. But, as your leader, I'm telling you to stay here with your group."

"Is that an order?" he quips.

"Yes." My voice is flat, devoid of any emotion. I think it gets through to him because he takes a step back.

"Yes, ma'am." He salutes me - a little over the top - and walks out.

Sigh. I take my phone out and text Bernard once again.

Must I come find you, Bernard? You brought me into this. Now I need answers. If I have to hunt you down, it won't be pretty. You know what I am capable of.

There. That ought to get a response. I'm not disappointed when my phone chimes mere seconds later.

I am sorry, Anala. I have been out gathering as much infor-

mation as I can. I can meet with you this Sunday afternoon. We will discuss everything. Shall I come there?

Two days. I suppose I can give him that time, though he better have satisfactory information for me. Besides, it will give me time to watch over my Hunters while they are out by themselves. I know it's not something I should do, but given the circumstances, I think even Papa would agree.

I text Bernard back, telling him I will meet him at his place on Sunday at four o'clock. I don't trust Bernard here in this house. Especially not after he asked me for more blood. There is something he is keeping from me. I intend to find out what that is on Sunday. Tonight, I will lose myself in Sam. I smile just thinking about him. Being with him has been exactly what I have needed. I've never felt so. . .human.

CHAPTER EIGHTEEN
"BEING HUNTED"

I'm nervous. It almost feels like I'm a mother sending her children out into the cruel world on their own. I can tell my Hunters are also anxious as they dress in their new duds (courtesy of Emily, a girl of many talents). I do my best to soothe their anxiety, but in reality, they won't feel soothed until they are out there and know they can do this on their own. I never had the privilege of experiencing it since I didn't hunt until after I was turned.

I suppress the pang of jealousy I feel. Feeling jealous of the kids who must feel they are going out to their impending doom is silly. They should again draw names from a hat - which I desperately wanted in hopes of separating Sam and Amanda. Still, they decided to stick with their original groups unanimously. The only addition was Jenna in this first rotation. Strangely enough, she volunteered.

"Just remember what you've learned," I tell them. "Stay focused and patient." I help Amanda put on her black leather trench coat, fitted with inserts to hold their swords in their sleeves. With a quick button push, the blades release smoothly, ready for action. They're ingenious really.

Zac rolls his eyes at me when I specifically look at him.

"I know, I know."

"No heroics," I continue. "Listen to your instincts. Always have each other's backs and, please, be careful."

"We got it, Mother," Jenna scoffs. I'm beginning to understand that she uses her rudeness to mask her nervousness. I'll let it slide because this is their first venture out by themselves. But part of me wishes I could pop her one.

"Help Zac take the rest of the gear out to the van, Jenna," I order coolly.

She huffs but doesn't argue - which probably saves her from actually getting popped.

I turn to Amanda. "Please be careful. And listen to your gut. You have the best defense by knowing they're near. Don't doubt yourself. Understood?"

"Yes," Amanda nods and hugs me quickly. She catches me glancing at Sam and silently slips away.

"You be careful, too," I tell Sam when we're alone.

"I will."

"Come back to me," I whisper.

"I promise," he says, his voice low and full of emotion. Sam feathers a finger down my cheek. With a quick check to see if we're alone, he leans down and kisses me softly. "I promise."

I dress in my hunting gear, thankful that the others have chosen to go home to be with their families tonight. I fill my belt with stakes, sheath my daggers, and grab my swords, placing them in the sheaths at my thighs. Taking a deep breath, I wrap my cloak around me and watch my face disappear in the mirror as I lift my hood.

I'm perched on a roof, observing my Hunters. I'm pleased to see Zac and Amanda walking together while Sam and Jenna venture ahead of them. They keep the chatter to a minimum and listen intently to their surroundings. I take a moment to put my senses to use, sniffing the air while tuning my ears to hear any irregular sounds. There are innocents around, but they are few. There's a stench of Hybrid. However, I cannot pinpoint the location.

"Just let them do their job," I scold myself. I crouch, following them as they patrol the alleyways, careful not to be seen. When I reach the end of one roof, I effortlessly and silently jump to the next. I think, briefly, of what it would look like if one of them happened to look up as I was in mid-jump. My cloak flowing behind me, a dark shadow flying through the air. I stifle a chuckle but sober immediately. Something isn't right.

My Hunters are being hunted. I turn my attention to the two figures stalking my group. Sam and the others are oblivious, and I understand why now. The figures are human.

"Shit," I mutter vehemently. They don't have time to worry about damn humans! Don't you people know they're trying to save your damned lives? My internal rant is doing nothing to help the situation. I run back, jumping to the building between the Hunters and humans. Soundlessly, I drop to the street.

The internal rant becomes an internal debate. What to do about the humans? I can't kill them. But, they intend to harm what is mine. Then, I see the glint of metal. Guns! Well, hell! In the span of a millisecond, I gauge my position and become aware that I'm closer to my group. A millisecond is all the time I have because, without warning, the human raises the gun and fires at the same time I run to Amanda.

Sam and Jenna, who are ahead of the others, whirl at the sound. Zac's blades are out and ready, and his head whips around, trying to find the origin of the sound.

I raise my cloak, swallowing Amanda in it as the bullet sinks into my back.

"Humans," I whisper to her, deliberately masking my voice. "Run."

She freezes for a moment while the others are yelling, dodging bullets. "Go!" I growl and push her away, staying in the path of stray bullets.

I pivot and run toward the humans. I wonder what the code is when they're trying to kill us.

"They're humans!" I hear Amanda yell to the others. "No! Zac, we can't! The code!"

I ignore everything else and focus on the humans. They keep shooting, and it takes everything I have not to engage my swords and sweep them across their necks. Bullets are biting into my skin, burning. They won't kill me, but damn if they don't hurt! I lift my arms, bringing my cloak up, and just as before with Amanda, I envelop them, wrapping my arms around their throats.

They struggle against my hold as I drag them away from the others but get nowhere. Not so tough when you can't use your guns, I think in disgust. When I know I'm far enough away from my Hunters, I let them go, throwing them against the alley wall.

Stupidly, they try to raise their guns. With a deft move, I disarm them both with blinding speed.

"Who are you?" The bald one, covered in tattoos (does everyone have tattoos?) demands.

"Who I am does not matter," I answer, my voice gruff. "Who are you?"

"Screw you!" This gem is from the bald one's partner. Blonde and, unfortunately for him, stupid.

I click my tongue, shake my head and backhand him. He, fittingly, slumps into the trash at his side.

"Let us try this again, shall we?" I say sweetly. "Who are you?"

"No one! We're no one!" Baldy is scared, but something about how he says, 'no one,' intrigues me.

I kneel before him, pinning him against the wall with one hand around his neck. With my other hand, I lift my hood enough for him to see my eyes.

"Who are you?" I ask again. I put the power of compulsion into the words and see his eyes glaze over.

"C-Cue. Er...Cody, but they call me Cue," he stammers. "That's 'Casper.' Eddie."

"Who calls you Cue?"

"My bros, um, gang."

"Why did you try to kill those kids earlier?"

"We were told to." His eyes are flat. He is entirely under my control. Susceptible? Or is this a sign that someone else has been controlling him?

"Who told you to?"

"I don't know. Just orders." Baldy is beginning to sound like a zombie. I soften my gaze, knowing he wouldn't know who they were if someone with my abilities got to him. He automatically tilts his head for me when I let go of his neck.

"What are you doing?"

"I am here to serve you," he whimpers and closes his eyes, waiting for me to feed.

I have to admit. I'm tempted. Very tempted. But, as I lean in, a peculiar tattoo catches my attention. It was a very simple tattoo. However, the message was anything but. Two small black rings with red ink in the shape of drops of blood dripping from them. Quickly, I check the neck of blondie and confirm my fears. He has one, too. Well, this can't mean anything good.

I shake - what was it? Casper? - until he is awake and fix my gaze on him.

"You will forget me and everything else that happened tonight. Do you understand?"

"Yes."

"You will not hunt Hunters anymore." I turn my gaze up. "Anyone who hunts Hunters will die. Whoever attempts to kill Hunters will feel like they are burning from the inside out. Get that message out. Is that understood?"

He shivers. "Yes."

I don't know if that will work, but I take the chance anyway. They've been used so badly that I'd actually be surprised if it didn't work. Besides, whoever did this to them can't be as powerful as I am. Right?

I catch up with Sam and the others in time to see them fighting Hybrids. This is what they were trained for and what they're good at. I can tell they're still shaken by what occurred earlier, but they are doing a great job of not letting it affect them. I don't need to interfere, and I'm happy about that. It means they are more than capable of taking care of themselves. I realize that I will have to have a conversation with the entire group about what to do with the humans that are apparently helping this new breed of Cursed Ones. I just don't know how to handle that situation. Yet.

Another presence catches my attention. Not human, but not a Hybrid either. A full blood.

"What in the hell is going on?" Because talking to myself will get my questions answered. I shake my head, disgusted, and watch the Cursed One closely. He's observing my Hunters and keeping an eye on his surroundings. "What are you looking for?"

Again, I'm talking to myself. If I want answers, I need to get them. I devise my plan while descending from my post. This needs to be done quickly and quietly. Another distraction for my group could spell disaster.

I know the shadows won't hide me from my target, so I time my approach between his surveillance. I pounce when I'm close enough, grabbing him from behind, my hand over his mouth, and plunging a stake in his heart before he even knew what was happening. I feel the pain in my own chest once more, but I don't take the time to analyze it. I pull him further into the shadows of the alley.

I touch my chest over my heart absently, crouching in front of him. No tattoos, I notice. He's quite beautiful, actually, with a mane of black hair and an angel's face. Immediately, and perhaps foolishly, I feel guilty for thinking that. Why the guilt? Because of Sam?

I mentally shake myself, chastising myself for being even momentarily distracted. Taking a sword from its sheath, I press the button to release the blade.

"You won't feel a thing," I say, then plunge it into his right shoulder through the building behind him. It won't hold him long after I take the stake out, but it'll buy me some time.

He wakes up sputtering and hissing when I remove the stake - not so beautiful now - then freezes when he sees me.

"You!" he snarls and makes a grab for me. Confusion sets across his face when he can't move far.

I cock my head. "Me?"

"Cloaked One! You're mine!"

I push my hand on the sword's hilt, penetrating it further into the brick behind him.

"I would say you're mine," I counter. "What do you want with me?"

He hisses in response.

"Well, hissing will get you nowhere. Tell me, and perhaps I'll set you free."

"Set me free, and I will stake *you*," he retorts.

A full sentence! I'm completely caught off guard by his response so I almost don't notice he's dislodging the sword.

"Ah ah ah." I wag a finger at him before taking a silver dagger out and driving it through his hand. "What do you want with me?" I ask again, ignoring his growl.

His response is a slow, maniacal laugh, and I imagine I won't get anywhere with him.

"To hell with this." I rise, taking out my second sword. "Any last words?"

"You can't hide forever, Cloaked One. We will find you."

"Technically, you won't. You'll be dead."

I slice my blade through him, disconnecting that pretty head from its body.

I make my way back home way before the others. I need to at least give them a little time to themselves and trust them completely.

I hate sewing. Even more, I hate having to dig damn bullets out of me. In my room, I peel off my gear and frown at the holes in the fabric.

"Barbaric invention," I grumble as I sit naked in my bathroom, readying myself. I take out a blood bottle and drink half of it immediately.

Gingerly, I dig my fingers into one of my wounds.

"Son of a...." That bites. My fingers finally find the bullet, and I pull it out. I place it in an empty vial. No way I'm getting rid of these.

I was hit six times—perfect—and that's not counting the one in my back that was intended for Amanda. It's going to be interesting trying to get that one out.

I drain the rest of the blood and start on a new bottle. It's more than I've had in a long time, and if I'm not careful, I will begin needing more. I finish fishing out the bullets in the front - my wounds have already healed - and look in the mirror at my back. Right in the middle. Of course. I reach back, and though I can touch it, it's just barely.

"Well. This gets better and better, doesn't it," I say to my reflection. With a sigh, I grab my elbow with my other hand and push, dislocating my shoulder enough to reach the wound. A guttural moan escapes from me involuntarily as I dig the bullet out. I quickly reset my shoulder, leaning on the counter, panting slightly. I felt the change occur when dislocating my shoulder, so I don't bother looking at myself in the mirror.

I take deep breaths, calming myself. The pain has already subsided. Now it's just a matter of returning my appearance to normal. What a night, I think as I glance at my cloak and shake my head. To be continued tomorrow night with the next group. I can't help but wonder how Mum and Papa did this. Then again, they didn't have to deal with humans trying to kill their Hunters with guns.

My thoughts are interrupted when I hear the others come in, animated, full of adrenaline, and talking over each other about the night's events. I dress quickly and go to meet them in the training room.

"Ana! You won't believe what happened tonight!" Amanda practically runs to me and throws her arms around me. "We were *shot* at!"

"Shot at?" I frown, feigning ignorance. "Hybrids are using guns now?"

"No! Humans!"

Amanda is much too excited about being shot at. Has she lost her ever-loving mind?

"Humans?" I look questioningly at Sam, and he shrugs.

"I don't really know what happened," he confesses. "It was all so fast. One moment we were patrolling, all was quiet, and the next, bullets were flying, and...."

"And?"

"And," Amanda continues for him, "someone saved my life! I don't know who it was, but I mean, it was so cool! They had like a cape and a hood!" She grabs the sides of her trench coat and twirls, the coat flying out behind her. "They wrapped the cape around me, then told me that it was humans shooting at us and to run!"

"Really? And you don't know who this person was?"

"Nope! But it sounds like the Cloaked One I read about in the journal! What if he came back? Is that even possible?" Amanda continues to twirl her coat, and I raise my eyebrows at her.

"Is she okay?"

"Just excited," Sam answers. "She's weird."

"Whatever. *You're* weird! How could you not think that was cool?"

"Because they could have killed you! They could have killed *all* of us!"

"But they didn't so relax." She turns her attention back to me. "The caped person, I'm going to pretend it *is* the Cloaked One, ran after the humans and took them away!"

"You didn't follow?"

"No. We can't do anything about humans, though Zac wanted to go after them."

"Thanks, Amanda," Zac says grumpily. "They were shooting at us. I feel it would have been justified to kick their asses!"

"Hmm." It was a noncommittal response from me, and I'm aware then that Jenna has been extra quiet. "Are you okay, Jenna?"

"You didn't warn us that we were going to be hunted by humans," she snaps.

"How could I possibly know that?"

"And, what the hell is this caped person about? What the hell is going on out there? None of this was in our training."

Oh boy. She certainly isn't shy about speaking her mind.

"We will talk about the innocents and our course of action should this happen again. This is a learning experience for us all, Jenna. Things are so different now than they were before." I hope she doesn't notice that I skip over her question about the 'caped person.'

"They weren't innocent, Ana," Zac interjects.

"He's right," Sam agrees. "Guns make them our enemies."

"Wait. Just wait!" I exclaim. I cannot let this fight get out of hand. We have enough to worry about with the Cursed Ones. Bringing humans into the mix will just complicate things even more. Besides, Hunters have a code not to harm innocents. That means *humans*, whether they're trying to kill you or not. "We are bound. . ."

"Screw the code, Ana!" Zac yells, and I was on him before he knew

161

what hit him. I push him back against the wall, fisting my hands in his shirt.

"*You* do not speak to me like that," I growl. "I am your leader. We are Hunters, Zac, not murderers. These codes have existed for centuries, and it is not up to you to question them. If you go against the code, you will give me no choice..."

I purposefully do not finish my sentence. It'll give him something to think about when he tries to figure out what might happen to him. Judging by his expression, he's already afraid of me. Good. How dare he speak to me like he did?

"Ana?" Sam places his hands over mine, gently coaxing me to let go of Zac.

"He dares to defy me," I snap, still holding Zac.

"He's a hothead. Zac is just trying to get used to all of this," Sam reasons.

I reluctantly release Zac. "Get out," I tell him.

"Ana, please, I'm sorry!"

"Get out. I don't want to see you back here until you get it through your head that I am in charge. Reread the damn journal. Learn the code, back and forth. When I see you again, you shall recite it to me verbatim. Am I clear?"

"Yes."

I turn my back to him. I need him to get out of my face before I do something I will regret.

"That was harsh, Ana."

"I do not care, Amanda. He needs to learn that he must follow the rules of the society. Rogue Hunters get themselves killed, or worse."

I catch Amanda's eye, and she looks at me curiously. I take a moment to calm myself. I must be more careful and learn to curb my anger.

"You should sleep. I will hear the rest of your story tomorrow. Then we shall discuss what to do about the innocents." I emphasize the word.

Jenna and Amanda walk away without another word. Only Sam lingers, watching me intently.

"Ana."

"Not tonight, Sam," I whisper and leave him.

I decide to halt further patrol until I can speak to Bernard. I can't possibly be there for every scouting, so I need more information before I get my Hunters killed.

I arrive at the address Bernard gave me on Sunday at precisely four o'clock. I'm slightly surprised that he gave me the address to his home, though I'm not sure why.

"Anala. Please, come in."

I raise my eyebrow at the name he uses. Obviously, he does not take my objections seriously.

"Ah, right. It is Ana now. I do apologize." Bernard smiles, but there's something off about him.

"Nice place," I mutter. It isn't really, but my parents always taught me to be courteous. The apartment is small and drab. Dark. He has every window covered in heavy, red velvet, and not a drop of sunlight could seep through. Books - old and filled with a language I have since learned - are strewn over a desk. Papers, some stacked, some disheveled, covered red velvet chairs and settee. The only light came from a small lamp on the overcrowded desk. Seriously, the place was a disaster.

"You must excuse the mess," he says with a chuckle. "As I told you, I have been trying to gather information."

I say nothing as I wait for him to clear a spot for me to sit. He empties two chairs and moves them so they face one another a few feet apart.

"Please, sit." He gestures, and I notice a slight tremor in his hand. "Could I offer you some tea?" Yes, something is definitely off with Bernard.

"No, thank you. I cannot stay long."

"Of course. You are here for information?"

He is distracted and fidgeting.

"Yes. First, I need to know if the Cursed Ones are contained here in this area."

"I believe so, yes. I cannot imagine they have ventured too far..." his voice trails off.

"Are you feeling okay, Bernard?"

"Yes, yes. I am fine." He laughs again, and it gives me chills.

"Why here?" I ask.

"I'm sorry?"

"Why did they show up here? And you? Why are you here? Something does not fit about all of this. Why wait until Hunters are found to make an army? You said they should all be contained here, but why wouldn't they build their army wherever they came from?"

"So many questions!" He snorts. "I am going to need a drink! Are you sure you won't have one with me?"

I decline, noting he has not answered any of my questions. "What is it you are not telling me, Bernard?"

"I do not know what..."

"Bernard!"

"Anala, I do what I have to do in order to survive," he says quickly, and I realize then that he looks like someone jonesing for another hit of their drug of choice.

"What does that mean?"

Bernard stands at the bar with his back to me. I think, fleetingly, that it's taking him a long time to pour a drink but forget about it when he sits back down. He drinks—whiskey from the smell—and watches me. Is he weighing his options?

"I brought them here," he confesses.

"You - what?"

"They agreed to keep me alive if I helped them find what they seek."

"They agreed?" I can't believe what I am hearing. I have seen how they have evolved, but so much that they can make deals with humans? "I do not understand, Bernard. How are you communicating with them?"

"They are not as primitive as you may remember, Anala. Especially the one..." he stops as though he is about to reveal too much and waves his hand through the air. "The point is, we made a deal. I was told to search for Hunters, and I found them. Found you."

I frown. "Cursed Ones *wanted* you to find Hunters? That makes no sense. We are the only ones that have the ability to kill them."

"But, you also have the ability to bring out the one they seek," Bernard said matter-of-factly.

"The Cloaked One," I whisper, horrified.

"Yes! You know of him? Do you know him personally?" He sounds so excited, like a child with a new toy.

"One of the Cursed Ones that I killed spoke about the Cloaked One," I answer.

"I see." Bernard is disappointed with my answer.

"Why, Bernard? Why do they want...the Cloaked One? And what is your involvement?"

Bernard smiles sardonically and rises to get another drink. "Dear Anala. It's all about the blood."

"I do not understand." It feels like this is the theme of this entire conversation. I'm completely in the dark, and it's annoying!

"Your father stumbled upon something back then," he says, sitting back in front of me. "I do not know if it was by accident, but his findings were astounding! Youth in a bottle! Everlasting life! A miracle...and extremely profitable."

"You have got to be kidding me." Incredible. Not just his story but that he's actually sharing it with me voluntarily. "Why are you telling me this, Bernard?"

"Your parents have been gone for centuries, Anala. You no longer have to keep up pretenses."

"Pretenses?" I'm too astounded by Bernard's audacity and intrigued to know where he's going with this not to hear him out.

"Money, Anala. Judging by your estate, you have needs. I can offer the world if you help me."

I raise my eyebrows. "Why would you need my help? It sounds like you have an army of Cursed Ones at your disposal."

He waves his hands in dismissal. "They are unpredictable. You know that. But your knowledge and expertise could help me keep them in line!"

"What are you asking of me, Bernard?"

"Blood," he says, leaning forward and resting his elbows on his knees. "You must have some left if you are still alive. I've been trying to recreate your father's formula." He reaches over to grab a book from the desk and passes it to me. It's Papa's. "I've done everything he says there, and it doesn't work. I thought I must be missing something...."

"Where did you get the blood to experiment with?"

"Hmm? Oh, I needed test subjects, of course. So, I made my own test subjects."

"You. . .this is your fault? You *created* more Cursed Ones?"

"You seem surprised." He tilts his head, studying me.

"You told me you didn't know how they returned! You blamed *me*! I am a Hunter, Bernard! Why do you think it would be acceptable to me that you would create what I was born to kill?"

Again, he dismisses my anger with a wave of his hand. "I know, Anala. I helped him, so it is okay to be straight with me."

"You've confused me again, Bernard."

He regards me closely once more. "You do not know?"

I give him a blank stare, keeping my mouth shut. If I can keep him talking, I may discover things I've wondered for centuries.

"Well, well," he chuckles. "Your father is not the saint you wish him to be, my dear girl. He is the reason Cursed Ones existed in the first place."

"That is a lie!"

"Of course he never told you. You thought the world of him." He clicks his tongue. "Good ole Henry Geil, Leader of the Society of Hunters. Maker of the ones Hunters hunt."

"Explain your lies now, Bernard, before I rip you apart," I say, my voice menacing as pain courses through my body.

"Please, Anala," he smiles that wicked smile. "You are a true Hunter. Bound by the laws of the Society. I am human. What you consider an innocent. You cannot harm me."

So, that's why he thinks he can say these things to me. He thinks I cannot harm him.

"Henry was the most sought-after medicine man in the land, Anala. He was known for his talents and was rumored to be efficient in magic. The king ordered your father to find a cure when the Black Death struck. I was his apprentice."

Bernard sits back in his chair and rests his ankle over his knee. I can almost see him going back hundreds of years. It was story time in his mind.

"Henry did not believe there to be a cure, but he tried everything. He put himself in danger, being around those retched souls, trying to cure them." He steeples his fingers at his chin, tapping them rhythmically. "He created a monster that craved blood and could not die."

"No."

"Ah, yes. Oh, he tried to correct his mistake. Told the king he had failed, but I could not let him squander this opportunity." Bernard leans forward, excitement dancing in his eyes. "Could you imagine the wealth? Instead of doing the king's bidding, we would *live* like kings! But Henry was a stubborn man. You get that from him, you know."

"What did he do?" I ask, ignoring his comment. This is it, I think. This was what the falling out between my father and Bernard was. Papa had promised to tell me one day, but that day never came.

"He warned the king that Cursed Ones would bring as much destruction as the Black Death, perhaps more. Then, he formed the society, hoping to 'right his wrong.' He ruined my chances at living a good and prosperous life...."

"A good life at the expense of the lives of innocent people," I interject heatedly.

"All good things come at a price, my dear Anala. But your father just could not let me have that. I tried to tell the king that his armies would be indestructible. *He* could be immortal! He laughed at me, calling me mad. By then, the curse had begun to spread, and he saw that none could be commanded."

Bernard takes my father's book from me, tossing it back on his desk. "I was run out of town because of Henry. When he called upon me to help him, I was shocked, to say the least. He truly must have been desperate. Seeing you alive now, I see how desperate he was."

"You know nothing," I scathe.

"Seems to me I knew more than you about your precious father."

I grip the arms of my chair to keep from lunging at him.

"But you are right in one aspect," he continues. "I do not know the secret to his formula. The only variable I have not tried that may have been available to him back then is the blood of the Cloaked One. That is what I am looking for and what the Cursed Ones are hunting for."

"Why did you have me train Hunters, Bernard?"

"The Cloaked One helps Hunters," he answers with a shrug. "It was the only way I could lure him out."

"What made you so sure...he was still alive?"

"I was not sure." He smiles slowly. Creepy. "But he has been seen now, so it is only a matter of time. If you bring him to me, I can spare your Hunters' lives."

"I will not help you."

"Stubborn, like your father," he sighs. "Look what happened to him and your mother."

My head snaps up, and I stare at him in disbelief.

"Did you kill my parents, Bernard?" I whisper, feeling sick to my stomach.

"All he needed to do was give me the formula, Anala." He reaches behind him, bringing out a gun and pointing it at me. "I would have given him a cut of the money I could have made. But he refused to help me. Again. Now, his daughter refuses me. It is a shame that I must rid the world of the last Geil."

"One more question before you kill me, Bernard." My patience astonishes me. Perhaps it's because I've spent so many years knowing in my heart of hearts that Bernard was responsible for what happened to my parents. Finally, hearing the truth almost brings me peace. Not as much as killing him will.

"Make it quick."

"How did you get the Cursed Ones to kill them and not you?"

"It's all about how you handle them, Anala. I offered them your parents and my servitude." He cocks the gun.

"Where is the Maker?" I ask quickly.

"You said one question, Anala. Besides, I do not know. They refused to tell me for fear it would be used against me. But I know how to get in touch with them," he scolds and pulls the trigger.

I feel the bullet drill through my forehead, and I have to bite my tongue not to cry out - I really do detest getting shot. My head slams back with the force, only pissing me off further. I level my head and stare at a shocked Bernard.

"H-how!" he stammers, struggling to get to his feet. Before he can react, I have him by the throat, pinning him against the bookshelf as his chair topples below him. "You are a Hunter, Anala! You can't hurt me! You are bound by the code!"

I cock my head to one side. "On one hand, I am a Hunter. Sworn to protect humans, innocents. On the other hand, I am Cursed." I bare my fangs and feel my eyes burn as they change. Bernard pales to a sick, pasty color. What a sight I must be with blood trickling down my face. "Which side should I choose, Bernard?"

"You're not a murderer!"

"You're right. I'm not. But is it murder? I mean, you did *shoot* me," I say, pointing at my head. "Do you see the blood I've lost? Now, I'm just angry. . .and hungry."

I sink my teeth into his neck, feeling the rush of live blood. I see Mum's and Papa's faces as I drink, solidifying that I'm doing the right thing. Bernard was a threat - to me and my Hunters - and murdered my parents. He is no innocent, and I feel no guilt as I tear his throat out.

CHAPTER NINETEEN
"YOUTH JUICE"

I drop Bernard's limp body before me and kneel beside him.

"Well, I did not enjoy that one bit," I say to his corpse. "You are - were - a very bitter man."

In fact, I feel lightheaded and a bit queasy after feeding off of him. Perhaps his blood did not age as well as he did. I shrug off the feeling and check his pockets for anything useful.

I never considered myself a murderer, yet here I am, going through a dead man's pockets—a man I killed.

"You brought this on yourself."

I'm unsure if I'm trying to convince myself or what's left of Bernard. Either way, I don't think it's working. I find a phone - looks like a burner phone - in his breast pocket and flip it open. Only one number is listed. It's probably a burner as well, but I keep the phone just in case it can be of use.

I find nothing else of use on Bernard, so I start rummaging through the endless papers on the desk.

"Useless!" I utter. I irritably fling papers and books to the side, barely registering what they are until I come across a piece with my name. Only then do I look at what's in front of me.

Most of it came from my father. Notes, formulas, and secret codes are all in Papa's handwriting, bringing me back to when I was in his lab, frustrated by all the tests I had to endure. What I wouldn't give now to endure all of that once again, just to have Mum and Papa back.

A low sob escapes as I'm unable to hold back angry tears. The last time I was in Papa's lab, my parents lay dead in front of me, victims of the likes of me. And of Bernard.

"Ah!" The rage I feel smothers me, making it hard for me to breathe. I don't even think about what I'm doing when I pick up the desk and throw it across the room.

My tirade is interrupted by an eerie crackling sound coming from the direction of Bernard's body. Curiosity wins over, and I walk to him. His body changes before my eyes, becoming wrinkled and weathered, then mummified and eventually turning to dust. I'm not sure if I should be shocked or happy.

"Easy cleanup," I whisper to no one. One less thing to worry about. Then again, perhaps I should worry about my total lack of compassion for this man. No. He killed my parents and brought Cursed Ones back into this world. I did everyone a favor by ending his life. Besides, he technically shouldn't have been alive anyway. *Neither should you,* my conscience sneers.

I discovered nothing of actual use at Bernard's about where the Maker could be, but I recover most of what was stolen from my parents. I'll have to study Bernard's notes when I get a chance, but he was either lazy or had no idea what he was really doing, as they are pretty jumbled.

Dropping everything on my bed, I strip, thankful to finally be out of my bloody clothes. Bernard's blood was beginning to smell putrefied. I toss the soiled garments into the trashcan in the bathroom and light them on fire. Mesmerized, I watch the dark flame consume them and what was left of my past.

"Good riddance," I mumble and step into the steaming shower. Sigh. The hot water feels amazing on my skin, washing away the day's events. The lightheadedness is better, as is the nausea, thank God, though it lingers. Ugh. Maybe if all blood tasted like Bernard's, I wouldn't have such a problem staying away from it.

I can't think about him anymore. I need to concentrate on finding the Maker and getting rid of these things once and for all. Again. With Bernard out of the way, it'll make that task easier. And if that's what I must tell myself to get through this, then so be it.

Okay, so I lied. The nausea isn't better. Either the shower steam or the reality of what I did has gotten to me. I have to sit on the edge of my bed to try and regain my equilibrium. Hell, it took most of my strength just to get dressed without getting sick.

"Come in, Sam." His smell almost makes it better, but not quite. My head is spinning.

"I'll never get used to that," Sam says as he enters. He kneels in front of me in seconds, taking my hands—which were holding my spinning head—in his. "Hey, what's wrong? Baby, are you okay?"

The endearment startles me enough to have me looking up at him, eyebrow raised.

He ignores my look, pushing a strand of my hair behind my ear. "You look pale. Do you feel sick?"

"Yes. Feeling a bit nauseous."

Sam's hand drops, and he turns pale himself. The look on his face is —comical.

"Relax, Sam, I'm not pregnant," I chuckle.

"A-are you sure? I know we've been careful, but nothing is a hundred percent."

I doubt it's even a possibility. "I'm pretty sure. It's probably just something I. . .ate." I see his color returning to normal. "Besides, I don't even know if we've been together long enough for me to feel those effects. But, it's nice to know where you stand on kids."

"Ana, that's not...I didn't mean. . .it's just that you're so young. . ."

"I was joking. Sam, we've only known each other for, what, a few weeks? Talking about babies is the furthest thing from my mind."

"Well, you know, if you ever want to discuss it, we can," he says sheepishly. "We never really talk about the future."

Wait. What? What's with the total about-face? One minute he's paler than I am, and the next, he wants to discuss *babies* and the future?!

"I. . ." I am at a loss for words. That's what I am. How do I discuss a future with him when I know there isn't one? There can't be. What I am prevents that. Damn it. I knew better than to get involved like this. Why couldn't I have just kept my heart out of this? "Sam, I -"

Whatever I am about to say is interrupted - mercifully - by arguing I hear in the training room.

"Something is wrong."

"Huh? What is it?"

I know he can't hear what I hear, and he's confused by my reaction. I grab his hand and tug him along with me.

"Zac, you can't do this!"

"She doesn't want me here, Amanda. Fine. I'll do it by myself."

Zac is throwing weapons into a duffel bag when Sam and I finally make it to the training room.

I'm standing behind him when he turns.

"No, you won't," my hand is solid against his chest, making him stop abruptly.

"Ana!" Zac's surprise is apparent. I don't know where he thought I'd be. This *is* my house. "Look, you don't want me in this Society. You've made that perfectly clear."

"I never said that, Zac." Patience I didn't know I had keeps my tone calm. "I said you needed to learn the code. Did you?"

"I know the code."

"Then tell me."

"Ana..."

"The code, Zac. Now."

"A Hunter's fundamental duty is to protect innocents at all cost - even if it means their own death," he recites stoically. "A Hunter *must* kill any Cursed Ones he or she comes across, even if it is family. If you know someone has bitten, you must make sure they are dead by either beheading them or setting them on fire. Never, under any circumstances," he pauses. "Kill an innocent. And never break any of the rules."

"I do not want you to leave. I merely want you to follow the rules."

Ugh. This nausea is really getting worse, and Zac acting like a petulant child is not helping.

"Those *innocents* are not following any rules!"

"They cannot help it."

"Really?" he scoffs. "Everyone has a damn choice, Ana."

"Not everyone," I say quietly. "They are being compelled."

"That's real?" It was the first time anyone else had said something since I entered the room.

I turn my attention to Amanda, and even that slight movement has me feeling dizzy. "Yes. I believe they're also being drugged."

"With what?" Sam asks. "The lab didn't find any trace of any known drug."

"Because it isn't known. I think they're being drugged with the blood of Cursed Ones."

"Wouldn't that turn them?" Emily shudders.

"No. Mere drops won't turn you." I sigh. "I'm still trying to figure all of this out, but these humans, these *innocents* don't know what they're doing. Killing them is not an option."

"What would happen?" Zac questions. "You never said what would happen if I broke the code."

I study Zac for a moment, trying to read his thoughts. Does he really want to kill a human? I can't imagine that would be true.

"The last ones to break the code were murdered," I tell him somberly, thinking of my parents.

I don't know how much longer I can handle this repugnant feeling, but being a leader, it is my job to be here for my team.

Sam clears his throat, breaking the deafening silence that fills the room. "So, what can we do?"

"Incapacitate them. However you do it, just make sure they stay alive."

"Wait, this is bullshit. I didn't sign up for this!" Jenna pokes her finger at me, full of contempt. "*You* never said we would have to deal with brain-washed humans with guns and orders to kill us! I'm a cheerleader," she huffs. "I cheered at football games, went out with friends, and had great sex with my college boyfriend. Ex-boyfriend, since I no longer have time for him. I would never have agreed to this if I'd known what we were up against! And, now, I'm stuck here!"

"You are not stuck here, Jenna. You are free to leave at any time." I feel a twinge in my stomach. This can't be good at all.

"What?"

"I'm not forcing you to be here."

"But, you said we were bound. . ."

I gasp as the twinge becomes a full-blown pain.

"Ana? Are you okay?" Sam takes a step forward, but I stop him.

"I'm fine. Bound by the rules, not the Society," I raise my eyebrow at Jenna. "It is your destiny as a Hunter, but it is also your choice." I turn to them all. "I will never force your decision. This is a dangerous, life-threatening duty. If you don't want to be here, I encourage you to leave."

"So, I won't get murdered if I leave?"

"Oh, I didn't say that, Jenna. Cursed Ones know who the Hunters are. Whether you are in the Society or not, they will come for you. Ugh!" I double over, pressing my hand against my stomach, hoping to relieve the pain. "But it's your choice who you want next to you when they do," I'm breathless and sick. Oh God, please don't let me be sick in front of them.

"Ana?" Amanda reaches for me, and I push her away. I'm going to be sick whether I like it or not.

"I'm sorry, excuse me." I run out of the room, praying I make it to my bathroom in time.

Slamming the door, I bend over the toilet just in time. Are you kidding me? I haven't been sick in almost six hundred years! In fact, the last time I remember being sick, I had—my retrospect is interrupted by another bout of retching—just been bitten.

I hate vomiting with a passion. I don't want to hear it, I don't want to see it, I don't want to smell it. . .and I certainly don't want to be doing it. Absently, I wipe my mouth and am surprised to see blood coating my hand. Blood? That's what I'm spewing? And I get sick again.

"Ana?" Amanda knocks lightly on my bathroom door.

"Go away," I croak, my throat burning.

"Do you need something?"

Yes, to stop getting sick!

"No."

But that's not true. I need blood. Ever since I - drank from Bernard, I haven't been feeling right. I grab a bottle from the fridge and drink half of it, hoping to keep it down. The feeling reminds me of a commercial I saw once for that pink antacid, the one that coats the stomach and provides relief. Blissfully, I drink more.

I am a damn immortal. I can be shot, stabbed, and pretty much anything else - with the exception of having my head cut off - and be just fine. One *drink* from Bernard, and I'm brought to my knees. Okay, so technically, it wasn't *one* drink. But I can regenerate. I shouldn't be sick.

Maybe...

I lean on the sink, close my eyes, and am willing myself to change. I feel the change, and it's peculiar how it seems to be happening in slow motion. Opening my eyes, I watch in the mirror as my eyes change color. The red ring is brighter, thicker. My mouth opens involuntarily as my teeth grow. Are they longer, or is my mind playing tricks on me? I shake my head, drink more of the bottled blood and wait. Turning makes me regenerate faster, and I feel my stomach begin to settle even more. With luck, my headache will go away as well.

Just as the thought enters my mind, my head explodes with pain. I grip the sink to keep my buckling knees from giving out on me. "Ahh!"

"Ana!" Sam bangs on the door - totally not helping me - his voice full of concern.

The pain subsides as quickly as it came on. I catch my reflection and am startled by my appearance. The red ring is even bigger! It nearly covers all of the eerie white that being Cursed gives me.

"*Shit.*" I try relaxing, turning back to normal, but the red is still visible. Well, this certainly will not do.

"Ana, answer me, or I'm breaking the door down."

"Go away, Sam!" I snap, grabbing my hidden key. Papa's elixir has to work. Please, let it work!

"I'm not going anywhere until I know you're okay!"

"*Did you do this to her?*"

"*What?*"

"*Is this your fault?*"

Oh, come on! Are Sam and Amanda really talking about this now? I hope against hope that they're alone, but I can smell the others. Fantastic.

Even through the ache of my burning insides from drinking the elixir, I notice Sam hesitates. Does he still think I'm pregnant? I want to scream at him that it's not possible. Hell, I want to scream! Instead, I quickly rinse my mouth, splash water on my face, and ensure I am clean.

"She seems to think it's not. She says it's something she ate."

"I swear, Sam. If you did this. . ."

"Look, Amanda, whatever is going on between. . ."

I open the door quickly to stop him. "Really?" I scorch both of them with a look. "You all did not have to stand here and listen to me getting sick."

"Are you dying?"

"No, Jenna. Thanks for your concern."

"We *are* concerned, Ana."

Eric's voice is so soft. I almost don't hear him. I flash him a smile.

"Food poisoning."

Amanda and Sam don't look convinced, but oddly enough, I think it's actually true.

"Well, you look better," Zac affirms. "You're not as pale."

"I feel better. Now, since you all witnessed that, and I'm completely uncomfortable, we should go to the dining room and discuss what I found out at Bernard's."

I spread the books and papers I took from Bernard's on the table.

"What is all of this stuff?" Amanda picks through the papers and flips through the books.

"This is everything I found at Bernard's." Minus the phone, but no one needs to know that. "Most of it is from my f...um, family. My ancestors. They contain formulas and notes."

"I don't get it. How is this supposed to help us?" Jenna has gone back to smacking her gum.

"Knowledge is always helpful, Jenna."

"You can read all of this?" Emily asks. She is changing slowly and subtly, but her confidence is growing.

"Yes."

"Wait," Jeremy interjects. "You said formulas. What kind of formulas are we talking about?"

Here goes. I open one of Papa's books I had not seen before I took it from Bernard.

"Back then, the country was being plagued by a disease called the Black Death."

"Anala!" Eric gasps, and I think my heart literally drops, stops, or flips - who knows which, but it was bad.

"What?"

"I read the journals. The Black Death is what Anala died from."

Good Lord! Don't people know they're not supposed to scare old people? Cursed or not, I think I could have died just then.

"Um, yes. Ironically, her father," I almost say 'my father,' "spent much time trying to find a cure before...she was even born." I flip through pages in the old book, stopping at the page I want. "It says here that the king sought, um, Henry, Anala's father, out requesting - or rather ordering - him to find a cure. Magic, back then, was more science than anything else, so the formulas you see here were for elixirs or potions if you will."

"He obviously failed," Jenna says quietly, and I give her a nasty look. "I'm just saying, his own daughter died of the damn disease. . ."

"He did everything he could," I say coolly. This is the part I'm afraid to talk about. I haven't even had time to process it myself. "He talks here," I point to a paragraph in the book, "about experimenting on two patients. He would administer two different medicines and record the effects, if any. Patient one was given what he called 'Antidote A,' but after a time, it was clear it did not work. When he goes to give Patient two 'Antidote B,' it is too late. The window of time to work with those with the Black Death was very short," I explain.

"Without another patient ready, Henry has no choice but to administer 'Antidote B' to the first patient. The effects were...not what he intended. What he created was. . ."

"Cursed Ones," Amanda finishes in a whisper.

"Yes."

"Your ancestors created Cursed Ones?" Jenna asks as though it's too unbelievable to be real.

"Yes. Then created the Society."

"To try and correct their mistake," Sam announces.

"Exactly. But he had an apprentice who wanted fame and fortune more than anything else. He tried to convince the king that Cursed Ones were a good thing."

"Did it work?" Amanda asks. They all look to me, completely taken by the legend.

"Thankfully, no. He was run out of town, humiliated." I flip further to notes about me. "When Anala got - sick - Henry sought out his apprentice for help in finding the cure." I tread carefully here.

"Why would he bring that creep back?"

"Because she was his daughter, Jenna. He would do anything to help her." Oh, yeah. Emily's confidence is certainly growing.

"He thought he had no choice," I say. "The apprentice knew how Henry worked and was talented in his own way."

"I'm sorry to interrupt, Ana," Eric says shyly. "But does it say in the book why he thought he could find a cure for Anala when he couldn't do it before?"

To say that hearing my Hunters say Anala is disconcerting is the understatement of the year.

"He speaks of having the blood of Cursed Ones to work with. Vampires can regenerate. They do not get sick," Unless they drink putrid blood.

"Ah, I see. That makes sense."

"They did not find a cure to the Black Death, though. What Henry did find was, well, the Fountain of Youth, essentially."

I place a vial that consists of my blood on the table.

"A drop every now and then can give eternal life."

"As a human or Cursed?" Amanda asks, curious.

I give her my attention. "Human. You do not become immortal but ageless."

"Seriously? So, a drop of this makes you young forever?"

I grab Jenna's hand before she can touch the vial. My eyes bore into hers. "Yes." I slip the vial back into my pocket. "But, once again, Henry's apprentice sees fortune and fame." I look pointedly at Jenna for an instant before continuing.

"Henry restricted his access to everything. He had no idea how long-term use would affect anyone using it, so he could not allow it to get out." I pause. The day I found my parents lying there, motionless - dead - fills my mind. "The apprentice would not be denied again," I whisper. "He had my family killed and took everything. Vials, potions. . .books."

"Oh, my God. Bernard."

I nod, affirming Amanda's assessment.

"Bernard? He was your ancestor's apprentice?" Sam asks incredulously.

"Yes."

"So, he took the 'youth juice,' and he's here from the 1400s?" Jeremy is completely enthralled. This has to be even better than the Sci-Fi movies he watches. 'Youth juice' tickles me, even if this is the furthest thing from a laughing matter.

"I guess we know it has no adverse side effects," Jenna says smugly.

"Is that what you think?"

"He seemed normal to me."

"Hmm. He created more Cursed Ones."

"He's responsible for this?" Sam demands.

I close Papa's notebook and reach for another.

"This is Bernard's. The first few entries were made centuries ago. He talks about his dealings with Henry and his suspicions that Henry was keeping something from him. When he discovered what Henry had created, he began plotting."

I turn pages.

"He grilled Henry about the, er, 'youth juice,' wanting to know the formula, with no luck. He risked everything by going to a Cursed One. *I am astounded by their ability to speak,*" I read. "*'Once I convinced them I was there to help them, it was easy. I offer them the Leaders of the Society of Hunters in exchange for their help. Of course, they want more. I cannot make the mistake of trusting them completely. However, I will help them find what they call "The Cloaked One." It is worth it for the use of their blood.'*"

My heart aches reading how he gave up my parents without even the slightest hint of remorse.

Amanda gasps. "They were searching for the Cloaked One? Why?"

"The Cloaked One was killing them off faster than any group of Hunters combined. But Bernard was right not to trust them. They did not live up to their end of the bargain. *They deny me their blood!'.*"

"What did he do?" Zac, who has been extra quiet, asks.

"He created his own."

"How?"

"My. . .Henry had stashes of Cursed blood everywhere in his lab. Bernard used that."

"Does he say who he used it on?" Sam is hopeful that the books will tell us who the Maker is.

I flip to a tear in the book.

"That page is missing."

They all groan at the same time. Believe me. I know the feeling. Nothing can ever be easy.

"I think Bernard went mad."

"Why do you say that? I mean, besides him creating monsters and all."

I slant a look at Amanda. Monsters. Still hurts.

"If you look here in his notes, in the beginning, they are comprehensible. As the years go by, the notes become more chaotic and deranged. They don't make sense and then just become unreadable."

"What was he like when you spoke to him," Sam asks.

Crap.

"He - wasn't there," I lie. "I tried contacting him, but it's like he just. . .disappeared." Okay, so that part is actually true.

"Fantastic. Now we have some maniac on the loose. Maybe I should call the station and put out a BOLO."

"I don't think that will be necessary. He fulfilled his purpose and exposed the Cloaked One. I don't think Bernard was useful to the Cursed Ones anymore."

"You think a Cursed One killed him?"

I hold Sam's gaze. "Yes."

"What do we do now?" Amanda asks.

"We continue to hunt."

"Now that you know how old the Maker is, will you let us hunt for him with you?"

I know Sam wants this, thinking he can keep me safe. Even Zac perks up at the question.

"No. Absolutely not."

"Ana..."

"No, Sam. Given how old this Cursed One is, none of you are qualified to hunt for it."

"But you are?" Zac snaps.

"More than you," I snap back. "Just as Cursed Ones get stronger and faster with age, so do Hunters."

"Ana, you're talking about a centuries-old vampire versus an eighteen-year-old Hunter," Sam adds.

Of course, that's all they know. That I'm just some kid that happens to have trained my whole life. All eighteen years of it.

"This discussion is over. You will hunt with your regular groups in your regular shifts."

"You're being unreasonable, Ana."

"Enough, Zac!" I can't stop the power in my voice. I should learn to control my anger, or I will regret it one day. I can already see the confusion and - is that fear - on my Hunters faces. "Please. Just do as you're told and let me do what I need to do." I take a deep breath, calming myself. "Who is going out with the second group tonight?"

The group ends up being Zac, Emily, Eric, and Jeremy. It's a strong group, though I worry about Zac. My trust in him is wavering, which is never good. If I can't trust him to go hunting and follow the rules or keep his group safe, what should I do with him?

As with the first group, I follow them, dressed in my full hunting gear. I hope the night goes smoothly, and honestly, be quiet. Judging by Zac's mood, I'm not sure he would hesitate to break the rules.

Friday night in LA. Humans flock to the area, looking to get drunk, laid, or both. I'm curious how my Hunters will handle being surrounded by innocents while trying to remain inconspicuous. Not an easy task when you're dressed similarly and in all black. But they seem to be doing an excellent job at not drawing attention to themselves when it's necessary for them to be among the crowds.

I keep my distance when I have to be on the ground, waiting for my chances to get to higher turf. I sense the Hybrids—four that I can distinctly identify—immediately. When they turn down an alley, I silently leap up, scaling the wall until I get to the roof.

I'm surprised by the fact that they don't have a victim. They just seem to be. . .waiting.

"Well, this can't mean anything good," I whisper. Yet, I keep my distance, ready to see how my Hunters react.

"*There they are,*" Zac whispers to the others.

"*What are they doing?*" Jeremy mutters.

"*They're waiting for us,*" Eric answers, then looks at Emily, who nods subtly. He then points at Zac, directing him to one side and Jeremy to the other.

Hmm. I don't think I would've guessed that Eric would take charge or the other boys would let him, but they followed his unspoken instructions.

They fan out, with Zac watching their backs, as they approach the Hybrids.

I scan the perimeter, sharpening my senses to everything around me. I can hear the faintest sounds and smell the most imperceptive smell. I relax—somewhat—when I don't sense a full blood.

To my utter shock, Emily enters the area alone. The Hybrids turn to her curiously, then show their fangs. It's a move meant to frighten her, but she stands her ground without a flinch.

On the other hand, I can't help but be fascinated - not to mention baffled - by the Hybrids' behavior. They never hesitated before. Never used scare tactics. Just went for the prey. Yet, here they are, taunting my Hunter.

They begin to spread out, just as the Hunters, looking to surround Emily. Without a word, Emily sprints towards the Hybrid farthest away from her and literally runs up his body, jumping off his shoulders. Mid-air, she releases her blade, twists her body, and kicks him toward Eric, who slices his sword through the Hybrid's neck. She lands gracefully, and they are on to the next Hybrid.

Very impressive.

Zac and Jeremy fight their own battles with formidable foes with strength and agility. They make quick work of the Hybrids and move on.

Their rhythm with each other is remarkable. Even Zac is oddly cooperative and efficient. Overall, I'm completely impressed with them.

A movement catches my eye, and the scent strikes me a split second later. A full blood. He is on the roof opposite of me, perched and waiting. For what? I ready myself for any attack it plans for my Hunters, but there is none. He just watches. He doesn't sense me, which is as curious as his indifference to my group. When he leaves, I follow him.

Cursed Ones, obviously, have a keen sense of smell and awareness, but he could be human with his total obliviousness to me. Or, I could be walking into the best trap ever. It's quite easy following him as he has no idea I'm even there.

I stay on full alert as he enters an area through a rusted, chain-linked fence. Deciding not to take any unnecessary risks of making noise, I leap over the fence, landing silently beside an old, broken column. I touch it inquisitively. It's not real. What the hell is this place?

I catch up with the full blood, still puzzled as to why he has not detected me. Don't look a gift horse - and all that stuff - I think. Keeping my distance, I survey my surroundings. It seems to be an old Roman coliseum. Wait, it's *the* Roman Colosseum! I am confused, as I have seen the Colosseum myself, and this does not have its grandeur.

"Hollywood," I murmur, realizing I must be in some old, unused studio lot. I stealthily vault to higher ground and zero in on the object of my interest. He stops inside an arch that blocks my view. Creeping forward, I position myself to get a better look and almost fall from my post at the sight.

There have to be close to one hundred full bloods! *Shit!* This is worse than I thought. How will I, with only seven Hunters - virtually newborns themselves - compete with this?

"Where is he?" The one I followed here speaks clearly, and, oddly enough, with an English accent! Their voices still hold that distinct growl of a Cursed One, but they have certainly evolved.

Are you kidding me? Not only are there far more than I expected, but they are communicating! Forget communicating. They're plotting and planning - and who knows what else they're doing!

"Off creating more," another answers. They are all dressed nicely. I don't know why I find that odd, but I do. If the men aren't in suits, they wear black jeans and long-sleeved shirts. The women - which look to be about half their population - also wear black, with their hair pulled back in severe ponytails. They're an army.

"We do not need more," the first one scoffs. "We are ready!"

"They are mere distractions. For him and the Hunters." An elder joins the one I followed, placing a hand on his shoulder. "You should not defy him, Nyle."

They have names!

"I will not. I merely want to get this over with so he may live in peace."

"He knows what he is doing. Did you find the Cloaked One with the Hunters?"

My ears perk, and I instinctively reach for my swords.

"No. The Cloaked One has left them to fight for themselves. They are good, Ward. Very good. They have been taught well."

"As have we. Do not worry. The new ones he creates do not possess the skills we do. Their accomplishments mean nothing against them." He smiles - I think it's a smile - and takes Nyle's arm. "Come. It will be light soon. We need to save our strength. The Cloaked One will come, and we will win."

After they all retreat inside the faux Colosseum, I sit there for a long while. None of them were aware that I sat there above them, listening. It's almost as baffling as everything I heard them say. *Say*! Clear, concise, intelligent sentences! Okay, they threatened me and my Hunters, but they did it intelligently! Ward, the elder, had said they had been taught well. What in the hell does *that* mean? In all of my knowledge of Cursed Ones, none of them - us - were *taught* to hunt or kill. It's just instinct. Survival. My mind reels at all of the information I learned tonight.

The horde is great. They communicate, are trained in something, are ready for my Hunters, and are nothing if not loyal to their Maker. The odds seem stacked against me and my Society. However, I do have advantages. They cannot detect me, and I know where they are. And knowing where they are, means I know where their Maker is.

CHAPTER TWENTY
"THE TRUE MAKER"

I sneak back into the house and immediately go to my room. I know the others made it back because I can smell them. Good. That's one less thing to worry about.

I carefully fold my cloak, lock it in the trunk at the end of my bed, and sit with my head in my hands. What am I going to do? I've fought many Cursed Ones in my time, but never this many simultaneously. Going in there alone could be suicide. Taking my Hunters with me could mean their death. I can't possibly do that to them. They're so young, just barely starting their lives. No, it is up to me to fix this problem and keep them out of it. I'm just not confident that I will be triumphant. In fact, I'm scared. After almost six hundred years of life, the possibility of death now stares me in the face. Am I strong enough to confront it? Am I strong enough to leave a love behind that I never thought I'd find?

"You left Thomas," I whisper in the empty room. But that was different. Thomas and I never had a chance to begin before my life changed. With Sam, I'm afraid I've lost my cold heart to him. It hurt to leave Thomas, but the thought of leaving Sam is devastating. I never should have let this happen. I knew what the outcome would be, knew there would never be a future for us. How could I let myself fall. . .

His scent fills my nostrils, and it's intoxicating. I walk to the door—

still in my hunting outfit—and open it to his beautiful, slightly bewildered face.

"I didn't know if you had made it back. . ."

I interrupt him by crushing my mouth to his and pulling him inside directly to my bed.

Even though my kiss is - let's say spirited - he is still gentle with me, easing me down onto the bed.

"Sam, I won't break." I stare into his eyes, willing him to understand what I need from him. "You're not going to hurt me."

He gets the message loud and clear as his kisses become more passionate. He fists his hands in my hair and tugs my head back to deepen the kiss. This is what I need. Hell, it may be my last night on this earth after so many years of excruciating loneliness. Spending it like this, with Sam, will be worth it.

I unbutton his shirt, slipping it off him as he deals with the zipper on my suit. It's halfway down when I inhale deeply, reluctantly breaking the kiss.

"What is it?" He's breathless, wanting more, but there's concern in his eyes.

"Amanda is here."

Sam groans and rolls off of me as I get up, zip back up, and open the door before Amanda can knock.

"Oh! Hey, I didn't even know if you were back yet. I. . ."

Amanda looks past me and sees Sam, and her demeanor changes instantly. She takes a deep breath, nostrils flaring, and I know she's angry. But, to her credit, she says nothing about him being there.

"Can I speak to you? Alone, please," she asks tersely.

"Of course." I glance back at Sam.

"I'll meet you in the dining room," Amanda huffs, then turns on her heel and marches down the hall. Great. My potential last night on Earth just got bad.

"Do you want me to come with you?" Sam asks, standing all half-naked and gorgeous in front of me.

"You heard her. She wants to talk alone. Just remember I'm in the dining room if I don't return for some reason."

"You want me to stay?"

"Stay," I whisper, kissing him briefly before heading to my impending doom. This may be scarier than the horde of Cursed Ones.

"Amanda?"

"Robby called," she begins, holding my attention. "He asked if I would go to the movies with him."

"That's great."

"Tomorrow night. I told him I couldn't. I mean, obviously, I can't tell him that I would love to but have to hunt vampires, so I just made up some stupid excuse. I don't think he will wait for me much longer."

"Amanda. . ."

"Why do you get someone," she interrupts. "Jenna lost her boyfriend. I'm probably losing mine. Why do you get Sam?"

I am at a complete loss as to how to answer her. I haven't had *someone* for a very long time. I'm not even sure she wants an answer from me. I have to avert my eyes because I'm too cowardly to hold her gaze.

"Forget it," she says quietly. "I asked you here because I've been reviewing all this." She gestures to all of the journals and papers on the table.

Surprise knocks my cowardice out.

"Going over it? How? It's in a different language."

"That's what the internet is for, Ana. I mean, there are all kinds of translators out there." Her temper is still there, but she seems to be thawing out a tiny bit.

"I see. What did you come up with?"

Since I haven't had the chance to go over the journals in depth, I'm genuinely curious about what she's discovered.

"Okay, well, this is just a theory. But, from what I can understand, do you think the Maker could be the Cloaked One?"

"What?" I swear, these Hunters will be the death of me! If I don't get myself killed by a horde of vampires, I may just die of a heart attack. "That's impossible." I should know.

"Hear me out. Bernard was searching for the Cloaked One. So are the Cursed Ones. There has to be a reason." She continues when I say nothing. "Your ancestor, Henry, is said to have had access to Cursed blood, right?"

I nod.

"Bernard assumed that the Cloaked One's blood is what Henry used to create what Jeremy calls the 'youth juice.' If that's true, that must mean the Cloaked One is also Cursed."

Smart girl.

"I mean, if he's back after all these years, if it's the same Cloaked One, then he has to be Cursed, right?"

"Or, the Cloaked One could be using the elixir," I say carefully.

"Well, I thought of that, but he didn't seem crazy when he saved me."

"Neither did Bernard," I remind her. "But you bring up another point. The. . .Cloaked One helps Hunters."

"Exactly! I haven't figured that part out yet, but it would make sense that that's how Henry got his blood. I mean, how else would he have gotten Cursed blood? Unless it was given to him freely?"

"He could have captured a Cursed One."

"True," she mutters, unconvinced. "But let's say I'm right for argument's sake. Wouldn't that mean we would have to kill the Cloaked One?"

Hmm.

"I mean, you're looking for the Maker. I think the Cloaked One may be the Maker. Maybe not by choice or intentionally, but if it's his blood that Bernard stole, that means it's his blood that made Bernard's crop of Cursed Ones."

Well, hell. I sit heavily in a chair and now think about how my chest hurts when I stake a Hybrid or full blood. I think about how my head pounded when I shot the Hybrid I had brought in for my Hunters to see. Absently, I touch my chest. She has to be correct.

"Ana? Are you okay?"

"Just thinking."

"So, I could be right?"

Amanda looks frightened like she wants desperately for me to tell her no.

I nod.

"The Cloaked One saved my life," she says softly. "Will killing the Cloaked One get rid of the others or return them to normal?"

I give her a puzzled look. "Did you see that in a movie?"

"The Lost Boys," she answers sheepishly and shrugs.

I give her a small smile. "No."

"Do you know that for sure?"

I open my mouth to answer, then close it again. No, I don't know that for sure. It certainly seems plausible if I can feel their pain. But I just can't believe that would be true. I killed the one that made me, and most certainly his Maker. If it were true, wouldn't I have changed or died?

"I'm sure," I say decisively. "The Cloaked One can't be the true Maker. If that blood was used, it was only used to make one. That one then made others. So, he would be the true Maker."

"But the bloodline begins with the Cloaked One," Amanda argues.

She's right. Which means what I've feared all along is true. Bernard may have done this, but the fault is mine. My parents' deaths, and this new outbreak, are all because I was distracted for one moment that fateful day. And still being alive today.

"If what you are saying is right, and we follow the code of the Society, then yes, you will have to kill the Cloaked One," I say softly, and Amanda gasps. "But, let me deal with the one making all these Hybrids first. The Cloaked One can still be of help to us."

"I don't want to kill the Cloaked One," Amanda sighs.

I don't want you to either.

"I think I have an idea of where the Maker is," I say aloud. "Let me take care of him, and then we will decide what to do about the Cloaked One."

"Okay."

"You did amazing with all of this."

"Thanks. I've been getting pretty good at deciphering *all* of the journals."

The connotation of the statement makes me frown.

"I don't even know if all of the translations were right. I'm kind of hoping they're not. Maybe when you go through them, you'll find different answers."

I doubt I will. But I smile and tell her goodnight when she's ready to leave.

"Ana." Amanda pauses at the door. "I don't want to be mad at you about Sam. Or jealous. I'm trying to be happy for you. I don't really think you would hurt him intentionally. But, as we're learning, things happen even when we don't want them to."

She leaves me alone then with that to think about. Amanda Logan is turning out to be...way more than I expected.

I walk back to my bedroom and open the door finding Sam sitting in bed, resting against the headboard, reading. He glances up at me and smiles, and I want to surrender to him completely. I unzip my suit, shut the door, and walk to him.

"I don't know how she expects me to focus on hunting tonight when she's going off alone." Sam begins his patented pace when I walk into the training room.

"Maybe we could force her to take us with her." Zac paces next to Sam.

"Do you really think you could *force* me to do anything, Zac?"

Both he and Sam spin around to face me, clearly unnerved by me hearing their conversation.

"Ana, please rethink this. You need *someone* with you." Sam's eyes plead with me, and as much as I would love to give him everything he wants, I can't give him this.

"No."

"Unreasonable," Zac grumbles.

"Realistic," I respond. "You are not ready. Not for this."

"So, you don't have faith in us. That's what you're saying."

"Zac, please. I have faith in you to help and keep each other alive. That's what I need you to do."

"And who will watch over you?" Amanda asks.

Great. Her, too? I wonder if she's told them I may know where the Maker is. Somehow, I don't think she has, as Sam isn't fighting me as much as I thought he would. In fact, he is being oddly complaisant.

"I need you all to focus on each other and your hunt tonight. Believe in me as I believe in you."

Sam's phone chimes, interrupting.

"Ah, I'm going to need someone to go in my place tonight," he says distractedly. "I just got called in to work."

He's willing to let his sister go hunting without him? It must be an emergency.

"Get Jeremy," I order Jenna - only because she hates taking orders from me. She salutes me sarcastically and marches out. "Is everything okay?"

"Hmm? Yes, just a case I'm working on. We've got a lead."

Sam rarely speaks of his work. I didn't even know he was working on a case. Why does that bother me?

"Well, be careful." I turn to Amanda and Zac. "And, you guys, be extra careful. Please. Stay focused, and don't worry about me. I'll be fine." Of course, that could be a bald-faced lie. How the hell do I know if I will make it out of that faux Colosseum alive?

I hug Amanda. "*Stay safe. And keep Zac under control,*" I whisper to her. She nods and mouths, 'stay safe' to me.

I hug Zac, surprising him. "Keep your temper in check. Remember that innocents don't know what they're doing. Remember the code."

"I will," he mutters.

When Jenna and Jeremy come in, I hug them again, to everyone's surprise, and tell them to rely on their abilities and be confident. I send them off, hoping I will be able to see them again.

Sam wraps his arms around me. "I don't like this."

"I know. I'm sorry."

He kisses my forehead. "I promised no distractions, so it's good I got called in."

Truthfully, I wish he had gone with Amanda and the others. I trust him to keep Zac in line, and I know he would never let anything happen to Amanda.

"*I have to go,*" I whisper against his lips.

He cups my face in his hands. "No unnecessary danger," he commands. "If you find any of these full bloods, be careful. Don't take on more than you can handle."

Oh, if you only knew, Sam. My response is a tender kiss on his mouth. I hug him tightly for a moment, then release him, grab my gear, and rush out. My mind, body, and every part of me want to tell him how I feel about him. But how cruel would it be to say 'I love you' to him and never return?

With extreme stealth and dexterity, I jump, climb, and crawl into the horde's detected hideaway. I find a good vantage point above them and observe with my hood pulled low over my face. Why aren't they out hunting for food? I half expected the group to be thinned out - at least somewhat - trolling for humans. But the numbers seem to be as great as they were the night before. Perfect.

Still, I don't see anyone, in particular, being singled out as the Maker. They should act differently toward him, right? Okay, so I technically don't know how this works, but I imagine I could distinguish who was in charge if he were there. Perhaps he is inside. I weigh my options, choosing who in the crowd seems the weakest. Looks can be deceiving, but I can tell with the little nuances in their posture or facial expressions who the newest is in the bunch. They are a good jumping-off point, so to speak.

I open my bag, filled with extra stakes and daggers, and put as many in my belt and boots as possible. I'm careful not to weigh myself down too much so I can't maneuver. With a deep breath, I zero in on my first victim.

She's about two inches shorter than I am—a slight thing with blonde hair. Typical California girl, I think as I make my way around the columns toward the back of the group. She couldn't have been more than Amanda's age, give or take a couple of years. Too bad for her that eternity will be far shorter than she bargained for.

I grip my swords, jumping silently to their level. They're about one hundred feet away from me, yet they still don't detect me. Is it because they have my blood in them? Not something to think about now!

"Where is she?"

Sam! No! He can't possibly be here!

"Get out of here!" I growl, hoping the Cursed Ones are too distracted to hear us or sense Sam. I keep my back to him, watching the group carefully.

"I'm not leaving without Ana. Where is she?" He positions himself in front of me, in my line of view. *"Is she in there? Do they have her?"*

Sam! You idiot! You're going to get both of us killed!

"Get out!"

Our argument catches the attention of my intended first victim and a couple more around her. They bare their teeth and hiss. And, to my utter shock and horror, they pull out swords! Are you kidding me? *This* is what they've been trained in? Swordsmanship? I don't think this night could get any worse. And, as soon as that thought enters my mind, they charge us.

"Shit!"

I release my blades, stabbing them into the ground as I grab Sam's arms, pressing the mechanism that releases the blades of his swords from his coat. I keep my hands on his hands, spinning us around so that I'm in their direct path to him. I feel two Cursed Ones approaching us first, and I use Sam's swords - still in his hands - thrusting them into each of them. I bring the swords up, essentially cutting the Cursed Ones in half. Two down.

They begin to surround us, coming towards us from Sam's rear. I clutch my own swords, plucking them from the ground and ramming them into two more Cursed Ones behind Sam. As with the first two, I cut them in half length-wise and watch them fall to dust. I spin Sam around until we're back to back, and we fight off more Cursed Ones.

With precise blows, I slice through necks, stave off attacks and try to keep Sam as close to me as possible. I smell his distinct smell, then, only magnified intensely. He's been cut and is momentarily distracted. Keeping my back to his, I lift my swords, bringing them behind me, and use them as a shield against the subsequent blows toward Sam. I have to get him out of here! I pivot, once again turning Sam towards me. I just need to see if he's okay. I have less than a second to assess his wound before another attack ensues.

I slice through three more Cursed Ones behind Sam as he takes care of a couple behind me. Their advance falters slightly when they see they're not making much progress. I take the opportunity.

"You have to go!"

"No! I'm not leaving without Ana!"

"You're going to get yourself killed!"

A few more brave, or perhaps stupid, souls (do they have souls?) attempt their barrage. Sam and I make quick work of them, and again, the onslaught of Cursed Ones hesitates.

"Sam, you have to get out of here!"

He looks down at me, confused. I don't bother disguising my voice anymore. I lift my hood.

"Ana?"

A sword pierces through my back, and I cry out.

"Ana, no!" Sam reaches for me, then stops abruptly when he sees my face.

I take hold of the sword and pull it out. My eyes are burning, my teeth ache. And, by the look on Sam's face, I know I look like the monster he is destined to kill.

"Go!"

He's frozen, unable to comprehend what he's seeing or what I'm saying. I have no other choice. I turn up the heat in my eyes, compelling him to do as I say.

"Run, Sam. Don't look back, don't tell the others where I am. Just run!"

Sam blinks a couple of times. I push him a little, and he finally does as he's told. He runs with swords in hand, ready to fight off Cursed Ones that stand in his way.

They let him go. It's me they want, and with Sam gone, they begin to swarm. I glance quickly at my surroundings, trying to find anything to help me. There are fallen columns surrounding me. I wonder how sturdy they are. I decide to find out when I run to one, jumping on it, pushing myself off, and over the group surrounding me.

When I land, I dig stakes and daggers out of my belt and boots, throwing them at the oncoming horde, hitting my mark every time. And, every time, I feel the pain in my own chest. A few Cursed Ones get through and run toward me. I make another leap, twisting my body in the air, dragging my swords through them, and landing on another column.

"Enough!"

The voice was booming and full of authority. Without hesitation, the group stops its advance.

"I will deal with this."

The booming, authoritative voice echoes throughout the Colosseum into my head, and I turn slowly.

Everything inside me wants to reject what I see.

"Thomas?"

CHAPTER TWENTY-ONE
"I'M STILL ME"

I heard the Irish brogue. I see the sun-kissed hair, just a tad lighter than the wheat that grew in our fields, and I look into his beautiful golden eyes. Yet, I still can't accept it. Carefully, I make my way to him - slightly surprised that none of the Cursed try to stop me.

"Thomas?" I say, again.

He tilts his head and looks at me curiously. He grips the sword in his hand a little tighter as I get closer.

"Thomas, it's me."

His brows knit together as though he's trying to decipher what I'm saying.

"You're dead," he declares, but his voice holds uncertainty.

"I'm here."

"Anala?"

My heart pounds painfully in my chest. He remembers!

"Yes, Thomas. It's me."

He raises his sword and points it at me. "You're killing us," he accuses, looking at my cloak.

"I'm a Hunter, Thomas. So are you."

"No! Hunters killed Anala."

What?

"I don't understand, Thomas."

"He told me. He said they killed you because they didn't want you infecting anyone." He lowers his sword but still grips it tightly. "He said he could help me not feel the pain anymore. He could help me with revenge."

Oh, Thomas! If Bernard weren't already dead, I would surely kill him for this.

"Thomas, I'm here. They didn't kill me. I'm. . .like you."

His head cocks to the side again as he studies me. "You will help us," he demands.

"Help you what?"

"Kill the Hunters."

"No, Thomas. This has to stop. You can't make more Hybrids, and you can't kill my Hunters."

"I am the leader here!"

"*You* are made from my blood!"

He stumbles back as if I punched him. "You're here to take everything away from me. Again!"

"No, Thomas. I'm here to do what I was born to do."

"You want to kill me."

"I don't. God help me. I don't want to kill you." I step closer. "I've missed you."

"Lead with me." He sweeps his arms, indicating the Cursed Ones standing before us. "They are all yours, too."

"Thomas, I can't."

"I love you, Anala."

For one second, I see the boy I once knew in him. I can't stop the tear that escapes.

"I loved you, too, Thomas."

He frowns. "You don't anymore."

No. I love Sam.

"I can't lead with you, Thomas. They can't be here. You know that. You know what I must do."

Thomas's eyes darken with fury. He lifts his sword at me again. "Kill her!" he commands.

Before I have a chance to go after Thomas, the entire horde runs toward me. I fight off as many as possible, but I know I will be killed if I don't find a way out of here. I can't let that happen yet. I need to find Thomas.

I'm older, faster, and stronger than these Cursed Ones, but their number can overpower me if I allow it. I leap to the balcony above me, fashioned as the imperial box the emperor would sit in while watching gladiators kill each other. I suppose it is a fitting arena for what's happening now. A few try to follow me, but I strike them down before they can even land. My objective is to get out of here alive and ensure I'm not followed.

I have the added benefit of being undetectable to these Cursed Ones. I can use that to my advantage once I'm out of this death trap. I will figure everything else out after that. Jumping up, I swing my legs onto the beam above me and climb until I reach the imitation Colosseum's top. A quick look back lets me know that the Cursed Ones are having problems following me. They're all trying to carry out their Maker's wishes at the same time—another advantage for me as they stumble over each other or fight each other, trying to get to me first.

I drop down a few stories to the ground and run, getting beyond the gates as quickly as possible. I hide in the shadows until I'm confident I'm not being followed. Staying hidden, I go home.

I'm exhausted. I don't think I've ever felt this worn down before in all my years. I could blame it on the fight or even seeing Thomas - Cursed. But, if I'm honest with myself, it's all about Sam. He saw me. He knows what I am. I don't want to think of what will happen if he tells the others. However, that isn't what saddens me the most. It's the way he looked at me. Fear and confusion filled his eyes. Can I blame him? Of course not. Still, I can't help but worry about what this will do to *us*.

I find I'm still hiding in the shadows when I get home. A Cursed One willingly going into a house of Hunters. I say willingly, yet, I'm sneaking into my bedroom like a thief in the night.

Once again, I carefully fold my Cloak and lock it away. At this moment, I don't know if I'll ever wear it again. Hell, I don't know what tomorrow will bring or if I'll still have a group of Hunters left. Perhaps they'll all try to kill me. Isn't that a thought. I sigh heavily and plunk down on the trunk.

"Why can't I sense you?"

I jump up, reach for my swords and nearly scream the expletive that fills my head. Am I so weary that I couldn't even smell Sam's scent when I walked in?

"You scared the hell out of me." I toss my swords on the bed and clutch at my pounding heart.

"I didn't think that was possible," he says dryly.

"Apparently, it is," I mutter.

"You didn't answer me. Why can't I sense you?"

"Sam," His eyes flutter closed for a second when I say his name. "What you sense is evil. Do you think I'm evil?"

He doesn't respond right away, just continues to watch me. His gaze is so intense. I imagine if it were possible, it would set me on fire. Maybe he thinks I will turn into the devil at any minute and eat out his insides. I realize that I'm holding my breath, waiting for his answer.

"You're one of *them*," he says finally.

It isn't a yes, but it certainly isn't a no, either. And it hurts more than I could have imagined.

"I'm still me, Sam. The same me I've always been."

He slowly walks to me, almost timidly. I'm careful not to make any sudden movements. I remember Mum and Papa being like this when they first realized what I was. I can understand Sam's hesitance. He touches my cheek, just a feather of a touch, and I press my face into his palm. I just want him to know I would never hurt him.

"Ana," he whispers, his eyes filling with tears.

The pain explodes in my chest, unlike anything I've ever felt before. My heart slows, and I have half a second to look up at Sam, my eyes wide with disbelief.

"*Sam.*" It is the only thing I have time to say before the darkness takes over and I lose consciousness.

204

The pain is almost unbearable like molten iron being ripped from my chest. I can't control the guttural wail that frees itself from deep in my throat as if it has been trying to claw its way out for days. I feel myself change from the pain, and I can only hope it speeds up the process of easing this torture. Though, I know that the real pain in my heart may never heal.

"*Oh my God.*"

"*Sam! How could you. . .*"

"*Has she been. . .*"

The pain makes it difficult to distinguish who makes each comment. When I am able to focus - barely - I become aware that my hands and feet are shackled by *my* silver cuffs to *my* silver chair in *my* holding room. I test the shackles against my strength but have been greatly weakened. I lift my head and see all of my Hunters staring at me from the other side of the glass wall. All except Sam, who stands before me, the stake he just removed from my heart in his hand.

"Sam, what have you done?" My voice is harsh and raspy. I could certainly use a drink. . .or two.

He doesn't answer, and I can't read the expression on his face. He looks sad. Or mad. Maybe even both. Sam drops the stake and leaves the room, locking me in.

I slump back in the chair, willing myself to change to normal despite lingering pain. The silver is not helping with my weakness.

"Ana? Are you alright? Sam, I can't believe you did this to her!" Amanda doesn't even wait for my response before she lays into Sam. "How could you?"

"You saw what she is, Amanda," Sam answers wistfully.

"I see *who* she is, Sam! And *you*, of all people, should, too! She has saved my life. She has saved all of our lives!"

"She's right, Sam," Eric affirms. "I don't think this is necessary."

"It's necessary!" Sam barks. "We need answers, and she will give them to us!"

"If you wanted answers, Sam, all you had to do was ask." My breathing is labored and painful, but I put as much malice as possible in my statement.

Sam walks up to the glass and addresses me. "Who are you?"

205

"You know who I am."

"*Who* are you?" he asks again, slamming his hand against the glass.

I don't flinch. I will not give him that satisfaction. Instead, I sit up, lift my head and look him in the eye.

"My name is Anala Geil. I am the daughter of the Leaders of the Society of Hunters."

Gasps come from everyone on the other side of the glass. Except one.

"Anala?" Emily whispers. "But she died when she was. . ."

"Eighteen," Jeremy finishes, looking at me with pity.

"What happened?" Jenna asks, genuinely interested.

"I was on patrol," I begin. "With a boy. . ."

"Thomas?" Amanda asks.

"Yes. His little sister must have followed us out to where we were and hid. When we heard rustling in the bushes, we thought for sure it was a Cursed One." I pause, trying to catch my breath. The damn pain just won't go away. "We almost killed her," I continue. "When Thomas left to take her home, I was distracted for one minute. Thinking about him. A Cursed One got to me before I even knew what was happening."

I take shallow breaths, hoping to alleviate the torture going on inside me.

"Why did your parents let you live?" Sam's voice is harsh again. Perhaps he was jealous when I spoke of being distracted by Thomas. Good. Let your heart hurt for a bit, I think bitterly.

"Because she was their daughter!" Amanda sneers. "Some people just have better judgment!"

"But they were the Leaders of the Society. There are codes that we must live by," Sam explains.

"He's right," Zac says quietly. They are the first words I have heard from him since waking up.

"I was not like the others." I glance at Zac. "I was an anomaly. I *am* an anomaly. My parents had no idea I had been turned until they saw how my eyes had changed. Everything else about me had remained the same. I never tried to hurt them. Just as I would never hurt any of you."

"How can we be sure of that?" Sam asks.

"She has had many chances," Emily interjects. "If she wanted us dead, we would be dead."

"And, why train us to kill, well, her if she wanted to hurt us?" Jenna adds.

"We don't know what her true agenda is!" Sam tries to hold on to his anger, but his confusion seems to be winning the battle. I lower my head, unable to look at him anymore - and unable to deal with the pain anymore.

"Are you serious? I can't believe you could do this, Sam. Or believe that she is capable of hurting us. You're *sleeping* with her, for chrissake!"

Another groan escapes me, this time from Amanda's words as much as the pain. I did *not* need everyone to know that! I hear Zac's sharp breath intake and risk looking at him. The hurt and accusation in his eyes are too much for me, and I break the gaze. Without a word, he walks away. My sigh is ragged and full of agony.

"Ana, what is it?" Amanda's voice is so full of compassion that I see no reason to lie to her.

"Your brother staked me," I tell her because, frankly, that *is* the biggest problem. "With a silver splintering stake. My heart is trying to regenerate around it but can't."

"Sam!"

He looks authentically shocked and self-reproachful. "I. . .It was a mistake. I didn't know I had chosen one of those..."

"He is a Hunter, Amanda. He followed his instincts." After everything, I wonder why I am still willing to take up for him. "Actually, what he should've done was kill me."

"Don't say that!"

"It's true." I turn my attention to Sam, who can barely look at me. "I have to finish what I am destined to do, Sam. I know who the Maker is. I just have to find him. After that, I will lay down my swords and let you do what you are destined to do. Kill me."

He pales.

"No. I won't let him!"

"It is the code, Amanda."

"I don't give a damn about the code! Not if it means killing you, and not if it means Sam has to do it! Whether he wants to admit it or not, he cares for you. He can't kill you!"

Cares for me? The silver splinters in my heart beg to differ.

"Who is the Maker, Ana?" Eric asks, trying desperately to change the subject.

"A boy I once knew." I can't disguise the sadness in my voice.

"Oh, Ana! Thomas?"

I nod my confirmation to Amanda and slump in the chair again. I will be too weak to do it if I don't get these splinters out soon.

"Sam, open the door!"

"I can't, Amanda."

"Open the damn door! She needs help!"

Sam stares at me, tears pooling in his eyes. After briefly hesitating, he drops the keys to the floor and walks away. Amanda waits for a split second, and no one makes a grab for the keys.

"You people are pathetic!" She scolds, picking them up herself. "All she's done for you, and this is how you repay her?"

The rest of them lower their heads in shame and follow Sam.

"Miserable excuses. . ." Amanda mumbles a string of expletives as she unlocks the door and walks over to me.

"Don't be hard on them," I tell her weakly. "They don't know how to react to all of this."

"How about like your *friends*!" She yells the word, hoping everyone hears her.

"They're Hunters," I explain as she unlocks one wrist. "I am what they are born and trained to kill. Leave it." I place my hand on hers before she can unlock the other wrist. "Just so you know you're safe."

"I already know that," she huffs and unlocks the cuff anyway.

"Very well." I lift my hand to my chest, ready to dig out the damn silver splinters. "You may not want to be here for this."

"I'm fine."

I shrug, and it sends a pain shooting through me. I take the opportunity to dig my fingers into my chest and pull out the first fragment. I try not to groan and succeed but I can't help the change. I fully expect Amanda to run from me in fear. However, she doesn't even flinch. She just holds her hand out, waiting for me to give her the splinter.

I go in for another one, gripping the arm of the chair with my other hand, bending it with force.

"You knew," I state, trying to think of other things. It's not working. I exhale through my teeth as the splinter slides out.

"What?"

"You knew who I am. How?"

"Why do you think I knew?"

"You're not surprised, for one." I start on another fragment. "You've dropped hints. How did you know?"

"I read the journal," she says simply.

"So did everyone else," I counter.

"People tend to read without comprehending."

Who is this person? This is not the same Amanda Logan I met two years ago. She has grown up exceedingly in the past few weeks. I hand her another splinter and eye her suspiciously.

"I wrote the journal. I still don't see how you deduced that I am Anala."

"Ana, you wrote that Anala - or you - died when she was eighteen. Your parents were murdered not long after that. There's no one left. It is impossible for you to be a descendant of the Leaders since they had no other family."

Well, hell. I freeze in the middle of having my fingers pushed halfway through my chest. Not a comfortable position, I might add.

"Hmm." I continue digging. "You will have to change that."

"Me!"

"Yes. When I'm gone, I want you to continue writing the journals."

"Ana, don't say things like that!"

I hand her the last fragment and breathe deep when the regeneration starts to ease the physical pain.

"Amanda, I have lived. Many, many lifetimes. I'm ready."

"Well, I'm not! And neither is Sam!"

"He staked me. I'm sure he'll be just fine."

"He did what he did because he's confused and angry. It was stupid, and he should've thought before doing it, but he cares!"

"Maybe he did, Amanda, but...."

"No. He *does*. I mean, I know Sam. I've never seen him like this."

"It doesn't matter." Only it does. It matters a lot. "Amanda, please. Let me go. If Sam can't do it, I need you to."

"Ana. . ."

"I have been alive for almost six-hundred years, Amanda. Do you have any idea how lonely that is? I can't stay here much longer, or people will begin to notice I don't age. I move from place to place, lose people I love, and I'm tired. *Help me.*"

Tears begin to flow down Amanda's face.

"*Please?*"

"You still look weak." She avoids giving me an answer. "What do you need?"

"Blood," I sigh.

She flushes. "Oh. How, er, where...."

I smirk at her obvious discomfort and can't help myself. "It needs to be from a live person."

She goes from bright pink to pale white in a matter of seconds.

"I'm kidding, Amanda. I have blood stocked here."

"Oh. Are you sure?"

"Am I sure I have blood?"

"Are you sure it doesn't need to be...live?"

It's my turn to blush...though I'm honestly unsure if I can.

"Actually, that would be better and faster."

"Then take it from me."

"Absolutely not."

"Why?"

"No, Amanda."

"Will it change me? Or, kill me?"

"No, I can control that. But I will not drink from you."

"Why not?"

"Because Sam really will kill me if I do, and I need to find Thomas before that happens."

"You can't fight Thomas unless you're at your best. Live will do that. Let me help you."

"If you want to help me, kill me when this is all over. I'm not taking your blood." I stand abruptly, effectively ending that conversation.

"Do you love him?" Amanda calls to me when I reach the door, and my step falters. "Do you love my brother?"

I keep my back to Amanda, not wanting her to see my tears.

"Yes."

What a damn night. I've been exposed for what I really am, Thomas is cursed and wants me dead, I doubt my Hunters trust me anymore, and the man I'm in love with *staked* me. Is it any wonder I am fragile and vulnerable? I honestly, for one split second, thought about taking Amanda up on her offer. Just to get *some* of my strength back. She's right, I will never defeat Thomas like this, but I can't drink from her. Everything about that feels wrong. The blood I have stored here will have to do. I hope it's good enough after everything I've been through.

"Ana?"

Immediately on alert, I back up into the door I just closed behind me.

"Get out, Sam!"

He holds his hands up. "I don't have any weapons. I'm not here to hurt you."

"I don't care why you're here. I want you to leave!" I don't have the strength to fight him, physically or emotionally. Not that I'm going to let him know that. "Actually, first, I want you to tell me how you knew where I was and why you were there."

"I put a tracking device on one of your swords," he says guiltily, and I swear I can feel my blood boil. "You wouldn't let me go with you, and I was worried! I lied about having to work. It was the only way I could be there with you. Ana, please. I came to apologize. . ."

"Apologize?" I snort. Seriously? I'm so mad right now. I don't think he can say anything to help the situation. "So? Let's hear it. 'Hey, sorry I betrayed you. Sorry, I staked you'."

Sam takes another step toward me, and I step back. Am I really afraid of him? At this moment, being as weak as I am, yes. Again, he lifts his hands.

"I don't have any stakes, Ana! No swords, no daggers!"

I eye him suspiciously. "I didn't think you did before, either. When you *pretended* to care, touching my face only so you could get close enough to me."

He flinches at my words as if I slapped him - or staked him. "I never pretended. Not even then."

"Just get out, Sam." I keep my distance from him, glancing at his hands. I will be ready for him this time.

"Jesus, Ana, I don't have any weapons!"

"You'll forgive me if I don't believe you."

With an exasperated sigh, he begins to unbutton his shirt.

"Whoa, what are you doing?"

"Showing you that I have nothing," he says, stripping his shirt off.

Well, crap. Now I know I'm still attracted to him despite what he did to me. I look away.

"I don't care if you have a weapon," I snap. "You'll never get close enough to me again to use it. All I want is for you to go."

Sam drops into the chair he sat in the first night he came to my room and rubs his hands over his face. For the first time, I see the fatigue. His usually clean-shaven face now sports stubble, and dark circles take up residence under his eyes. As much as I try to stop it, my heart melts a little for him.

"Let me try to explain..."

"Explain how you *staked* me?"

"Ana!"

"Don't like it, Sam? Try being on the pointy end!"

"I was confused! And angry," he says, reiterating Amanda's words from earlier. "You *made* me run! You compelled me to leave you there!" He looks up at me, and I see the question flash in his eyes.

"How dare you! Do you really think I compelled you to sleep with me?"

He runs his hand through his hair but takes too long to answer.

"*You* came to me, remember? Do you think I *wanted* this? *Any* of this? I wanted a *normal* life! As normal as I could get! I didn't want to be doing this again or putting those kids' lives in danger," I point in the general direction of the other Hunters. "I didn't want to get involved in something I *know* can't last! And I certainly didn't want to get staked by someone I'm in..." I take a shaky breath.

A tear runs down his cheek, and the ice in my heart melts once again.

"I know I came to you," he says quietly. "Of course I know you didn't compel me, not in the way you think. I didn't want to hurt you." He pauses, taking a deep breath. "What I did was unforgivable, and I don't blame you if you hate me forever. I want...I need to make it up to you."

"I don't think you can."

His head falls. "Please don't say that. I screwed up, Ana. Bad. I heard you talking to Amanda. I know what it is you need. Let me help you."

What I need? I asked Amanda to help me...he's willing to kill me. If this is indeed what I want, why does it hurt so much that he wants to help me?

"You know I can't let you do that until after I've defeated Thomas."

Sam looks up at me, confused. "After?"

"Yes. I have to finish this before I let you kill me."

"Kill you? Jesus, Ana! I don't want to kill you!"

"Then what are you talking about, Sam?"

"I want you to drink from me! I want to make up for what I did. I want to help you."

This time, I'm taken aback. Drink from him?

"No."

"Ana. . ."

"No. Get out."

"Why? I can help you."

"Is this some sort of test? Are you trying to prove that I have no control over my cravings?" Because, truthfully, I'm not sure how much control I have. Drinking from Sam is so incredibly tempting.

"It's not a test, Ana. I *need* to do this for you. I need you to know how sorry I am."

"Fine. I get it. But I'm not taking your blood."

He sighs and sits back in the chair. "I thought that's what you would say. I lied before," he confesses, watching me.

Damn, I could use some blood. Each passing moment makes me

weaker and hungrier. I take a second to close my eyes, indulging in the relief it gives my tired, aching head. "About what this time?" I mutter.

"Having a weapon."

My eyes fly open at the same time Sam brings the blade of his pocket knife to his throat and slices. With a speed I didn't think I could muster, I was at his side.

"What did you do?" I clamp my hand around the wound, trying not to think of how amazing his blood smells.

His head falls forward a little before he catches himself. "I think I cut a little too deep," he slurs.

"Son of a bitch, Sam! Look at me!" I deliberately change as he's watching. I want him to really see what I am and what I am capable of. He doesn't look away. Probably because he's losing too much blood and can't comprehend. Holding my breath, I bring my hand to my mouth and bite my palm. I touch my blood to the wound on his neck, and it closes immediately. "Idiot," I mutter, making myself return to normal and move to stand up.

Sam grabs my hand and pulls me. My current state of weakness has me stumbling until I'm sitting bestride him.

"Ana." He caresses my face. "I'm so sorry. I know my words mean nothing, but they're true nonetheless."

He tugs me closer, brushing his lips on mine.

"Sam. . ."

He kisses me again, deeper.

"*I love you,*" he whispers.

The words melt my heart, and the rest of me heats up beyond my control.

"*I love you, Anala.*" He kisses me more, swallowing my moan.

"*I love you, too,*" I confide between kisses. I can't fight him. I don't want to. This is what I want. This doesn't hurt.

Sam breaks the kiss and tilts his head. "Please."

"I can't. You don't know what you're asking of me."

He holds my gaze. "Yes, I do. I trust you, Ana. I didn't know if I could, but I saw you with my sister. You *are* still you. Let me help you." He angles his head again.

Seeing the blood there, still wet and smelling delicious, demolishes my resolve. Tentatively, I lick his neck with the tip of my tongue. The taste is intoxicating, and I turn again immediately. The sensation is too much for me, and I try to get up, but Sam holds me steady.

"It's okay," he murmurs. "Look at me."

I shake my head, and he lifts my chin with his finger.

"You're beautiful." He looks at me fully, taking in my eyes with their red ring and my sharp teeth. "Drink from me, Anala."

The use of my proper name is my undoing. I sink my teeth into his neck and drink the sweetest, most provocative blood I've ever tasted.

CHAPTER TWENTY-TWO
"DIFFERENT"

I awaken abruptly, my eyes flying open at the sensations I feel inside. Sitting up, I inhale deeply. What a remarkable feeling. Everything inside me seems to be more. . .alive. Supersensitive is the only way I know how to describe it. The affliction in my heart has completely vanished, and it feels strong. My muscles contract under my skin when I reach up to touch my chest. I feel as though I could fight every one of the Cursed Ones under Thomas by myself without complication.

Touching my chest reminds me I am naked, and I hear Sam snoring softly beside me. The sound makes me smile. I have no idea how we ended up here, but I do know I enjoyed it immensely. I lay back down, facing Sam. Without much thought, I bring my thumb to my mouth, opening the skin with my tooth. I touch my blood where I bit him. The wound promptly closes, and Sam stirs awake.

"Hmm, hi," he smiles sleepily.

I grin back at him. "How are you feeling?"

"Lightheaded. And, amazing."

"You need to eat something."

"Mmhmm." He leans into me and kisses me.

"I'm going to go make you a sandwich," I tell him between his sweet kisses. He holds on when I try to get up.

"Don't go."

"You need to eat, Sam."

"Later."

"Hey, I did what you asked. Now it's your turn."

He sighs but gives me a crooked grin. "Fine." Sam narrows his eyes and studies me. "You look different."

I feel different.

"You're lightheaded," I quip. "I'll be right back." I kiss him quickly and get up. I wrap my robe around me, well aware that Sam is watching me. I look back and wink at him before heading off to the kitchen. I haven't forgotten what he did to me, but I can try to forgive. How would I have reacted had the tables been turned?

I scour the refrigerator for anything I can piece together for a sandwich. Turkey looks good. I pile condiments and vegetables in my arms, then grab the bread.

"Would you like a sandwich, Zac?"

He has been standing there watching me since I came in but saying nothing.

"How do you do that?"

I turn to face him, laying my contents on the kitchen island. "I'm a vampire," I smirk.

He doesn't return my smile. "You look different."

"Because you know what I am now."

"No, that's not it." He shakes his head, changing the subject. "Why Sam, Ana? Why not me?"

"Zac, please don't do this."

"I need to know. Why did you stop that night in your apartment?"

Sigh. I don't want to be having this conversation with Zac when Sam is waiting for me. Hell, I don't want to have this conversation! Especially now that I'm aware we're being listened in on.

"I wasn't myself that night, Zac. I'm sorry if I led you on. It wasn't my intention."

"You weren't yourself? Meaning you really didn't want to kiss me?"

"What I wanted was to hurt you," I tell him honestly. "I almost did."

"I would have let you. I love you."

Well, crap. "You don't love me, Zac. You barely know me."

"I know how I feel. And I've known you a lot longer than Sam."

This can't be good. Zac's feelings for me could be a major distraction while hunting. He inches closer to the island. To me.

"Maybe now, after what he did to you, you'll give me a chance."

I lower my gaze, unable to look him in the eye. How do I tell him that I'm still with Sam?

"That sandwich is for Sam, isn't it?" he asks, reading my thoughts.

"Yes."

"Really, Ana? After everything he did?"

"Really, Zac? Can you stand there and tell me you wouldn't have done the same thing if you were in his shoes?"

He opens his mouth to answer but has none. I round the island and walk to him.

"Zac, you don't love me." It may not be right to take someone's feelings away from them, but it's for his own good.

His brows furrow. It's like he's fighting me. "Yes, I do."

I try again, putting more power behind the suggestion.

"You don't love me. You're a friend: a *good* friend and a great Hunter. You won't let feelings distract you from that. Do you understand?"

His eyes glaze over, and I know my compulsion is working.

"Yes."

"Good. You need to get some rest." I walk back around the island and begin making Sam's sandwich. "Goodnight, Zac."

"Goodnight, Ana."

"It was necessary," I say to Amanda as Zac leaves.

"I wasn't going to argue. That's freaky, by the way. How you know people are here. How do you do it?"

The discussion has me thinking back centuries ago when I explained to Mum the different scents people have. I tell Amanda the same thing.

"Wow. I mean, that has to be pretty cool being able to do that."

"It has its perks."

"You look different," she says, cocking her head, scrutinizing me.

"Why do people keep saying that?"

"Um, because it's true. Come here."

She drags me to a mirror, and my reflection makes me gasp. I *do* look different! My hair is shinier, my eyes brighter, my skin as smooth as alabaster. There's a red tint to my lips, a soft blush to my cheeks, without the help of makeup. And, though it's barely noticeable, I can see the faded red circle surrounding my iris. When I change, I can only imagine how bright it will be. This is a far cry from how I felt after. . .Bernard.

"Is this what it's like after you've had live blood?"

I inhale sharply and look at Amanda. Shit. How am I going to explain what Sam and I have done? "I. . ."

"It's fine. I had a feeling Sam would come to you."

"You're not mad?"

"Is he okay?"

I smile. "Yes. He just needs some food, which I'm bringing him. *If* I ever get this sandwich made." I return to the task, slapping mayonnaise, tomatoes, turkey, and lettuce onto the wheat bread I chose for Sam.

"Then, I'm not mad. What made you say yes to him?"

I pause, thinking about the answer. "I don't know. At first, I said no. He told me he loved me, trusted me, and I just—gave in. The answer to your first question, by the way, is no. This isn't what happens when I drink live. Although I've never drunk from a Hunter before."

"Have you fed from someone you're in love with?"

I frown. Hmm. Could it be that? "No."

"How do you feel inside?"

"Different," I tell her after a moment of consideration.

"Tell me."

"It's hard to explain. But I feel. . .stronger. Everything inside me is hyper-sensitive." I grab a plate for the sandwich, some chips, and a can of soda. "Come with me. I want to try something."

I lead Amanda to the training room and into the holding room. "Here, hold this." Handing her Sam's food, I walk to the silver chair. "Silver greatly diminishes our strength. I'm not sure why."

"What does it feel like when you touch it?"

I pick up a silver chain and try to describe it. "It feels like your strength is literally seeping out of your body. I can feel the pull, like a magnet. It's almost like being considerably fatigued, and the energy just keeps draining out."

"Do you feel that now?"

I test the chain, rolling it around my hands. "A little," I divulge. "But not like it was before." I don't want to think about the last time I was in here, so I move on with my experiment. "It depletes our energy so much that we cannot break through silver chains or cuffs. That's why they are used."

I take the chain in both of my hands and pull. It takes substantial strength, but the chain breaks in two. Well. . .that's interesting. Bernard's blood left me ill. Sam's gives me a greater power than I've ever had.

"You broke it! Sam's blood did this to you?" Amanda asks, echoing my thoughts.

"I guess so," I answer, distracted by the two silver chains in my hands. I still feel the pull of it trying to drain my power, but just barely. Is this what happens when you feed from a Hunter? I shudder to think of what would happen if other Cursed Ones found this out.

I take the food from Amanda. "I should get this to Sam. Will you do me a favor and tell everyone I would like to meet with them in the dining room tomorrow morning?"

"Sure." She's confused by my abrupt need for departure but doesn't question me.

"Amanda? Thank you. For everything."

I'm nervous. I have no idea if anyone will show up this morning - except Sam and Amanda, of course. But the others? Will they accept me? Trust me?

At least some of my fears are laid to rest when I open the double, ornate doors and find all of my Hunters waiting for me. I breathe a sigh of relief and smile at them.

"First, I would like to thank you all for still being here," I begin, standing at the head of the table. Amanda is to my right, with Jeremy and Jenna next to her. Zac is on my left, followed by Emily and Eric, and Sam sits at the other end. "I know this may be difficult for you to come to terms with, but I *am* the same person I was before you knew...*what* I am."

Eric rises from his seat and addresses me. "I think I can speak for us all when I say we would like to apologize for our behavior yesterday."

"There's no need. . ."

"Please," he holds his hand up to stop my protest. "The way we just left was shameful, and Amanda was right, pathetic. We have no reason not to trust you. I hope you can forgive us."

No one argues. They simply sit there quietly.

"Eric, I lied to you about who I am. I can only imagine the shock you must have felt. I do not hold any grudges against you. Please do not apologize or feel shame. How about we agree to forgive each other?" I smile sweetly at him, and he returns a shy smile.

I gesture for Eric to take a seat as I sit.

"Before we begin, can I ask something," Amanda raises her hand as if she's in school.

"Of course."

"What do we call you now?"

What an unexpected question.

"Um. . .I'm not sure. I have hidden my true identity for so long. The only people who have ever known what I am are my parents and now the people in this room. I would love to be Anala again if you're comfortable with that." I think momentarily of how it felt when Sam called me Anala last night, and it makes my heart jump.

"Anala it is, then," Amanda interrupts my flashback, bringing me to the present. I can't help but grin.

"Now, there are two issues that we need to discuss today," I say, getting down to business. "Beginning with the Maker. I don't know how much Sam told you..." I pause, looking at Sam, who shakes his head. I guess he hasn't said much to them. "The number of full blood Cursed Ones surrounding their maker is overwhelming. More than I expected."

"What are you going to do?" Emily inquires.

"We," I correct. "I realized with Sam that I was completely underestimating you. I will need you all if I'm going to defeat Thomas." I stumble ever so slightly on his name. I wish there were some other way. . .but there's not. I am a Hunter, and I must carry out his fate as much as it may hurt me to do so. And, no, the irony is not lost on me. "You will train with me, with what I am, so that you can get the feel of what it will be like to fight against a full blood. They are also trained to use swords." Gasps fill the room. That is precisely how I felt when I found out. "We don't have long, so training must be quick. Is everyone okay with that?"

I get agreements from everyone, and I hope I am doing the right thing.

"Once I am convinced you know what you're up against, we will head out. You *must* pay attention and keep your head in the game at all times. These are not Hybrids. They're stronger, faster, and can kill or turn you with a single bite."

Their courage falters slightly, but not enough to make them back down. They're up for the challenge. I hope I am, too.

"On to the next order of business. Once Thomas and the others are defeated," I hesitate, taking a deep breath. I'm assuming we're going to win. My confidence in my Hunters supersedes the abilities of the Cursed Ones. "I need one of you to finish the job."

"Ana. . ."

"Sam, there's no way around this. All of this happened because of me. My parents kept me alive and look what it has done."

"*It's brought you to me,*" he whispers. No one at the table acknowledges that he said anything. The words were for me only.

I hold his gaze for a moment before continuing.

"It is the code. You may not like it, and to be honest, I'm scared as hell, but it is what must be done."

"You want one of us to kill you," Jenna's tone is full of objection.

"Yes," I answer simply. "I have asked Amanda and Sam to do it, but - well, Amanda is my best friend. And Sam?" I look Sam in the eye, making sure he's paying attention. "It is unfair of me to ask someone I'm in love with to kill me."

Sam inhales sharply.

"Whoa. You guys are *that* serious? I thought you were just, you know, screwing."

"Nice, Jeremy."

He shrugs at Jenna's chastise. "I'm just saying. It's sad."

"You're not helping."

I clear my throat, cutting off Jenna and Jeremy's totally awkward conversation. I take my sword and place it on the table in front of me.

"My father made this. It is the first of its kind. And it is what I would like used."

"Anala, we can't do this! You're asking us the impossible," Emily cries.

"I can."

Everyone turns their attention to Zac. I didn't notice before now how quiet he has been.

"Zac!" Amanda practically shouts at him, but his eyes don't leave me.

"Let's get it over with now."

Zac grabs my sword before I can comprehend what his saying and releases the blade. The others are up, going after him in seconds.

"Leave him!" I yell, ducking the blade that barely misses me. I leap up and do a backflip to escape his next attempt.

"Zac, what are you doing!" Sam brings out his own sword, ready to fight.

"Sam, don't! He's compelled!"

I can see the vacant look in his eyes, and I know this isn't my work. How did they get to him? Whatever happened, I'm grateful that all they did was compel him and not change him. His eyes may be dazed, but they are still Zac's golden eyes. He lunges at me, and I block his attempt, pushing him away. I don't have my other sword to aid me, which may be a blessing. I don't want to hurt him.

"Anala, you have to help him! He wouldn't want to do this!" Amanda's voice resonates.

"If I undo it, I undo it all, Amanda," I tell her between jumps, ducks, and blocks.

"Then undo it all!"

Sighing, I force Zac to retreat toward the table. "You will have to restrain him."

Jeremy and Sam quickly round the table, grabbing Zac and avoiding the blade of the sword. He fights as though his life depends on it. I'm curious if they made him think it does.

"I will *kill* you!" Zac snarls.

Sam pushes him down in the chair, perhaps a little too harshly.

"Careful. I must have made him more susceptible," I say, mostly to myself. I pull up my own chair and sit in front of Zac. Whoever did this to him laid it on thick. The poor boy is out of his mind. "Zac?" I lean in, turning up the heat in my stare. "You don't want to kill me."

"Yes, I do!" He struggles against Sam and Jeremy's hold.

Well, this is going to be more challenging than I thought. It's going to require. . .sigh.

"Don't be afraid of me," I tell the group before closing my eyes and ordering myself to change.

When I open my eyes, my Hunters see the eerie white and blood-red ring. When I open my mouth to speak, they see the fangs. To their credit, they don't recoil.

"Zac, enough. Calm down." In my Cursed form, my power of persuasion is intense, and Zac ceases his struggle. "You don't want to kill me. Do you understand?"

His brows knit together as if he's trying to fathom what I'm telling him.

"I release you. Of all coercion."

Zac's eyes begin to clear, but he's still confused.

"What's going on?" He notices my appearance. "Ana? What's happening?"

Deliberately, I change back. I don't want to make Zac any more uncomfortable than he probably already is.

"Did you go out last night?" I ask him.

"What?" He tries lifting his hand, but the guys still hold him down. I nod to both of them, and they reluctantly let go. Zac's head is throbbing so much I can hear it. He rubs his temples where the veins are pulsing.

"Zac? Did you leave the manor last night after we spoke?"

Sam eyes me curiously. I failed to mention last night when I got back to him that I had talked to Zac. I imagine he's not happy about that.

"I - I can't think."

"Try."

"Yes. I went for a walk, I think."

"Where? Did you see anyone?"

225

"Nowhere in particular." He squints as though he's trying to recall what happened. "I don't remember seeing anyone."

"They told him to forget," I state.

"Who? What is going on?"

"Zac, you just tried to kill Anala," Sam snaps.

"I did not! And you should talk!" Zac stands up a bit too quickly and wobbles. I grab his arm to steady him, but he jerks it away. "Don't! This asshole *stakes* you, and you're *still* sleeping with him!"

"Careful, Zac," Sam warns.

"Screw you! Oh, wait, Ana's already doing that."

Sam punches him, hard. I can't say that I blame him or that I would have stopped him if I had the chance. Hell, I wanted to punch him myself.

Zac curses vehemently, wiping blood from his nose and mouth. "I see how it is. Sam gets away with anything because he's sleeping with the *leader*."

"That's enough, Zac." My voice is quiet but holds authority and more than a touch of anger. He turns to me, ready to argue with me, until he sees the look in my eyes. "Your anger and inability to control yourself are making you a liability to this Society."

"You're kicking me out?" He backs away as if I bit him. "A Society of Hunters that is led by a Cursed One, and you're kicking me out?"

"Your attitude and lack of respect for me and your fellow Hunters make you dangerous."

"Anala?" Emily's soft voice takes my attention away from Zac. "Perhaps he just needs some time to calm down."

"I agree," Eric chimes in. "Zac's feelings for you have made him forget what he is meant to do here."

They know how Zac feels about me?

"I don't have any feelings for her," Zac mumbles. His lie is highly unconvincing. "You should be kicking *him* out!" He jerks his thumb towards Sam.

I stand between them when Sam goes for Zac again.

"I said enough! Everyone else, out. I want to talk to Zac alone."

"Anala. . ."

"Please, Sam."

He doesn't argue but sends Zac a clear message with the 'hurt her and you're dead' look.

"*Are you going to compel him again?*" Amanda whispers as she passes me. I shake my head in answer and wait for them to close the door behind them.

"Get over it." I don't raise my voice. In fact, I'm desperately trying to hold my anger in check for fear that I may hit Zac myself.

"What?" He asks, gruffly.

"These feelings you think you have? This disrespectful attitude? Get over it. And, quick."

"It's as easy as that? Maybe for your kind it is, but not us humans."

I take a deep breath, and with monumental strength, I keep calm. Seriously, I should be commended for my effort.

"You are trying my patience as no other has before, Zac," I say evenly. "If I am such a monster to you, you should probably watch your step. Who knows what I could do if you make me angry enough."

"I don't think you're a monster," he mutters grumpily. "You just broke my heart."

He sits heavily in one of the dining chairs and leans his elbows on his knees.

Sigh. I pull a chair close to his and sit with him.

"Zac, do you really think I don't understand feelings? Centuries ago, I was infatuated with a boy, and he with me. We never got the chance to explore those emotions thoroughly, and now I find myself faced with having to kill him." Just the thought of that turns my stomach. "I care about you. Don't get mad at that," I say when he huffs.

"'I care about you' is the equivalent of 'I'm just not into you.'"

"Perhaps it is. I'm not trying to be mean, Zac, but I've never felt that way towards you."

"You *kissed* me."

"In a state of weakness."

He leans back and groans, rubbing his face.

"I'm sorry that hurts you. I truly am. However, I need you to know this so you can move on. If you feel I've led you on, I apologize. You're my friend, Zac, and a great Hunter. I want you here with me, by my side, as I do the hardest thing I will ever have to do in all my years. But that can't happen if you harbor these feelings towards me and Sam."

He winces when I say Sam's name. "Why him? Can you at least give me that answer?"

"Honestly? I don't know. I felt an immediate connection with him, even though he infuriated me. Maybe it's because he's a descendant of Thomas," I shrug. "All I know is I have fallen in love with him against my better judgment."

Zac frowns. "You don't want to love him?"

"Love is difficult for someone like me, Zac, especially in this situation. I have to move often in order to keep my secret hidden. Sam is established here and has family here. I'm immortal, and Sam is not. I am Cursed," I say quietly. "Sam is a Hunter. So, you see, this would have been better for everyone had I not let my feelings get in my way."

"I guess I never looked at it from your perspective." He looks at me guiltily. "Did I really try to kill you?"

"Yes," I chuckle. I can't help it. The mood in the room needs to be lightened. My Hunters are stressed enough. "Lucky for you, I'm just too good."

A slight grin replaces the scowl he has been sporting for too long now.

"Lucky for *you*, I was compelled and not at my best."

"Ha! Keep dreaming, Connor!"

"Can I stay?" he asks soberly.

"I don't know, Zac. Can you? Can you come to terms with everything, recognize that I am with Sam, and treat your fellow Hunters with respect? Can I trust you?"

"Yes," he answers without hesitation. "Look, it's going to be hard for me seeing you with Sam. Especially after what he did, but I'll deal. If you can forgive him, I guess I can." He looks at me, and I see the sincerity in his eyes. "I want to be there for you when you have to face Thomas. Give me another chance? Please?"

"This is the last one, Zac. You need to get a grip on your anger. If you do anything to put the others, or yourself, in danger. . .I cannot tolerate that. Do you understand?"

"I do. Thank you." He gets up, heads for the door, and stops. "It's real? What you and Sam have?"

"Yes."

"You know he won't let anyone kill you, right? This plan you have for ending it all? You may have to come up with a different plan."

He leaves me with that thought. It sucks because he's probably right. Sam will never allow someone to cut my head off, at least not without a fight. The damndest part of it all is I have finally found a reason to live.

CHAPTER TWENTY-THREE
"ONE LAST TIME"

"Again!"

Three Hunters come after me at once, slashing their swords, creating a distinct clank as their blades meet mine. They're getting better, closer to actually cutting me each time. I know they still hold back, not wanting to hurt me, so I am harder on them.

I'm in full Cursed mode, wanting them to be aware of everything they will be up against. I use my swords, fight hand to hand with them, and even border on biting them if they allow me to get too close - though I never cross that line.

They are tired and winded, but they keep fighting, swords clanging.

"Come on, Amanda! Don't hold back!"

"I don't want to hurt you!"

I snarl at her and charge. She duels with me as I snap at her. Scared, she pushes at me, but I don't budge. I just keep coming at her. Somewhere in the brawl, I accidentally clip her nose with my elbow, and she begins to bleed.

"Son of a bitch!" She rounds on me and, finally, puts everything she has into the fight. She's good. Fast and furious, agile and smart. Amanda ducks one of my attacks, somersaults, and comes up behind me. She lunges at me, and I fail to sidestep the advance feeling the blade ramming into my stomach. With a strangled cry, I drop to my knees. Holy hell, getting stabbed is *not* fun!

"Oh my God! Oh God, Anala, I'm so sorry!"

"Amanda! What did you do?" Sam runs towards me, dropping beside me.

"I'm sorry! I thought she would deflect it like she usually does! Oh, Ana!" She reverts back to the name she's more comfortable calling me.

"It's fine," I manage and expel the breath I was holding in. "I'm fine. Just give me some room."

Sam backs away slightly - okay, he scoots like two inches from me. I take hold of the hilt of Amanda's sword, pulling it out of my stomach. I really do try not to whine, not wanting Amanda to feel worse than she already does. But I fail miserably.

"I am *so* sorry!"

"Don't be." I hand Amanda her sword, stained in my blood. "You did very well."

"But I stabbed you!"

"I know," I chuckle. "Believe me."

She looks down at her sword. My blood drips from it, and she throws it to the ground as though there is a massive spider on it. "I can't believe I did that."

I lift my blood-soaked tank, showing her my belly. "Look. All better." I pat her on the shoulder. "I'm fine, Amanda. You should be proud of yourself. You got through to me."

"Well, you bloodied my nose," she says grumpily.

I laugh at her petulance. "Now, that *was* an accident. Sorry about that."

"Are you sure you're okay?" Sam inches back to me, cradling my face in his hands.

I smile at him. "Yes."

"Alright, let's get on with it before these two start making out in front of us," Jenna complains.

Just for that, I kiss Sam - a nice, juicy kiss - before getting up.

"Ugh. The dude stakes you and still gets to. . .stake you."

"Don't be crude, Jenna," Emily scolds and rolls her eyes at Jenna, who is sticking her tongue out.

And we're back to being high schoolers.

"Next wave," I bark, ordering the next group to come at me.

"You don't want to rest?"

"No, Zac. Let's go."

I end up with a few more cuts as training continues, which I consider progress. My Hunters are exceptional. If they can get to me, I have no doubt they can defeat Thomas's army with a bit more training.

Exhausted, I step into the shower to wash the dried blood off me. There's not a scratch on me. If it weren't for the actual blood itself, there would be no indication I had been hurt at all. I dollop body wash on my sponge, and smile when I smell him.

"Can I help?"

"Be my guest."

"You took a lot of hits tonight."

"Yes," I smile broadly. "You all did very well."

"You're probably the only person I know who would be happy to be cut so many times."

He shakes his head, gently washing the blood off of me.

"I don't feel it, you know. It's like it never happened. You don't have to be so timid."

Sam touches my abdomen, where Amanda's sword went through me. "It really is amazing."

"Thanks, I work out." I wink at him, and he laughs.

"I meant how you heal. That's not to say your abs aren't amazing." He pushes a strand of my hair behind my ear, gazing at me. "You lost a lot of blood."

"I have more." Uncomfortable with the conversation, I try distracting Sam with a kiss.

"*So do I,*" he whispers.

"Sam, I can't."

"Why?"

"Because it would be very easy for me to get hooked on you," I confess.

"What's wrong with that?"

Everything.

"Anala, I told you before, I trust you. I know you know when to stop."

"It's not that, Sam. I - I don't want to need you."

He backs me up against the shower wall. The coolness of it - and the closeness of him - sends chills throughout my body.

"Maybe *I* want you to need me." He kisses me until I'm lost in him. When he feels the fight leave me, he tilts his head, exposing his neck to me.

Without another word, I sink my teeth into him once again.

We spent the entire week training harder and longer. They are ready. Hell, if I'm honest with myself, they were prepared days ago. I'm stalling the inevitable. On more than one occasion, I've scoped out Thomas's hideout. I say it's to ensure they are still there and haven't gone into the wind. But I know I want to see Thomas. I want to reaffirm that he has changed. I just can't wrap my mind around this sweet boy becoming a... monster. Every night, though, I'm reminded by the bodies they bring in to feed on or offer to Thomas, and I watch as he tears them apart. As much as it hurts, it also helps me come to terms with what I must do.

Now, as I sit alone in my training room, I must try and forgive myself for not helping those innocents. All for the greater good, I try telling myself. But it does nothing to ease the guilt. That coupled with what I must do to Thomas and what should be done to me, I'm pretty stressed.

"Anala?"

I hadn't realized I was sitting on the floor, my back against a weapons crate, with my hands in my head, until Amanda sat beside me.

"Hey." I smile at her and push myself onto the crate, helping her up.

"Do you want to talk about it?"

I know she's not alone. All of my Hunters are here, seeing me this way. Do I pretend to be strong or tell them what I'm feeling?

"I think you're ready," I answer. "It's time to end this." In more ways than one.

"Are you ready for that?" Eric drags another crate over and offers his sister and Jenna a seat.

"Honestly? No." Truth it is. "I have all the confidence in the world for all of you. It's me that I am uncertain about."

"You're the strongest of us all," Emily suggests. "Why would you doubt yourself?"

"Because I don't want to kill Thomas."

"Then don't, Anala." Amanda's voice holds such benevolence I feel tears threaten. "You've lived this long being who you are. Can't you teach Thomas to do the same?"

"I can't. Amanda, despite *what* I am, it's who I am that prevents me from doing that. I was born a Hunter. I know it sounds hypocritical of me to say, but I can't let him live."

"Let someone else do it," Sam says quietly. So many emotions play on his face. Pity, sadness. . jealousy. How odd for him to be jealous of a boy I have to kill.

"I have to do it."

"Why?"

"It's what Thomas would want. He would be appalled if he understood what he has become."

Sam approaches me, kneeling to look me in the eye.

"Do you love him?"

"Sam," I sigh. "I care for him. I loved him." Sam bowed his head, pain etched across his face.

"It's not the same," I tell him, touching his cheek. "But I feel responsible for him. What happened to him is my fault. He allowed himself to be turned because of me. And, then, there's the fact that he is your family. Yours and Amanda's. I have to do it," I repeat.

"You're sure this is the only way?" Emily asks.

"He's too far gone. He's killed too many, turned too many. I can't allow that to go unpunished." It's the truth, and I know I'll use the same argument about myself. "We will go out tomorrow night to finish this. And, I mean finish it, Sam. As a Hunter, it is your duty to kill *all* Cursed Ones."

"Forget it." He pushes away from me and begins pacing. I almost missed his pacing. I even missed his arrogant attitude. A little. "You're different."

"Am I? Do you really think I haven't killed an innocent in all my years?"

"Impossible. I know you. You wouldn't do that."

Here we go.

"The case you were working on when we first met? The gang that was murdered? That was me."

Sam inhales sharply, as do the rest of them. "You're lying. You're just trying to justify someone killing you. It's not going to work."

"I'm not lying." I frown. I'm not, right? "I don't remember it. I - I thought it was a dream. I had been feeling off, and I honestly can't recall actually being there in that alley. I only remember waking up in bed, and Zac was knocking at my door. . ." I trail off, trying to think what really happened.

"You hadn't been to school for two days," Zac confides. "When I came to check up on you, you didn't know what day it was."

"Why do you think it was you, then?" Sam asks.

"When your parents brought it up, and you gave more details. . .It wasn't a coincidence that my 'dream' matched your description, Sam."

Amanda takes my hand. "Why can't you remember? What happened?"

I have thought about it so many times, coming up with nothing—until I remember Amanda's theory.

"When you read the journals, you came up with the idea that the Cloaked One is the true Maker." I glance at Sam. His eyes widen with surprise. He has not disclosed who the Cloaked One truly is. "I think you're right, and that's why I started feeling the way I did."

"Is the Cloaked One *your* maker?" Jenna asks incredulously.

"Not exactly." I go over to the table where my cloak lays. If I'm going to be honest, I need to be honest about everything. I pick up the cloak, wrapping it around me in dramatic fashion. I raise the hood before turning to face them.

"You have got to be kidding," Jenna snorts.

Amanda comes to me, cocking her head to one side as she studies my cloaked figure in front of her. "You really did save my life."

I bring the hood down, returning her stare. "I thought you knew."

"I only suspected, but I didn't know for sure. So, Thomas. . ."

"Is of my blood," I finish.

"Wait, I don't understand," Zac interrupts. "Why would that affect you and make you lose days? He's obviously been alive for as long as you."

"I can only guess it's proximity. Bernard brought them here, which made me feel. . .unlike myself. Or, perhaps, it was even Bernard himself. Whatever the reason, with Thomas being of my blood, all of the ones he's made are of my bloodline. It's why I feel pain when they are staked or killed."

"You feel them?" Sam breaks his silence. His pacing halts for a brief moment.

"Yes."

"Maybe they killed the gang, then, and you just, I don't know, felt it through them?" He sounds hopeful.

I would love for that to be true, but I don't think it is. Though, I don't think I will convince Sam of that now. "I've killed before, Sam."

"Doesn't matter," he says, waving his hand in the air, dismissing my confession. "That's in the past."

"I killed Bernard."

"You said you didn't see him."

"I lied. I saw him and knew exactly what I was doing when I ripped his throat out."

"Ana! Sam, there's an explanation, I'm sure!" Amanda pleads, but Sam doesn't say anything. He's not mad or surprised or even daunted by my confession.

"Did you go there to kill him?" he asks evenly.

"No. I went there for information. He gave me more than I bargained for. He looked like he was high or needing to get high, shaky, and weird. Then, he just started telling me everything. How my father," I stumble on my words, wishing they weren't true. "My father created Cursed Ones, how he - Bernard - created his own. He told me how he had my parents murdered, then pulled a gun on me. He admitted every-thing to me, thinking I was like him. He had no idea I was immortal. He shot me in the head."

"Son of a. . ."

"I killed him," I interrupt Sam's tirade. "For my parents, for threatening your lives, for me. I'm not sorry. Especially after finding out about Thomas, I'm glad he's dead. I only regret drinking from him."

"Is that what made you sick that day?" Jeremy chimes in. For such a big dude, he sure can be quiet. I almost forgot he was there.

"I think so."

"Why? Was his blood like rancid or something?"

I silently chide myself for being impressed that Jeremy knows the word rancid.

"Apparently."

"Where's his body?" Sam asks, getting back on track.

"It disintegrated. I'm serious," I say when Sam gives me a look. "I started searching his apartment after I killed him and heard a strange noise coming from him. By the time I got to him, his body was changing. Mummifying, then, poof, it was gone."

"That's awesome." Jenna sticks her tongue out and blows a bubble when Sam glares at her.

"He tried killing you. Self-defense."

"Sam, are you going to find some way to exonerate me of all my wrongdoings?"

"I'll find any way I can to keep you alive."

"Whether you feel I have done wrong or not, I am Cursed. That is enough for you to kill me as it is."

Sam stalks off, punching a sparring dummy hard on his way out.

"You can't blame him for fighting this, Anala."

"I don't blame him, Eric. However, that doesn't change anything."

Eric lowers his head, saying nothing more. The others are also quiet, not sure what to say. I feel emotion well up inside me that I haven't felt since my parents were alive.

"Can you all leave me, please? I need to be alone for a while. You should eat. Make it a hearty meal with a lot of protein. Then, get some rest. Tomorrow is going to be hell."

They surprise me by hugging me on the way out - yes, even Jenna. No words are spoken, but I hear their message in a simple hug. The task I have put before them is not one they will take easily. If at all.

Inhaling deeply, I begin the meditation process. I try clearing my mind of everything and letting it go, but it's not working. No matter what I try, Sam is there. Sam. The way he looks at me. The way he touches me. The way he makes me feel. It's all overwhelming and wonderful. . .and incredibly painful.

I bury my face in my hands and begin to sob. What a cruel bitch fate is. I have lived for centuries wishing I could just end it only to get here when I wish to live but need to end it. I am so in love with Sam that the thought of leaving him hurts even my cold heart.

"Ana?"

Amanda sits beside me, draping her arm around me and hugging me close.

"You should be eating, Amanda," I say through sniffles.

"I was worried about you. What can I do?"

I give her a watery, sad laugh. "Put me out of my misery."

"Ana, don't say things like that. This is hard enough as it is."

"I shouldn't be here, Amanda. If my parents had done what they were supposed to do, none of this would be happening."

"They loved you too much to kill you. You can't blame them for that."

"They were the *Leaders* of the Society. *They* made the rules! You, Sam, and the others would be leading normal lives had they followed their own rules."

"Normal or boring?"

"Amanda, you are going to graduate soon. You had just started dating Robby. You have loving parents and a plan for your future. Now, you don't even know if you'll live beyond tomorrow."

"Do you know what I've learned these past few weeks? I've learned how self-absorbed I have been. I wasn't ready for what came after high school because I refused to grow the hell up. You helped me do that."

"It's called being a teenager," I say softly. "I envied that about you. You didn't have to deal with what I had to at your age. My innocence was taken away from me when I was just beginning to feel things a normal teenage girl was supposed to feel." Another tear rolls down my cheek. "And it will be taken away from me again."

"It doesn't have to be. You can live like this with Sam."

"And, what? Make him run with me? Moving every few years, never having a stable life? Watch him grow old? Watch him die?"

Tears pool in Amanda's eyes, and she squeezes me tighter.

"I shouldn't be here," I repeat. "I shouldn't exist. I'm not natural. My existence puts everyone in danger."

"Once we finish this with Thomas, there won't be any more danger," Amanda sniffles.

"That's what I thought ages ago. I was wrong. As long as I am alive, that possibility exists. Amanda," I cut her off when she opens her mouth to argue. "I've made up my mind."

I breathe in Sam's scent, and it pulls at my broken heart.

"Your brother is here."

"I'll leave you two to talk," she replies as he walks in. "But, you should know, none of us have made up our minds."

I catch the look they give each other before Amanda leaves us alone. It makes me nervous to think of what they may have in store for me. Sam leans down and kisses me, tilting my head up to look me in the eye.

"It unnerves me to see you crying," he murmurs.

Absently, I wipe the tears from my cheeks, not mentioning how his kisses unnerve me.

He sits on the crate in front of me, holding my hands and gently stroking them with his thumbs.

"I'm sorry I left earlier."

"I understand. It's a difficult situation."

"Difficult? Try impossible. You know how I feel about you, Anala. How do you expect me to let you go? I just found you."

"Don't you understand that this is hard for me, too, Sam? I've never opened my heart to anyone. For this reason. It's too painful."

"It doesn't have to be. We can be together, Ana. . ."

"Sam, please. I can't." I cup his face in my hands. "I don't want to think about any of this right now. Can we just be together?" At least for one more night, I add silently.

He leans in and kisses me again. "Okay."

"Did you eat? You need your strength."

"I did. Did you?"

"Not yet."

"Good."

"I can't drink from you, Sam. Not tonight."

"Why?" He frowns, disappointed.

I have to get up, away from his intense stare.

"Because, like I said, you need your strength."

"I'll be fine. Please?"

I turn to him and scrutinize him. "You're addicted," I accuse.

"To you?" he laughs. "I think you're right."

"No. To me drinking from you. What does it do to you?"

"Nothing."

I can tell he's lying because he blushes ever so slightly, and his heart-beat accelerates.

"What does it do, Sam?"

He sighs and walks to me. "It feels amazing," he says, feathering a finger down my cheek. "Unlike anything I've ever felt before. And, when we. . .when we're together, it intensifies everything."

"Why didn't you tell me?"

"Why didn't you tell me what it does to you when you drink from me?"

Amanda must have said something about my little experiment and how I felt. Damn it. She's supposed to be my best friend, keeping my secrets, not running to her brother.

"It's not right what I'm doing to you."

"What's not right about it? I offered. I want it. You're not doing anything wrong."

Whenever I drink from Sam, a war wages between the Hunter in me and the Cursed One, guilt versus pleasure. I always choose pleasure, but I can't do that tonight. I can't leave Sam weakened. And, honestly, I think guilt is closing in on me.

"I'm feeding from you! You're human! More than that, you're a *Hunter*!" I whirl away from him. "Papa would be so disappointed in me."

"Ana, look at me."

When I don't comply, he tugs my arm, turning me back towards him.

"Baby, I think your dad would understand. He loved you enough to keep you alive. I think he would accept that I love you enough to. . .provide for you."

Again, his endearment leaves me bewildered enough that I can't think of anything to say in rebuttal. To go from such a lonely existence to this, to someone who loves me, is almost too much.

Temptation sucks! No pun intended. I can't give in. Not tonight. Lord, help me. I need to be strong.

"Sam, I want to be with you tonight." So much. "But I can't drink from you." I put my finger to his lips when he begins to protest. "Don't. Don't ask, don't try to get me to do it. Please? Just be with me as if I'm a human. I just want to be human with you tonight."

For one last night, I want to know what it's like to be in love and to have someone love me. I want to have dreams of a future, be held like a lover, and forget everything that lies ahead of me tomorrow. Tomorrow, my existence could end. I need to feel human one last time.

CHAPTER TWENTY-FOUR
"LONG ENOUGH"

I have been staring at the ceiling for half the night. Sam is sleeping, snoring softly as he does. His arm is draped across my body, holding me protectively. I would love nothing more than to fall asleep with him and dream of rainbows and unicorns - okay, not really, but even that is better than what's in my head now.

I kiss Sam lightly on the forehead and gently pull away from him. He must be tired as he only grumbles a little and rolls away.

Dressing in workout clothes, I make my way to the training room. This isn't where I want to be. I'd much prefer staying in bed with Sam, but I don't think it would be fair to him in my restless state. So, I grab my swords and begin a vigorous assault on the sparring dummy. I try to imagine it's Thomas I'm fighting and realize I'm holding back.

"Damn it!" Wiping the sweat off my brow, I pull my hair back and secure it in a ponytail. "You're a Hunter, Anala! He is Cursed. . ." I punch the dummy hard enough to make it bend all the way back to the floor. It would have flown across the room if it had not been bolted down. I castigate myself for being such a damn hypocrite.

"What am I going to do?" I'm alone, so obviously, I'm not expecting an answer, though I could really use one.

"You do what you must, Anala."

The soft voice stuns me. I lift my swords tentatively to. . .to what? Fight the ghosts in my head?

"What is that?" I whisper. Of course. It's the one answer I need, and all is silent. *It's all in your head, Anala,* I think to myself. If I want answers, I will have to find them within myself. Sitting with my legs crossed, I breathe deeply and immerse myself in meditation.

The meadow is beautiful and tranquil. A rainbow of flowers are in bloom, and they perfume the air with their sweet scent. I remember this meadow. Mum and I used to come here when I was a child to pick bouquets for the house. It was our time together to talk and giggle like girls instead of being a stoic and strong Hunter. I loved these moments with Mum.

She stands by the enormous oak tree, dressed in the flowing cotton dress I knew so well. Though her back is to me, I recognize her instantly.

"Mum?"

She turns to me and smiles.

"Anala." She reaches out to me, and I come closer. Part of my subconscious knows this isn't real. Oh, how I wish it were.

"I miss you, Mummy."

"I miss you, too, my sweet girl."

Imaginary or not, her sentiment touches me, and I feel tears threatening.

"Tell me what to do, Mum."

"I cannot, honey. This must be your decision. You know who you are and what Thomas has become. Follow your heart."

"It is my heart that torments me. It is Thomas, Mum."

"Is it?"

She is right. I cannot think of the boy Thomas used to be. Easier said than done.

"What if I cannot do it?"

"Then you will have failed, Anala."

The harsh words cut me deep.

"You did not kill me, Mum. You and Papa chose to keep me alive."

Her expression changes from serene to troubled.

"Yes, we did. We loved you and thought we could cure you. We were wrong. Look at what you are doing. Feeding from a Hunter, Anala?" She lowers her head, unable to look at me anymore. "Your father and I made a mistake."

I'm ripped from meditation, wounded by the statement. It takes me a moment to recognize my surroundings. I'm back in the training room, alone and shivering from the experience. I know my consciousness put those words in Mum's mouth, but that doesn't help my agony.

Anger consumes me. I grab my sword, and with one severe blow, I bring it down on the neck of the sparring dummy with a warrior cry filled with misery. The sheer power behind it has the head plunging off the dummy, rolling to rest at my feet.

The day is filled with anxiety. No one is quite sure what they should be doing, what to say, how to act towards me. The awkwardness of it all is maddening. If I didn't think it would wear them out, I would have them take out their frustrations in the training room. Instead, I feel like we're just twiddling our thumbs waiting for the moment none of us want to think about.

Sam is quiet and keeps his distance except for the brief, intimate touches here and there. Zac can't bring himself to look at me. Jeremy, Eric, Emily, and Jenna try engaging in a game of cards to pass the time - or avoid me. Amanda's rueful glances are beginning to irritate me. If I don't do something productive soon, I will go crazy.

"Where are you going?" Sam's question stops me.

"For a run."

"Want me to go with you?"

"You wouldn't be able to keep up." I regret my tone instantly when his face registers hurt. I go to him and kiss him gently on the lips. *"I'm sorry,"* I mouth. I run to the balcony before anyone can say anything else and jump. I hear shocked screams as they race to the balcony to see if I am okay. I'm halfway across the massive lawn and out of their sight within seconds.

It feels good to run, which is paradoxical since I believe I've been running my entire existence. However, the unadulterated liberation of being out of that house and away from the responsibilities weighing me down is exhilarating. It's completely childish to run, I know. But it was the only thing I could think to do that didn't involve me going insane - or wearing out one of my Hunters.

I stop abruptly, pushing my hands through my hair. *My* Hunters. Mum and Papa would not run from those depending on them. I'm being a petulant child, and it's unfair to the others. Tonight is going to be the hardest night of their lives, too. I should be there with them, getting them ready. I sigh heavily and begin my trek back to the house.

"Follow me. We're going to train for a bit. Then you will rest and eat."

They all look at me with confusion etched on their faces. One second, I disappear. The next, I'm there ordering them around.

"I thought you wanted us to rest."

"Are you resting, Amanda? Or are you sitting here worrying about me and tonight?"

She shrugs. "I could beat something up, I suppose."

The others agree, and we're off to the training room.

"I don't want you to overdo it. Just get your adrenaline going. Use the sparring dummies. Maybe spar with each other."

"We won't be sparring with you?"

"No, Jenna," Sam answers for me. "She needs to keep up her strength as well, and us cutting her up probably isn't a good idea."

I roll my eyes at the interference - as does Jenna, but he's right.

"Dude, what happened to this dummy?"

Jeremy picks up the severed head I cut off last night in my rage.

"Sorry. That was me."

"Man, I didn't know these things could be destroyed!" He juggles the head for a minute, then rolls it across the room like a bowling ball. It lightens the mood in the room, and laughter fills the air. I can see them physically relaxing, letting the tension roll off their shoulders.

I chuckle with them, shaking my head. "Let's get started."

After the brief, semi-intense training, we all eat at the dinner table. There's a distinct family feel in the air, and it's lovely. Tonight, we feast on steak and baked potatoes. I threw in some spinach just to get some vegetables in there, and they didn't seem to mind as they devoured the fare.

I pick at my food, eating it slowly. It's good for me to eat with them, be like them, but this food isn't what I need.

"Does this do anything for you?" Amanda asks.

"What?"

"Human - er, regular food. Does it help you?"

"Did you just say *human* food?"

"No! Well, yes, but. . ."

My laughter halts her explanation and has everyone looking at me as though I've lost my mind.

"Sorry," I gasp in between fits of laughter. "I don't know why I'm laughing. I guess I never thought I'd be having this conversation." My sides hurt, and I almost snort when the others start cautiously giggling with me. Dabbing my tearful eyes with my napkin, I try to compose myself. No need to have the others think I have gone insane before such an important night.

"Ahem. Um, *human* food is fine. I can get some sustenance from eating it."

Amanda calms her own laughter but keeps a smile. "But blood would be better?"

She says it so nonchalantly that I'm taken aback. I haven't been open about my diet with the others, and I'm unsure how they will receive it. With a quick, embarrassed glance at them, I answer.

"Yes."

Out of nowhere, Amanda produces a bottle filled with the red liquid I crave.

"Here," she hands it to me as though it were the most normal thing in the world.

"I. . ." Again, I glance at the others. I'm mortified. This isn't a side of me I want them to see.

"It's okay, Anala," Emily voices what the others are thinking as they all nod their approval. "We know this is what you need. We're fine with it."

"It's kinda gross, but who cares as long as I don't have to drink it," Jenna declares.

"Take it, Anala. Please?" Amanda pushes the bottle into my hand.

Tentatively, I take it. Honestly, blood sounds so good to me right now, but with everyone watching me, drinking it feels weird.

"Go back to eating," Amanda commands, as though she read my thoughts. "We don't need to watch her."

"*Thank you*," I whisper, taking a long, thirst-quenching gulp. The tingle hits me immediately. My muscles vibrate, and my already-enhanced abilities intensify even more. I breathe in deeply, actually feeling the air - or the dust - tickle my nose.

"What did you do to this!" I want to grab Amanda, but in my heightened state, I'm afraid of hurting her.

"Is it making you sick?" She's alarmed by my reaction, reaching for me, but I pull away. "Ana? Are you all right?" She looks to Sam for help, and he starts to get up.

"I'm fine." I hold my hand up, effectively stopping Sam's approach. "It's not making me sick. What did you do?"

"Nothing. . ."

"Amanda! What did you do!"

"We - we just thought you could use a little boost." She begins to wring her hands, then stops and sits up straight, holding my gaze brazenly. "We used some of our own blood."

"You did what! Why would you do that?"

"I saw what it did for you, Ana," she says, using the name she's most familiar with. The name of her best friend. "We wanted to help you."

I open my mouth to argue, then close it. I have no argument. What do I say to something this. . .weird, yet, sweet?

"You need all of your strength," I mutter. It was the best I could come up with, and even that was said half-heartedly.

"We didn't use enough to harm us, Anala," Eric assures me.

"You didn't have to do this."

"We wanted to," Emily chimes in.

"Yeah, I think it's pretty cool that my blood can boost your awesomeness." Jeremy puffs out his chest - as he tends to do - and gives me a silly grin.

I haven't come to terms with how I feel about them knowing what Hunter blood does for me. It must mean they know about Sam, and I'm mortified all over again.

"You've done a lot for us," Jenna - yes, Jenna - says. "We just wanted to be able to return the favor." She must not be used to being nice because she blushes a scarlet red when everyone looks at her.

"I haven't done anything for you except put you in danger."

"That's not true," Sam counters.

"You made us strong, Ana. It was you who made all of us believe in ourselves."

"Amanda's right." Zac touches my hand briefly. "We may have had to grow up a bit faster, but now I feel ready for anything life throws at me. That's because of you."

The praise is making me uncomfortable. Sure, it's nice to hear. I just can't bring myself to believe it when I'm about to throw these kids into the lion's den to either fight or be eaten. Literally.

I clear my throat, hoping I don't cry in front of them. "Thank you. All of you. I don't know what else to say."

"You don't have to say anything," Amanda ascertains. "Just drink, and we'll go back to eating, and we'll all be normal for another couple of hours."

Normal? Somehow, I don't think the sight of me drinking blood from a bottle is normal. But I do as she asks, as do the others. The blood, again, magnifies everything inside me. The more I drink, the more intense it gets. I close my eyes, trying to restrain the response the Cursed One in me is having, but the change comes abruptly and unexpectedly.

"Sorry." I fight it, making myself change back through sheer determination.

My Hunters just smile at me and continue their dinner conversation as though nothing unusual is happening around them. I've never appreciated anything more.

249

I wish I could get rid of this feeling of dread. The others busy themselves with readying their swords or getting gear together. They're all dressed in their hunting garb and looking quite formidable. However, I still can't shake this feeling.

I'm surprised I don't feel worse. This *is* supposed to be my last night on earth. Of course, none of my Hunters have confirmed that they will indeed kill me. I glance in Zac's direction and find him watching me.

"Why don't you guys start loading up the van," I announce, startling them by breaking the silence. "Zac, hang back for a minute. I would like to speak with you."

Sam looks at me warily, and I give him a slight nod. After Zac tried to kill me, Sam wasn't too keen on me being alone with him. If he only knew what I intended to ask.

"Am I in trouble?"

"Of course not. As long as you don't try to kill me again. Yet."

He chuckles and then sobers abruptly.

"Yet?"

"Zac. . ."

"No way! Are you crazy? Sam will *kill* me!"

"Sam is the reason I'm asking *you*, Zac. He won't do it. Amanda won't either. And, honestly, I'd rather Jenna not do it because I think she would actually enjoy it." I take a step closer. "You care about me. So, I'm asking you to do this for me."

"It's seriously messed up that you're asking someone who *cares* about you to kill you, Ana."

"I know. But you understand why it has to be done, Zac. You know it's wrong that I'm alive."

Zac runs a hand through his hair, blowing out air in an exaggerated - and exasperated - manner.

"How can it be wrong? You're not evil. You haven't done any harm to anyone. . ."

"I have. I have killed innocents, Zac. My mere existence is what brought all of this to you and the others. I'm not natural," I say, using the words I used with Amanda, hoping they will sink in with Zac. "Please?"

"Damn it, Ana. Did you really think I would agree to do this?"

My hope deflates. With how he feels about me and Sam together, I had hoped it was enough to have him on my side about this. I guess I misjudged just how much he does care.

"Think about it. And know that what I'm asking is what I want. It's what I need. Six hundred years is long enough, Zac." I pause as I walk by him and lay my hand on his shoulder. With a brief squeeze, I walk away, keeping a shred of hope that he will do as I ask.

CHAPTER TWENTY-FIVE
"FAMILY"

The ride to Thomas's location is a somber one. Sam and I sit in the middle seats of the van while the others fill out the back. Zac is driving, which keeps him occupied and quiet - good for me. Amanda sits next to him, occasionally calling out directions.

He holds my hand tightly. I don't know if it's because he's nervous about the fight ahead of him or because of what I want after the fight. I can't have him thinking of anything except staying alive, so I squeeze his hand and smile reassuringly. It's the least I can do, even if I don't feel reassured myself.

We're a couple of blocks away when I order Zac to stop.

"They'll have a harder time smelling you if we don't drive right up to the front door," I explain, and take out the makeshift 'floor plans' that Eric helped me draw up. I lay them on top of a trashcan and beckon everyone to come and look.

"There's a small opening here," I point on the right side of the drawing depicting the Colosseum. "A very narrow corridor follows with openings here, here, and here," I say, identifying each doorway. "You will spread out, but not too far from each other. I want you to be able to help each other if needed. I will go in first. . ."

"Anala. . ."

"Sam, listen. They cannot detect me. I will climb up to this vantage point," I point to the perch I usually use to observe. "I will relay to you how many Cursed Ones are there and their approximate location. Then, I will look for Thomas."

"It's a good plan, Sam," Amanda says, and the others agree. Sam nods - reluctantly, of course, and we start unloading the van.

"Stay focused. The only thing you should be thinking about is staying alive. Let your training take over. You're prepared for this, and you've worked together long enough to know when someone needs help."

"We got this," Jeremy assures me, but even he looks a little worried.

"Make sure you do." I walk up to Amanda and hug her tightly. "Be careful. If you get into a difficult situation, do whatever you can to escape it." I address them all again. "Have each other's backs." I glance at Zac. *Have my back*, I think silently.

I wrap my arms around Sam and kiss him. "Please stay focused. Do not worry about me. Worry about yourself and Amanda."

"I will."

"Promise me."

"I promise, Anala."

"Stay alive."

"You, too." He kisses me again. "I love you."

"I love you, too, Sam."

With one last kiss, we start walking the couple of blocks to the hide-out. He doesn't want to let go of my hand, but when we're close, I slip it away and raise my hood. I motion for them to wait for my signal, then scale the wall until I sit atop.

"*That is so cool.*"

They are the last whispered words I hear from Jeremy before focusing my attention on the Cursed Ones below me. Not just Cursed Ones, I realize. Hybrids. Could it be possible that Thomas was expecting me, or is he just being cautious? Either way, he's brought in the cavalry.

I gesture down to Sam, making a five and a zero with my hand and an upward motion.

"*Fifty plus.*" I hear him tell the others.

Then, I make another gesture, hoping he understands what I'm trying to say.

"Damn. Hybrids."

I glance back at him and nod my head. I signal for them to move in, saying a little prayer for them as I do. I have no idea if some*thing* like me is listened to, but I try anyway.

"Be careful! Let's go!"

I hear Sam relay the order. Then I round the area to try and find Thomas. I know they're inside when I hear the clash and clanks of swords hitting swords. Trust them, I tell myself, trying to take my advice to 'stay focused.'

My adrenaline pumps, my Hunters' blood in me feels like it's coming to life. I drop down to the quarters below me, checking each room, each crevice for Thomas. When I don't find him, I make my way into the 'stage' area where I first saw him. Thankfully, my Hunters are holding their own and are still alive, but the sheer number of Cursed is overwhelming. I abandon my search for Thomas temporarily to help.

Even though these Cursed Ones are not as strong as I am, having them come at my Hunters from all sides can be daunting for the most seasoned Hunter like myself. Fighting me is difficult for my group, and I am only one. They are closing in on Amanda, and I can actually *feel* her fear. Before I have a chance to get to her, Zac is there. Together, they skillfully take care of the small crowd of Cursed Ones around them. I am almost mesmerized by the way they work together. It's like a well-rehearsed dance.

Shaking myself, I return to reality just in time to see three Cursed Ones running toward me. With a low growl, I greet them with a vicious attack of my own. They have no chance against me, especially not with this blood running through my veins. As the last of the three falls to dust at my feet, I find that I'm angry. Angry that I had to drag people I care about into this mess. Angry that I can't be with the man I love. Angry that Thomas is nowhere to be found.

"Thomas!" My shout reverberates throughout the coliseum, momentarily distracting all that are in there. "You are not a coward! Come out and fight me!"

I swing my sword behind me, beheading the Cursed One who dared to sneak up on me. Amateurs.

"Do you really want to fight me, Anala?"

I look up and find Thomas looming above me at the top of the structure. His accent makes my heart ache. He sounds so much like the boy I care about.

"It is my destiny, Thomas."

"Hunter's code," he mocks. "Bollocks is what it 'tis." He drops from his post, landing in front of me. I barely register that the fighting has completely stopped. My Hunters, Cursed Ones, and even the Hybrids are focused on the stage where Thomas and I are.

"The code is there for a reason. Cursed Ones should not exist."

"And, yet, here you are. *Someone* broke the code. You should be grateful."

My parents flood my thoughts, but I say nothing.

"Perhaps if they hadn't, none of this would be happening. You wouldn't be here killing innocents or creating an army. Why should I be grateful for that?"

Thomas lets out a low snarl. "You think I do not deserve to be alive!"

"Thomas, I have missed you and thought of you often."

He takes a step forward with something that resembles a smile on his handsome face.

"However," I continue, "I think it's wrong for you to be alive. And I still have a duty to fulfill."

He lets out a strangled cry and charges me. I cross my swords above me to block his from slicing through my skull. The force vibrates through my arms. He is strong. I push him, and he flies through some fallen columns across the stage.

Thomas gets up and shakes off the dust that covers him.

"I can defeat you, Anala."

"You never have before," I taunt.

"I'm stronger now," he growls.

He's delusional if he doesn't think that same strength - or more - runs through me. He circles, and I follow his movements. Incredibly, my Hunters are still watching the exchange, as are the others. I want to yell at them to finish the job, but I need to focus on Thomas.

"We could rule this world, Anala. What happened to your feelings for me?"

"Things change, Thomas. You changed."

"There is someone else."

It was a statement, so I don't bother answering.

"Who is it?"

"All that matters is what is happening right in front of you. Do you not recall your Hunter training at all?"

"Bollocks," he repeats with venom.

"Such hatred for what you were born to be."

"I was born for this," he retorts, gesturing towards his Cursed Ones. "I was born to lead."

"You're not even their true leader," I smirk. I see his eyes darken with rage. It's exactly what I want. I need him to be mad at me. If I have any chance of killing him, I need it to be in self-defense. I don't think I have the heart to do it any other way.

When I think he is going to charge me again, he changes directions and jumps out towards my Hunters. Before I know it, he has Jeremy in his grasp.

"Is it you?" Thomas grips Jeremy's hair and pulls his head back painfully. I know it's painful because I can feel it. I'm afraid that the slightest movement from me could mean a certain death for Jeremy. From my peripheral vision, I see Sam slowly move, inches at a time. He's trying to position himself behind Thomas and Jeremy.

"Does it make you feel better to kill those weaker than you, Thomas?" I am risking Jeremy's life by provoking Thomas. I'm hoping it distracts him enough not to notice Sam and to let Jeremy go in favor of fighting me. "Is that the only way you can win?"

"No, it's not you," Thomas smiles. "Not Anala's type." He picks Jeremy up and throws him across the arena. I can only pray he lives. It is a better fate than being bitten or having his neck broken by Thomas. He eyes Sam for a split second, and my heart stops beating then. For whatever reason - perhaps because Sam is partially hidden in the shadows - Thomas bypasses Sam and goes after Zac.

Without the element of surprise that Thomas had with Jeremy, Zac fights. *Stop fighting, Zac! He will kill you!* I plead silently. I'm astonished when Zac stops and looks at me in confusion. With the hesitation, it doesn't take much effort for Thomas to entrap Zac in his vice-like grip.

"What about you?" Thomas looks up at me, trying to read my emotions. I give him a blank stare - at least, I hope it's blank and not filled with the anguish I feel inside. "Is it him, Anala? Is he the one that has replaced me in your heart?"

"No one replaced you, Thomas. You drove yourself out by becoming what you are."

"She judges me when she is what I am," he says to Zac.

"She judges what you do," Zac responds.

Oh, Zac, please don't antagonize him.

"Who are *you* to judge me?" Thomas squeezes Zac's throat tighter, and I feel my air constricted.

"He's not judging you, Thomas," I say quickly, trying to distract Thomas with conversation. I think it works because he loosens his hold on Zac a fraction. "He's telling you how I feel. I don't like what you have become."

"This is what we are *meant* to be, Anala. Superior. Immortal. Not weak like them."

"This is not you, Thomas. How can you turn your back on what you once were? Not just a Hunter, but *human*."

"Being human brings nothing but pain."

"Pain is all I have felt in the past six-hundred years, Thomas. Losing my parents, being alone, never being able to have a normal life. Immortality is lonely."

When he looks at me, I see sadness in his eyes. And something else. Something that resembles pity.

"It's not lonely if you make more, Anala. I would have sought you out if I had known you were alive. We could be together. Build our family."

"This is not a family, Thomas!" His blatant disregard for life is aggravating me. "You don't know them. You don't care to sit down and ask how their day went. You make them kill for you, bring you humans to feed off of. If they do not satisfy your wishes, they are killed. Oh, but you can make more, so it does not matter," I say sarcastically. "You know not what a real family or real love is anymore, Thomas."

A darkness as black as storm clouds fills his eyes.

"You were always arrogant, Anala. Always had to be better than everyone else. This time, I am better. I do not let my emotions get the better of me."

"My emotions for you, Thomas, got me turned."

He hesitates for a split second at my admission, his eyes clearing. But, as quickly as it happened, it was over.

"It is your emotions that will *kill* you this time, Anala. What pain will you feel when I kill the one you love now?" He raises his sword and points at me. As though a switch was flipped, the Cursed Ones and Hybrids all turn to me and advance. They don't attack, but they are sure to surround me. Only a few stay back to ward off my Hunters if they try to ambush Thomas.

"Thomas, please!"

"Or, better yet, turn him."

"No!"

"It's not him! It's me!" Sam yells before Thomas can sink his teeth into Zac. "She loves me!"

Sam! No!

"He's lying," Zac manages through gritted teeth. "He wishes it was him. Anala loves me."

"Zac, shut up! Leave him alone. He's just a kid! Anala's heart belongs to me."

Sam comes into the light, and his appearance takes Thomas aback.

"Who are you?"

"My name is Sam Logan."

"Sam!" I put every ounce of myself into that one word, pleading with him to stop.

Thomas glances at me, seeing the agony etched on my face. I cannot hide it this time.

"You are mine," he says to Sam. "My blood?"

"Yes."

"Is this true, Anala? Is he the one you love?"

There is no way for me to answer this without a terrible outcome. If I answer yes, Thomas will go after Sam, family or not. If I answer no, I again put Zac's life in danger.

"Thomas, you know as well as I do that we are incapable of emotions like that," I lie. It is my only option, and I can only hope that Sam understands what I am doing. But it doesn't work.

"You lie! I saw your face." He looks bemused. "But, you looked distraught over this one as well. Do you love them both?"

"They are my family, Thomas—all of my Hunters. I love them all. If you hurt any of them, I will kill you. Without regret, without sorrow. I will bring the blade of my sword down on you with a vengeance so absolute your Cursed Ones will feel it."

"You will never make it to me in time to save him. Either of them."

"Oh, but I will make it to you. And, when I do, you will know that immortality does not truly exist."

Fight, Zac. Do everything you can to keep him from biting you. Use your training. Use daggers or stakes, anything to distract him until I can get to you.

Zac's eyes meet mine, and he blinks them once to acknowledge my request. I turn my thoughts to the others, assuming, praying, they can hear me as Zac can.

Do everything you can do to get to Zac. I will get there as fast as I can. Sam, you have to stay away from Thomas, or he will kill you, too. Help me with the others. Go! Now!

I'm assured that my Hunters hear me loud and clear when they begin charging the Cursed Ones at my command.

All hell breaks loose as the onslaught of Cursed Ones and Hunters begins. More than ten vamps charge me, and I charge back. I have to do everything I can to get to Zac. Swinging my swords precisely and accurately, I drop five vamps without a hitch.

"I got this," Sam yells as he runs up the stairs to meet me.

I nod and jump as he reaches me, pushing myself off his shoulders. Zac is fighting Thomas with every ounce of strength he has. As far as I can tell, he has avoided being bitten, but he can't keep this up for long. I push my way through vamps and Hybrids, shredding them when I can, immobilizing them when I can't.

"Thomas!"

With my focus on Thomas and Zac, I don't see Nyle approaching me until his sword slices into my side.

"You will die, now. You should never have come after our Maker."

"Such loyalty for someone who would kill you without hesitation." The pain sears through me, but I hold steady, keeping Nyle at arm's length.

"My Maker deserves my loyalty."

"Then give it to me," I growl, staring into his eyes.

He blinks in confusion.

"You? You are not. . ."

"You are of my blood. *I* am your *true* Maker. Stop him. Stop Thomas."

Thomas must hear my command because his attention is momentarily drawn away from Zac. His hold, however, does not loosen, and Zac is still trapped in the grip. Nyle glances at Thomas, then back at me, seemingly torn at what to do.

"Do not listen to her! She is nothing!" Thomas yells.

"You feel it," I counter. "You know what I say is true. You are mine."

Nyle turns to Thomas, baring his teeth. He retracts his sword - a tad too slow, I might add.

"Nyle, I made you!"

"Did she make you?" Nyle asks in return.

I welcome the distracted conversation between the two. Zac stands a better chance at surviving as long as they're engaged.

Don't struggle, Zac. Be patient.

Zac immediately stills.

"She did not make me!"

"Is it not my blood that made you, Thomas?"

"That means nothing! You did not make me!"

"So, it is true. It is her blood that runs through you? Through me? She is my true Maker?"

"I gave you immortality! It was me that gave you this life!"

"At what cost?" I ask Nyle. "What did he take from you?"

Nyle frowns. I don't know if he can remember his life before Thomas turned him, but I have to try.

"Anala, stop! Do not listen to her!"

"He does not want you to remember. Did you have a family, Nyle?"

The red ring around Nyle's irises begins to almost pulse with rage.

I'm curious as to what he remembers. I'll never know as he races toward Thomas. To my horror, I see Thomas position Zac between them—his human shield.

What happened next is a blur. I'm not sure I even truly know. When I look back, I wonder if I will see where I went wrong. All I can comprehend now is Nyle's ashes and a gasping, struggling Zac lying at my feet. From the top of the coliseum, Thomas looks down at me, at my Hunters (who have defeated his 'family'). He's angry, but an evil smirk forms on his blood-stained lips.

I catch Zac as he rises and lunges at me, snapping to get at my neck. I draw Zac to me with a quick twist, his back against my chest. My heart aches, but this time it's not only because I feel Zac's pain when I push the stake into his heart. I raise my eyes, burning with tears and hatred, to Thomas.

"I will come for you. I will find you, and I *will* kill you."

His smirk falters slightly, and then he's gone.

"Ana! He's getting away! We have to go. . ." Sam stops abruptly when he sees Zac slumped before me. "*No*."

"He has been bitten."

"Do something! Help him!" Jenna is hysterical. I didn't realize she cared so much. But then again, our eclectic little group has become more of a family than I thought possible.

"There is nothing I can do." I gently lay Zac on the ground and stand up. "It is too late."

Sam grabs my hand as I reach for my sword.

"You can't."

"It is what must be done."

"He's just a kid, Ana."

"So was I."

"Your parents let you live. They gave you a chance."

I whirl to face him. "And look what happened! If they had done their job, what they were *destined* to do, *none* of this would be happening! These kids would be worrying about nothing except graduating, Thomas wouldn't be out there killing people, and Zac. . ." I take a breath, hoping it will calm me. It doesn't help at all. "I never should have involved any of you in this. I can't let him live like this. He wouldn't want that."

"You think he would rather die?"

"It wasn't supposed to happen like this," I say, ignoring Sam's question. "I was supposed to kill Thomas, and then Zac would kill me."

"He agreed to that?" Amanda asks, quietly.

"Yes." I brush off Sam's sharp intake of breath. "But, instead, I'm faced with having to kill him, all while Thomas is still out there."

"Ana, please. Think of his mother. Give him a chance."

"A chance to what, Sam? Kill his mother the moment he sees her?"

"Maybe he won't be like that," Emily interjects.

"He is. He came after me. It's why I staked him."

"*You* staked him?" Sam's incredulity annoys me.

"*You* have no room to talk about *anyone* staking *anyone*."

"Teach him," Amanda pleads, cutting short my and Sam's stake debate. "Teach him how to be like you."

"No one taught me, Amanda. This is just who I am. I don't know why I didn't lose my humanity, and I wouldn't know how to *teach* Zac."

"The elixir!" Amanda clutches my arm in hope. "Your father's elixir. I read about it in one of his journals. You stated that it gave you memories of your childhood and made you feel humanity. Could that help Zac?"

I pace away. Part of me would love nothing more than to help Zac, to keep him alive. However, the Cursed One in me knows what kind of life this is. Why would I want Zac to experience this?

"You are asking me to go against everything that I believe in. And, yes, I realize how hypocritical that sounds coming from me!" I add, raising my voice at Jenna's scoff.

"Look, Ana, you need us to help you with Thomas," Jeremy begins.

"No, I do not. I need you to graduate and live full and happy lives. This," I gesture to Zac, "is my fault. I will make Thomas pay for it."

"Zac is our friend, too. Whether you let us fight with you or not, we're still going after him." Jeremy, and the others, give me defiant looks. "We think Zac should be a part of it, too. He deserves that. Try the elixir Amanda is talking about. Please."

Ugh! Teenagers can be extremely annoying and persistent! They are all murmuring their pleas, talking to each other, trying to convince each other it will work, and talking to me, trying to persuade me to give in. Their voices were like angry little bees swarming around my already pounding head.

"Stop! Just shut up." I take a deep breath and let it out slowly as I retract my sword. "Fine. I will *try* the elixir. But if it does not work. . ."

"We know what we have to do."

"You better, Eric. And I have one condition, so be sure this is what you really want to do."

"What is your condition?" Sam asks, wearily.

"When this is over, and Thomas is dead, you must complete your destiny. You have to kill us both. If you cannot agree to that condition, I will kill Zac now, kill Thomas when I find him, and then finish the job myself."

"You can't kill yourself." Where the hell did Jenna get the gum she is currently smacking? "What are you going to do? Cut off your own head?"

"Perhaps. Or, perhaps, I'll set myself on fire."

"Your survival instinct will kick in. You said yourself that you can't kill yourself."

"I'm a resourceful woman. I'll figure it out. That is my condition. Take it or leave it."

"Deal," Amanda speaks up before anyone can say anything else, yet they all begin protesting immediately. I ignore them and focus on Amanda.

"Your word, Amanda."

"You have it."

"If you are lying and do not willingly kill me and Zac at the end of all of this, I will make you."

"You would compel us to kill you?" Sam's disbelief hardly registers with me.

I lower my head, willing myself to change.

"No," I answer, feeling the change come over me.

I know the blood-red rings around my irises are brighter than ever.

My eyes change to the white, almost transparent color, an eerie contrast. My teeth are longer and sharper, scarier after feeding live. My appearance is threatening and precisely what I want when I look at my Hunters again.

"I will come after you."

ACKNOWLEDGMENTS

I have revamped (pun intended) this book and changed some things. But these are the acknowledgments that I wrote back in 2013, so I'm going to keep them. With the exception of a couple of additions and one omission.

———————

Being an author may seem like a solo 'job', but as they say, it takes a village! Most importantly, friends who cheerfully (hopefully not rolling their eyes) say yes to reading your very rough draft. To those friends (you know who you are), thank you so much for your feedback. It makes being an author much easier.

I don't have an agent, nor am I well known as an author to have bloggers or editors to acknowledge. However, I do have friends and family that have my back and help me tremendously.

My family, your continued love and support mean the world to me. We may not agree on everything, but how boring would it be if we did? We can't pick our families, but it turns out I would have picked all of you anyway.

Daisy, I'm blessed that you have the patience to put up with my multiple personalities and give me the room I need to write. Thanks for being cool. Also, thank you for reading Destined to Kill and playing "devil's advocate". You make me think about things that I wouldn't normally consider. I still think it's funny that someone who watches "The Walking Dead" and believes in aliens uses the phrase "that part's not believable" when reading a book about vampires. ;)

Wanda, Ivy, and the girls from my "Xtreme" group, I thank you for reading Destined to Kill and giving me your honest feedback. I take all you say to heart. Book nerds must stick together!

Melissa, when I came to you asking if you'd help me revamp this book, you didn't hesitate to say yes. I appreciate you. I'm glad we're friends!

Aven, you've been a godsend, bringing my characters to life! I couldn't imagine anyone else narrating my books. Thank you!!

To my readers. Every author dreams of having readers that love their characters. I hope you love Anala and her eclectic group as much as I do. Thank you for reading. I hope you'll want to come back for more!

———————————————————

I will be revamping the next two books of the trilogy. I hope you enjoy! Just one more chapter...

ABOUT THE AUTHOR

Jourdyn Kelly lives in Houston, Texas, with a beautiful zoo of pets ranging from furry to aquatic. Jourdyn attributes her passion for writing and sharing stories to the love of the written word she inherited from her mother, who always surrounded them in books. After losing her mother from Alzheimer's complications, Jourdyn started her own company, Jaded Angels, as a tribute to her and the strong women who have inspired Jourdyn throughout her life. A portion of the proceeds goes to alz.org in her mother's memory. Jourdyn collects Grogu merchandise with startling avarice, paints 3D printed models as a hobby, is a Dim Sum fanatic who loves going to the movies, and of course, penning her novels.

SOCIAL MEDIA

Connect with Jourdyn Kelly online
My Website
(http://www.jourdynkelly.com/)
Patreon
(https://www.patreon.com/JourdynKelly)
Twitter
(https://twitter.com/JourdynK)
Goodreads

(http://www.goodreads.com/author/show/2980644.Jourdyn_Kelly)

Facebook
(https://www.facebook.com/AuthorJourdynKelly)
Secret Society on Facebook
(https://www.facebook.com/groups/JoKels/)
Instagram
(https://www.instagram.com/jourdynk/)
Amazon Author's Page
(http://www.amazon.com/-/e/B005O24HK8)